Burning bridge

This is it, Hollister thought. The Golden Gate Bridge is in the midst of a *terrorist attack!*

For years, they had been reading about how the terrorists planned to target the bridge and bring down yet another symbol of America. He couldn't believe it. What hellish luck it was to be caught in the middle of a terrorist attack!

Coming toward him, southbound across the bridge, Hollister saw a solid wall of what looked like huge, burning spheres.

"Oh, my God, this can't be happening!"

There was only one thing to do—turn around, head back into San Francisco, and *outrun* them. The Porsche could do it. It had the power to outrun anything that those goddam Middle Eastern bandits could throw at him.

Hollister slammed on the brakes, jerked the steering wheel to the left and floored the accelerator . . .

RAPTOR FORCE
HOLY FIRE

Bill Yenne

BERKLEY BOOKS, NEW YORK

THE BERKLEY PUBLISHING GROUP
Published by the Penguin Group
Penguin Group (USA) Inc.
375 Hudson Street, New York, New York 10014, USA
Penguin Group (Canada), 90 Eglinton Avenue East, Suite 700, Toronto, Ontario M4P 2Y3, Canada
(a division of Pearson Penguin Canada Inc.)
Penguin Books Ltd., 80 Strand, London WC2R 0RL, England
Penguin Group Ireland, 25 St. Stephen's Green, Dublin 2, Ireland (a division of Penguin Books Ltd.)
Penguin Group (Australia), 250 Camberwell Road, Camberwell, Victoria 3124, Australia
(a division of Pearson Australia Group Pty. Ltd.)
Penguin Books India Pvt. Ltd., 11 Community Centre, Panchsheel Park, New Delhi—110 017, India
Penguin Group (NZ), 67 Apollo Drive, Mairangi Bay, Auckland 1311, New Zealand
(a division of Pearson New Zealand Ltd.)
Penguin Books (South Africa) (Pty.) Ltd., 24 Sturdee Avenue, Rosebank, Johannesburg 2196,
South Africa

Penguin Books Ltd., Registered Offices: 80 Strand, London WC2R 0RL, England

This is a work of fiction. Names, characters, places, and incidents either are the product of the author's imagination or are used fictitiously, and any resemblance to actual persons, living or dead, business establishments, events, or locales is entirely coincidental.

RAPTOR FORCE: HOLY FIRE

A Berkley Book / published by arrangement with the author

PRINTING HISTORY
Berkley edition / February 2007

Copyright © 2007 by William Yenne.
Cover design by Steven Ferlauto.
Interior text design by Kristin del Rosario.

ISBN: 978-0-425-21300-1

BERKLEY®
Berkley Books are published by The Berkley Publishing Group,
a division of Penguin Group (USA) Inc.,
375 Hudson Street, New York, New York 10014.
BERKLEY is a registered trademark of Penguin Group (USA) Inc.
The "B" design is a trademark belonging to Penguin Group (USA) Inc.

PRINTED IN THE UNITED STATES OF AMERICA

10 9 8 7 6 5 4 3 2 1

"**THE** Sultan of Brunei is dead. Long live the sultan!"

His passing hardly rated more than a brief reference on the evening news. Sultan Haji Hassanal Bolkiah Muizzaddin Waddaulah had been a geopolitical footnote. He was best known as having been, off and on, the world's richest man, and for such curious, but harmless, eccentricities as converting his large collection of Ferrari and Jaguar sports cars into station wagons. Despite his extravagant lifestyle and his disdain for democracy, the sultan was a generous man, offering his people free education and medical services, while abolishing taxes. He was a congenial man, and in the fraternity of absolute monarchs, a good man.

"The Sultan of Brunei is dead. Long live the sultan!"

Defying the assumed line of succession, Bolkiah's successor was his rotund distant cousin, Prince Omar

Jamalul Halauddin, best known on the back pages of society tabloids as an international playboy who threw around his considerable weight and his royal pedigree at Hollywood pool parties and the triple-A-list private club scene from London to Dubai. In the meantime, as his nights were filled with parties, it was whispered that his days were devoted to a small, but efficient, organized crime operation based in Marseilles.

Though he wasn't thought to be the direct heir, Prince Omar flew in from Cannes on his private jet the moment that Sultan Hassanal Bolkiah took ill. When the sultan died and the dust settled, Omar Jamalul Halauddin was on the throne.

"The Sultan of Brunei is dead. Long live the sultan!"

Nobody in the outside world took the new sultan seriously. Indeed, he was hardly mentioned in the global media, and that was a problem. As with Kim Jong Il, the eccentric playboy potentate of North Korea, it was soon evident that Omar suffered from a deep inferiority complex, and that would be a problem.

PROLOGUE

April 4
7:07 P.M. Pacific Time

RICHARD Morgan Hollister walked back to his corner office on the twenty-ninth story of Embarcadero Center Four and looked out across San Francisco Bay. The late afternoon sun-washed the tall buildings of downtown San Francisco and the towers of the San Francisco-Oakland Bay Bridge in its intense orange-pinkishness. Yerba Buena Island and the Oakland Hills beyond were beginning to twinkle with lights.

A powerful San Francisco attorney and an uncannily adept litigator, Hollister was relishing the glory of victory. Eleven people and a stenographer had just watched him reduce opposition counsel to tears. Eleven people and a stenographer had just watched him turn the Abernathy settlement conference into a $14.7-million victory.

There was much to celebrate, but this was just one of a string of killer wins for him, and for Roebuck, Springer & Seigal.

"Damn, I'm *good*!" he told himself out loud in the quiet of his private corner office with its panoramic view of the city and the bay.

He spilled some ice cubes into a tumbler and poured himself a splash of tequila. His ice bucket was replenished once an hour, like clockwork. It was one of the perks of senior partnership that Richard Morgan Hollister had come to take for granted. He relished the warmth of José Cuervo for a moment and turned to his Black-Berry. The Karlsruhe-Jamison case. Dammit. Those bastards never sleep. He answered the messages, shuffled some minor issues off to a junior partner, and checked his voice mail.

Hollister poured the last dribble of tequila into his glass, gulped it, replenished his ice, and poured the tumbler full of water from the chilled pitcher that always seemed to be on the low table next to his credenza. Oh, the perks of senior partnership.

Between e-mails and voice mails, it was nearly nine before Richard Morgan Hollister slipped on his silk-lined jacket, straightened his four-hundred-dollar tie in the mirror on the back of his office door, and made his way toward the elevator. Roebuck, Springer & Seigal was virtually deserted at this hour; only about seven attorneys and a dozen paralegals were still at work.

He walked past the smoked-glass wall that looked in on the conference room where eleven people and a stenographer had watched him reduce opposition counsel to tears and turn a settlement conference into a $14.7-million victory. There was still a pair of bifocals on the opposition side of the vast rosewood table. One of those wretched opposition attorneys must have been so distracted with the crushing, devastating loss that he just forgot his glasses.

"Damn, I'm *good*!" Richard Morgan Hollister grinned as he made his way toward the big double doors.

A young attorney who was hurrying past with an armload of file folders glanced at him with a puzzled expression. Hollister smiled and winked. She blushed. He had seen her in the hall and wondered in passing what her name was. She knew his name, obviously. He was Richard Morgan Hollister, *the* Richard Morgan Hollister, and she looked back at his smiling face with the appropriate awe and adulation.

She was young and attractive. With her long, honey-colored hair and her perfect body perfectly packaged in her lavender blouse and narrow gray skirt. She was young and tender, Hollister thought to himself. Tender in so many ways. He would have to get to know her—whatever her name was—before she became a hard-ened and seasoned attorney, or before she vanished from the halls of Roebuck, Springer & Seigal as so many of the young and tender ones did.

It was 7:50 by the time that Richard Morgan Hollister reached the garage level of the towering San Francisco skyscraper and tossed his handmade, wildebeest-hide attaché case onto the seat of his $100,000 Porsche 911 Carrera 4S Cabriolet.

As he headed down Columbus Avenue toward the Broadway Tunnel, he phoned home on his cell phone. Northbound traffic on the Golden Gate Bridge would be moderate at this time of night and he should be in Sausalito within a half hour or less. The housekeeper's voice sounded peculiar, and he couldn't tell why. It wasn't her Ukrainian accent, it was something else. It must have been the connection.

Hollister recalled that his wife was at one of her goddamn charity functions, so he'd have to dine alone. He told the housekeeper that he'd have the quail, and to chill a bottle of the Pinot Grigio. As he clicked off, he had the sense that someone was listening in on his call, or that someone was watching him. It was uncanny.

As he floored the accelerator and the Carrera dashed through the Broadway Tunnel, he glanced in the rearview mirror. The tunnel was awash in headlights, but nobody appeared to be following the Porsche. It had been a long day.

It was just a little after eight as he raced down Lombard Street and merged onto Doyle Drive. Hollister could see the floodlit towers of the Golden Gate Bridge in the distance. He glanced into the car on his right. It was the ugliest person he had ever seen, and it really startled him. No, it was a mask. Some sunavabitch was going to a costume party. Hollister couldn't believe that the man who had reduced opposing counsel to tears had been so unnerved by the sight of a guy in a mask. He could hardly wait to get home to a good stiff drink.

As the Carrera slid past the southbound toll plaza

and streaked across the Golden Gate Bridge, Hollister suddenly noticed that the sides of the bridge were *on fire*!

There were huge, blazing flames, dozens of them, everywhere. Huge tongues of flame reached up and seemed to be consuming the bridge.

This is it, he thought. The Golden Gate Bridge is in the midst of a *terrorist attack*!

For years, they had been reading about how the terrorists planned to target the bridge and bring down yet another symbol of America. He couldn't believe it. What hellish luck it was to be caught in the middle of a terrorist attack!

Coming toward him, southbound across the bridge, Hollister saw a solid wall of what looked like huge, burning spheres.

"Oh, my God, this can't be happening!"

There was only one thing to do—turn around, head back into San Francisco, and *outrun* them. The Porsche could do it. It had the power to outrun anything that those goddamn Middle Eastern bandits could throw at him.

Richard Morgan Hollister slammed on the brakes, jerked the steering wheel to the left, and floored the accelerator.

ONE

A MONTH EARLIER

March 4
10:17 A.M. Eastern Time

As Richard Morgan Hollister would be doing from his office one month later in San Francisco, Secretary General Baudouin Abuja Mboma stared out the window of his spacious apartment on East Sixty-sixth Street in New York City. It was a warm and beautiful early spring day, and he could almost smell the fresh young women in their flowered dresses on their lunch breaks down there on Madison Avenue.

Nine years in New York and the secretary general was getting used to the good life in America's most powerful and most vulnerable city. He had come to relish the fine restaurants and the way that so many people fought among themselves to wine him and dine him, to indulge him and beg him for favors. He had come to relish the most exotic of pleasures, and the young women in their flowered dresses. Especially, he had come to savor his diplomatic immunity, and a virtually unlimited expense account.

Baudouin Abuja Mboma had come a very long way from Djambala, the squalid back corner of the Congo where he was born and raised, and even from Paris, where he had gone to university and where he had reinvented himself as an urbane man of the world. As his lofty perch on the forty-fifth floor reminded him, he had reached the pinnacle of global power—and he liked it here.

Looking down from the forty-fifth floor, Secretary General Baudouin Abuja Mboma felt like he was the king of the world. Thanks to the extraordinary International Validation Treaty, he literally *was* the king of the world. Order and balance in the world was insured because the member states of the United Nations had subscribed to the notion that only the world body could issue an International Validation certification to permit any nation to act militarily outside its borders. Ultimately, Mboma had the power to pull the strings to grant or deny this certification.

A year ago, Mboma's longtime friend and colleague, Muhammad Bin Qasim, had headed the International Validation Organization. Like Mboma, Bin Qasim was a Third World success story. The son of an Egyptian college professor, he had grown up in Cairo. The two crossed paths at the Sorbonne in Paris, and a friendship began that survived as the two men climbed the pinnacles of power within a series of well-funded NGOs, and finally the United Nations itself. With the

International Validation Treaty, Bin Qasim had emerged as one of the most powerful men in the world. His power was second only to Mboma's. As head of the International Validation Organization, he could decide when and where nations could go to war, and over what issues.

A year ago, Muhammad Bin Qasim had headed the International Validation Organization, and all was well. Gratuities from supplicants crossed the palms of both friends. It was the prerogative of those within the apogee of power at the United Nations. It always had been. It was the way that business was done. If Bin Qasim kept a little more than he was entitled to, that didn't bother Mboma. From time to time, he might skim a little extra himself.

But suddenly things had changed. There were the terrorist attacks in Denver and Kansas City, and then in Downers Grove, near Chicago. The Americans came begging. President Thomas Livingstone came begging for an International Validation to attack Fahrid Al-Zahir and his international jihadist group, the Mujahidin Al-Akbar. Bin Qasim had the power to refuse, and so he did.

Mboma had smiled, as much for the thought of humiliating the begging Americans as for the $1.3 million that he made shuffling his oil portfolio when only he and Bin Qasim knew what would happen. Then came the jihadist mastermind, Khaleq Badr, whose mysterious Ikhwan Al-Jihad had emerged from nowhere to challenge Fahrid Al-Zahir.

Mboma had been stunned when he had gotten the news. Fahrid Al-Zahir was found dead, in a pool of blood on the floor of Muhammad Bin Qasim's Paris apartment. Bin Qasim had fallen to his death from the balcony a few feet away, and the French police had never determined exactly what had happened. Khaleq Badr, whose mysterious Ikhwan Al-Jihad had emerged from nowhere, vanished into thin air and was never heard from again.

The shock that Mboma felt gradually ebbed. Bin Qasim was dead, and his portfolio as head of the International Validation Organization lay orphaned. Mboma tried it on himself. He liked this. It was the silver lining to the death of his old friend and colleague. Why should Mboma create a successor to Bin Qasim with whom to share the power when he could keep it all as his own? He reshuffled the International Validation Organization bureaucracy, staffed it with supplicants, and became yet more powerful.

The bell rang, and Mboma's personal secretary picked up the intercom. Mboma smiled. His personal secretary was young, but not too young. She was blond, but not too blond. And she was efficient, very efficient.

"The doorman said that Mr. Quintara is here to see you, sir."

"Have him sent up."

Through the years, Enrique Quintara had proven himself as someone who could be trusted. He was the ultimate and stereotypical yes-man. He had no greed for the lifeblood of the back rooms of diplomacy. Money meant nothing to him. Unlike nearly anyone within Mboma's inner sanctum, money could not buy him. The son of a fantastically wealthy Chilean landowner,

Quintara had a unique perspective on wealth. He saw it only as a toy, a piece on a board game. He was a shy man who craved only the opiate rush of the unseen shadow world behind those who romped on the playing field of geopolitical power. Mboma satisfied this craving, and was rewarded with a cunning and able lieutenant who gladly delivered complete loyalty.

"Greetings, my friend," Mboma said, shaking the young man's hand.

"Good day, sir," Quintara replied, showing the senior official the appropriate deference that was due a man of his rank.

Without saying another word, he handed Mboma a Federal Express pack with diplomatic markings on it. The secretary general peeked into the pack—noting the bundles of banknotes sealed in plastic—and placed it on his desk. It was from the powerful foreign minister of a not-so-powerful East African nation. The secretary general had arranged United Nations funding for a major infrastructure project, the foreign minister had extracted approximately 40 percent for making the arrangements, and, of course, the secretary general required his commission for making the funding available. It was only natural. In some more westernized places, this would be called a kickback, but this wasn't one of those places, this was the United Nations. This was how things were done.

"Can you stay?" Mboma asked the younger man. "Could I pour you a drink?"

"We have a problem, sir," Quintara replied without answering the questions. He had a serious look on his face.

"What sort of problem?"

"It's Brunei, sir."

"Brunei? What about Brunei?"

"It's the new sultan, sir."

"Omar, isn't it? Omar Jamalul Halauddin? He's sort of a playboy prince with a great deal of money, is he not?"

"He's got a nuclear weapon, sir," Quintara said nervously. "Maybe several."

"What in God's name does he need with nuclear weapons? Who does he feel threatens him? Malaysia? Indonesia? He shares the island of Borneo with them. Does he fear that one or the other is going to push him into the South China Sea? Certainly they have bigger fish to fry."

"Tomorrow there will be an article in the *New York Times*. It was deliberately leaked to their man in Singapore, or maybe it was a stringer in Kuala Lumpur. In any case, it will say that Brunei intends to acquire the technology."

"There is certainly a wide gulf between acquiring the technology and possessing the weapons."

"My source in the Direction Générale de la Sécurité Extérieure, the DGSE, France's external intelligence agency, tells me that he already *has* the weapons. I'm told that he bypassed the step of acquiring the technology, and just bought the weapons. It was easier and faster."

"Where?" Mboma asked in amazement.

"Anywhere. Maybe the Pakistanis? Maybe the Iranians? Or maybe he just picked them up from an arms dealer in Dushanbe or Tblisi? You know as well as I do that there are hundreds, if not thousands, of Soviet-era artillery shells and tactical aerial bombs that were never accounted for."

"What does he intend to do with them?" Mboma asked. "Who will he use them on?"

"The DGSE thinks that he is taking a page from Kim Jong Il's playbook."

"How do you mean?"

"It is as old as the hills, sir." Quintara shrugged. "It's called extortion."

March 4
1:55 P.M. Mountain Time

PROFESSOR Anne McCaine wheeled the big Mercedes 660 into the broad driveway of the massive "executive home" on the bluff overlooking Boulder, Colorado, that she had shared with her husband for the past eight years. The two electricians unloading the gear from their van across the street looked up when they heard the sound of the door slamming. They could tell by the way that she strode up the curving walkway to the grand portico of the house that this was a very angry woman.

"Some dude is in *big* trouble," one man said as she slammed the big front door of the house.

"But *hell yes*," the other said, nodding in agreement.

Had he still been alive, Dennis McCaine would indeed have been in big trouble—*very* big trouble. Yet it was only in this house that Dennis McCaine was scorned. Except in this house, Dennis McCaine, or at least the memory of the late Dennis McCaine, still inspired acclaim and respect.

He was revered as a truly great man, a self-made man whose civic generosity had become a legend in Colorado. He had been the founding member of Nothal-Corp, who had gone on to buy out his partners at a most auspicious moment. From there, he had ridden the corporate skyrocket to unimaginable heights. As NothalCorp's CEO, he had built the company from a fragile startup into a multinational powerhouse. He had seen its stock double four times, and had seen its corporate headquarters rise above the Denver skyline as the tallest building between Chicago and San Francisco.

Anne had met Dennis at the University of Colorado in Boulder before all of this. Dennis was in the business school, and Anne was studying archaeology. When they met, two decades ago, they were both just undergraduates with the likes and lusts that define college kids as a species unto themselves. While Dennis climbed the corporate ladder with a single vision of the view from the top, Anne stayed in the academic world, with a professorship at the University of Colorado, and had soon achieved distinction in her own right as a globally recognized archaeologist.

Anne and Dennis had lived in their separate worlds, and more and more they were spending long periods of time apart. He worked sixteen-hour days, often flying out to New York or Los Angeles on week-long business junkets. She spent her time mostly teaching, also putting in long hours, and going off for months at a time to, as Dennis put it, "dig up old bones."

Despite this, Anne still loved Dennis and she believed that he loved her. She had never looked at another man, and she believed that he remained true to her as well. Though they were spending a lot of time apart, she looked forward to the time they could spend together. She looked forward to a senior professorship, maybe even head of the department. Then they could spend a lot more time together.

The dream was shattered on that horrible day last November.

It was the day that changed Anne's life forever.

It was the day that changed Denver forever. It was the day that the Mujahidin Al-Akbar terrorists destroyed the NothalCorp Tower, killing thousands of people. Dennis had been in his penthouse office. He never had a chance.

On that terrible day, Anne had been heading an archaeological team in Turkey, excavating the bronze-age temple of Teshub, the Hittite god of Tempests. She hadn't even been on the same continent as her beloved husband. Despite this, fate dealt her a rare opportunity almost never dealt to widows. She had been given the window of opportunity to avenge his death—and she had. She had fired the bullet and had watched as Fahrid Al-Zahir, the man who planned her husband's death, died a painful death at her feet.

Revenge was sweet, but it had done little to fill the void of emptiness that she had felt. She had come home alone to this big house. She had walked the heavily carpeted halls. She had looked at the pictures that hung in nearly every room, and at the mementos of two decades of marriage. She had looked into photographs of the smiling face of the man whose voice she would never hear, and she had cried.

Anne McCaine had cried for hours, just as she had cried twelve years ago when Janie, their little daughter, had died at the age of four months after a terrible battle with a congenital heart defect. At least back then, Anne could lean on Dennis. Now there was no one to hold her when the terrible echoes of Janie's cries reverberated through this huge, now empty, home.

Today was supposed to have been a day of going through the motions. The reading of the will was to have been just a formality. They had community property, and that was hers. There was more than $2 million in their joint stock accounts. There was this house, and the lodge at Aspen, and the condo on Kauai. But since college, they had also kept separate accounts. Anne's was a pittance, compared to his. Nobody gets rich as a college professor. She knew that Dennis was wealthy, fantastically wealthy. She knew that the stock value in NothalCorp had fallen after the terrorist attack, but its assets—and Dennis's—were spread widely around the world.

Anne was prepared for it to be painful, but totally unprepared for the shock that awaited her in the will. The attorneys—there were four—appeared nervous as they opened the large legal-sized document. They knew what was there, but they had shared nothing with Anne until the reading.

Anne listened as she received the preponderance of his estate. She had expected this. She thought of Janie, and the tears poured down her cheeks.

She listened, but only partly, as the attorneys

methodically listed all of the charities to which Dennis
had bequeathed this sum or that. The American Cancer
Society. The Boy Scouts. The Boulder Symphony.
Blah. Blah. Blah. Anne had expected this. She thought
of the generosity of the husband whose touch she
would never again feel, and the tears poured down her
cheeks.

What Anne had not expected was what came next.
Dennis had left a third of a million dollars to Miss
Kristee Lou Laval!

It was like a sharp knife had been plunged into
Anne's stomach. She gasped but could not breathe.
One of the secretaries in the room rushed to hand Anne
a glass of water.

Kristee Lou Laval!

Anne had seen her a time or two when the young
woman was an intern on the executive floor at Nothal-
Corp, but why did Dennis leave her a third of a million
dollars? It was a rhetorical question. In the split second that it took the knife to pierce her stomach, she
knew.

Anne didn't need the embarrassed attorneys to explain that Miss Laval had been Mr. McCaine's mis-
tress and that they had been there when he asked that
she be provided for. Anne didn't *want* the embarrassed
attorneys to explain that Miss Laval was deceased, and
that she had been with Mr. McCaine when the terrorists destroyed the NothalCorp Tower. They didn't say,
but Anne suddenly and painfully realized, that Miss
Kristee Lou Laval had died in the arms of Dennis Mc-
Caine.

As she slammed the big door of the massive

executive home on the bluff overlooking Boulder, Anne McCaine found herself surrounded by the artifacts of her late husband's greatness. On the wall near the grand entry to the vast executive living room, with its twenty-five-foot beamed ceiling and floor-to-ceiling windows, were numerous framed photographs of Dennis with this senator or that, Dennis with this governor or that, Dennis with former presidents, Dennis with the archbishop, and Dennis with the Dalai Lama.

Anne walked to the hallowed shrine and seized the large executive portrait of her husband and flung it as hard as she could at the opposite wall. As the glass shattered, she began pulling the other pictures of Dennis down one by one and crushing them beneath her three-inch heels. She took down his honorary doctorate from Yale and tossed it into the yawning maw of the massive executive fireplace.

She walked to the huge wall of windows and stared out at the panoramic view of Boulder and the skyline of Denver in the distance. When she had come back to Denver having watched as the man who planned her husband's death died a painful death at her feet, the sight of that skyline without the NothalCorp Tower had brought a surge of tears. And so it was today, but the tears came from a completely different place within her, within the tortuous and convoluted mix of emotions that she felt.

The face that looked back at her from the reflection in the glass was the tired face of an exhausted woman, used and spent and deceived. The gray streak in her hair stood out in the indirect lighting in the room, lighting that accentuated the lines that she imagined

seeing in her face. She thought back to the photograph
of Miss Kristee Lou Laval in the attorney's office.
Miss Kristee Lou Laval, with her perfect blond hair,
her perfect pouty smile, her perfect pink cheeks, and
the strand of pearls, a gift, no doubt, from the great
and glorious Saint Dennis McCaine. Anne stared at
the tired face of the exhausted widow, used and spent
and discarded without even knowing it.

Anne kicked off her shoes, sat down on one of the
vast sofas in the huge living room, curled her emotionally and physically drained self into a ball, and sobbed
uncontrollably.

She must have dozed off slightly, because when she
opened her eyes, it was nearing dusk. A stream of light
entering from the west had fallen across the mantel
above the fireplace and the small bronze sculpture of
the goddess Astarte that had been crafted by a Hittite
artisan around 2000 BC and 1000 BC.

Anne remembered the night in Paris when she had
first held this little bronze. It was at Gallerie L'Aiglon
on Rue de Varenne. Anne was masquerading as the
Cambridge-educated personal curator to a Bavarian
billionaire antiquities collector, who was actually a retired American Special Forces colonel. When she had
first touched this exquisite little artifact, she and this
trained killer were within an hour of that moment
when Fahrid Al-Zahir died his painful death at their
feet.

Anne remembered that night, in that tiny Paris
bistro an hour after the terrorist died, the tall man with
the auburn mustache, whom she hardly knew but had
come to trust like no other, had bashfully handed her

this little bronze. He gave it to her as a memento of a shared experience, a shared experience like no other.

Touched by the intensifying golden rays of the sinking sun, Astarte seemed to be looking at Anne and to be telling her that her old world was gone, abruptly and forever. Astarte also seemed to be telling Anne that if she listened to herself, she already knew where her new world would begin.

March 5
3:55 A.M. Eastern Time

"**G**O back to sleep, Tom," Joyce Livingstone moaned. "It's four in the morning. You can sleep for another hour and a half. *I* need another hour and a half. I *want* another eight hours."

President Thomas J. Livingstone had just entered his fourth year in office. It had not been an easy three years, and now he had to work double time to run for reelection. So far he had no challengers from within the party, but nevertheless, he had to appear in every state where there was a primary. He had to show the flag. He had to raise money for the fall, and this meant rubber-chicken dinners four or five nights a week. Some weeks, these were all in different states. So far, there was no clear front-runner among the opposition, but that was only temporary. Livingstone could not rest.

As he had discovered four years ago, running for president was more than a full-time job. However, so too was *being* the president. Now he had the dubious joy of doing *both,* and of dragging Joyce from one end of the country to the other. The only time they had seen their grandchildren since Thanksgiving was at photo ops.

It had been a hard four years. So far, the signature event of Livingstone's presidency had been the terrorist attacks last year. Fahrid Al-Zahir and his Mujahidin Al-Akbar had left smoking ruins in Denver and Kansas City, with thousands of Americans dead on their own soil. But the United States had been powerless to act. Without an International Validation from the United Nations, there was nothing that Livingstone could do.

In desperation, he had reached out to General Buckley Peighton, a retired Special Forces officer, whom Tom Livingstone had known when both men were just college kids. Livingstone reminded Buck Peighton of a story from more than half a century ago. General Claire Chennault was a former Army Air Corps general who went to China to set up the American Volunteer Group to fight the Japanese before the United States got into World War II. President Franklin Roosevelt used him to covertly fight the Japanese invasion of China at a time when the United States military could not yet act overtly.

Livingstone had asked Peighton to find him a Chennault, and he had. Livingstone did not know, and did not *want* to know, *who* it was, but Peighton had found a Chennault. Then, Fahrid Al-Zahir wound up dead, and Mujahidin Al-Akbar withered and collapsed. Livingstone's Chennault had done it, and Livingstone never knew the man's name, or how he did it. As far as the world knew, Al-Zahir was killed by a rival gangster named Khaleq Badr. Outside the shadowy clique of former Special Forces men that Livingstone asked Peighton to create, only Tom Livingstone knew that Badr was really an American, but that was *all* he knew.

The work had been done, and Livingstone's Chennault had simply faded away. That was probably just as well. If it came out in an election year that the president had created a secret private army, he could kiss reelection good-bye.

Tom Livingstone listened carefully. The rhythmic ripping sound from the other side of the bed told him that Joyce was asleep again, so he grabbed the remote off the nightstand and clicked on the news channel.

The talking head was chattering about a world tour by a Latina pop singer named Caprice. Another one of those little divas with one name. He remembered Cher, and Madonna, and Beyoncé—and, of course, Liberace. He was sure there were others, but he couldn't think of them. Caprice probably could.

There was nothing else happening yet, and it was obviously a slow news day. Everybody seemed to want to know this girl. Livingstone had heard the name constantly, but to him, it meant just another pretty, young face in an endless succession of divas with only one name. They seemed to come and go faster than he cared to keep track. Maybe his grandchildren had her on their iPods. Maybe not. He hadn't actually talked to them in three years. He only saw them at photo ops.

Suddenly, the screen changed.

A bulletin. A different talking head. The backdrop was a still of a pudgy man in a fez. It was what's-his-name, the new Sultan of Brunei.

The talking head started talking. There was breaking news. There was an article in the *New York Times*. The sultan was acquiring nukes! There was already a rumor that he already *had* nukes!

"Holy shit!" Livingstone shouted at the screen.

"Tom!" replied his wife, her head still buried in the comforter with the Early American motif that the White House decorators had insisted upon. The news reader on the screen had not heard the president's bellowing expletive, but *she* had. "What is it? Let me sleep."

"It's the Sultan of Brunei," he explained. "The guy has got nukes."

"Oh, no," Joyce Livingstone moaned, rolling over and grabbing her glasses to have a look at the screen. Her husband was already on the phone to Steve Faralaco.

"Steve," he shouted at his hard-working chief of staff, who was still asleep when the phone rang at his Alexandria town house. "Turn on your television right now. The *Times* is reporting that the Sultan of Brunei has got nuclear weapons. Why the hell didn't we know this? Get the director of national intelligence in my office in one hour. I want a briefing. Get Edredin in there too."

March 5
5:06 A.M. Eastern Time

SECRETARY of State John Edredin arrived at the Oval Office with his necktie askew. He had obviously been awakened as suddenly as the others at the meeting. He eagerly accepted the cup of coffee that Steve Faralaco offered. The president was fuming, and everyone in the room was on the hot seat, especially Director of National Intelligence Richard Scevoles.

"What in the hell happened here?" Livingstone asked, looking at Scevoles. "Why didn't we know about this, and what are we going to do about it?"

"On the scale of things in this world, Brunei has been pretty far down the list of problem areas," Scevoles explained. "It's somewhere between Andorra and Vanuatu. With the Middle East at a full boil and Africa on fire, we have really not had the agents and analysts to give every area of the earth the same sort of attention. And these stateless mobsters like Fahrid Al-Zahir and Khaleq Badr running around the place have been a much greater threat than countries."

"Okay, assuming for a moment that I accept this excuse for not knowing about this thing yesterday, what can you tell me about this character today?" Livingstone asked. He figured that he had made his point, and to push it farther would open the door for Scevoles asking for more money for his agency.

"Mr. President," the director began. "As we know, Omar Jamalul Halauddin took power in a back-room power grab when his cousin died, acquiring the money and power that comes with being more or less one of the world's richest men. He also took over one of the world's smallest and most marginally important countries. Like I said, it's been like Vanuatu. We think that he's out to use his money to buy some respect."

"So now we're looking at this clown as the Rodney Dangerfield of dangerous rulers?" Livingstone quipped. "John, what can we do about this diplomatically?"

"He hasn't actually threatened anyone," the secretary of state replied. "He hasn't actually said that he would attack anyone. The article in the *Times* says only that he intends to obtain the technology. The stories that are all over the cable channels this morning about him already having it are just rumors."

"Where there's smoke, there's fire," Livingstone told the men in the room. "We need to operate under the worst-case assumption and develop a plan for dealing with this."

March 5
7:02 A.M. Central Time

"I don't think he's going to make it, he's unconscious. Over," the voice cracked out of the big two-way radio base station speakers. "He needs to be medevaced out of here, like now! Do you copy?"

"We copy you, Delta Platform," the man at the console said nervously. "But we can't get a chopper out there in this storm, over."

"He's gonna die on us if you don't."

The storm had been lashing the Gulf Coast from Port Arthur to Lake Charles for about six hours and there was no letup in sight. Bobby Girardeau had been working on an offshore oil rig and he was suffering—and suffering was indeed the word—from appendicitis. With the storm tracking in, the rigs had been evacuated, but Bobby and two others had remained at Delta Platform to finish lashing things down. The storm blew in faster than anyone expected and there they were.

The rain and wind slammed the radio shack like a fist. People were talking, and comparing it to the Category 5 hell-storms back in 2005 that flooded New Orleans and leveled everything from Lake Charles to Biloxi. It wasn't nearly that bad, but it was bad enough to bring back nightmares. The thing that reminded people about the other storms was not so much the intensity, but the way this tempest just sat on them. It was like a heel grinding something into the ground.

The state police emergency helicopter crew up in Lake Charles was not willing to fly until things calmed down. Even the Coast Guard was still grounded.

"See this," Greg Boyinson said, pointing to the computer screen displaying the United States Weather Bureau satellite downloads. "These patches in the dark purple are breaks."

"Those aren't breaks, they're little patches of terrible weather in the midst of a solid mass of very terrible weather," his boss replied. "I hope you aren't thinking of doing something stupid."

"You know damned well what I'm thinking."

Greg Boyinson was the company chopper pilot, operating the Bell Jet Ranger between the base south of Lake Charles and the company's nine offshore oil rigs in the Gulf. He was no stranger to bad weather and no stranger to difficult flying. During his years in U.S. Army Special Forces, he had flown Rangers,

Delta Teams—and units that officially didn't exist—
in and out of tight spots on five continents. In the
cockpit of one chopper or another, he had triggered
weapons that killed bad guys in trucks, cars, SUVs,
tanks, and other helicopters. Last year, he had flown a
sniper in to kill a jihadi who was trying to blow up the
Eiffel Tower. Of course, he never talked about most
of this. He couldn't, and who would believe him if
he did?

Nor did he need to talk about what he had done.
There were an awful lot of people in the world who
owed their existence to his flying ability. Boyinson got
his flying jobs by word of mouth, and kept them by
proving that he was everything his reputation said he
was. On the other hand, his reputation said a lot about
his behavior on the ground, and he left a lot of broken
tavern furniture in his wake to testify to the "bad boy"
aspect of his behavior.

Today, the boss knew exactly what Greg Boyinson
was thinking. He was watching the storm on radar and
trying to find enough of a path to dash out to Delta
Platform and snatch Bobby Girardeau.

"You are *not* going out there, and that's final," Carl
Carruthers said sternly. "You'd be risking not only
yourself, but Bobby, if you crash on your way back."

"Bobby's dead for sure if I don't go, and you know it."

"So are you if you go out there, and you'll lose the
chopper too."

"The chopper's insured."

"Don't do it," Carruthers shouted angrily. Boyinson
was already zipping on his foul-weather gear as the radio crackled to life again.

"Delta Platform to Base, come in Base. Bobby is really bad. Can't you do something? Please. Over."

Boyinson and the radio man looked at the boss, and he said nothing.

The wind was so strong that it was difficult for Boyinson to push the door open.

March 6
8:07 A.M. Eastern Time

"**M**ORE coffee, sir?"

President Thomas Livingstone shook his head. Two days ago things were bad enough. He was running for reelection against the backdrop of a sluggish economy, and there were rumors that gadfly congressman from California was going to challenge him in the primaries. That was then. Now, things were spinning out of control.

Domestic politics were just a parlor game compared to what happened internationally. Bad economic data could be massaged. Sluggish economic factors could be finessed. Political opposition could be spun. But when somebody out there in the world beyond did something, it was hard to get ahead of the problem.

Overnight, Sultan Omar Jamalul Halauddin had let the other shoe drop. Yes, the rumors were true. Yes, he had nuclear weapons, and he was prepared to use them.

Two U.S. Navy Seventh Fleet destroyers had transitioned the Balabac Strait last week, traveling westward from the Sulu Sea into the South China Sea. They were threatening Brunei, asserted Sultan Omar Jamalul Halauddin.

"The bastard is trying to pick a fight."

Admiral Michael J. Felth, the chief of naval operations, did not mince words.

"Apparently," Livingstone agreed.

"The Balabac Strait separates Philippine waters from those of Malaysia's Sabah Province," Felth explained, pointing to a small map that he had grabbed on his way out the door of his Pentagon office twenty minutes earlier. "The Seventh Fleet passes through there all the time. Hell, we've been operating in those waters for more than a hundred years. We even did joint exercises with the Brunei Navy back in the nineties . . . the CARAT exercises . . . Cooperation Afloat Readiness & Training. We'd go in there and train them in at-sea maneuvering, command and control, diving and salvage, force protection, maritime patrol, jungle ops. Lots of things."

"The Balabac Strait looks a long way from Brunei," the president observed, staring at the map.

"It is," Felth replied. "Brunei is over three hundred miles away. Our ships were nowhere near his country. Not even remotely near his territorial waters, but yet Omar thinks he's threatened?"

"He's not threatened," Secretary of State Edredin interjected. "He's just posturing. This thing will blow over in a week or so."

"But we're still stuck with a sunuvabitch with nukes," Admiral Felth cautioned. "Just say the word and

I'll have a carrier battle group in there to put this sunuvabitch outa business."

"You know we can't do that, Admiral," Edredin chided. "Without an International Validation, we cannot attack anybody, and with the current leadership in the United Nations, that is not going to happen."

Everyone glanced at Livingstone. Of all the things he'd done in his first term, signing the International Validation Treaty was the one that he regretted most. In a perfect world, order and balance would have been insured because the member states of the United Nations had subscribed to the notion that only the world body could issue an International Validation certification to permit any nation to act militarily outside its borders.

Unfortunately, the world was filled with people who did not play by the rules. Livingstone had learned this when the Mujahadin Al-Akbar terrorists had killed all those people in Denver and Kansas City.

"Attacking Brunei would get this country in a lot of hot water around the world," Edredin cautioned. As secretary of state, diplomatically massaging the image of the country in the world was his not-so-easy full-time job.

"It's not like we don't already have that problem," Steve Faralaco added. "I was just looking at streaming news reports on my computer before I came in here. The demonstrations at our embassies in Nairobi and Djakarta have turned violent."

"Oh, great," Felth snarled. "This kook in Brunei is threatening the world with nukes and *we're* the bad guys!"

March 6
8:11 A.M. Eastern Time

"**I** thought I told you to hold my calls!" Secretary General Baudouin Abuja Mboma roared. He was the most powerful man in the world and in times of global crisis, *everyone* in the world thought they needed to speak to him. He thought of them all as being like the people that he saw swarming along First Avenue far below his huge corner office in the United Nations World Headquarters. They were like ants, and he was the most powerful man in the world. He told his secretary not to let them bother him.

Mboma had been just as startled as President Livingstone when Sultan Omar had rattled his nuclear sabre. The secretary general was never disappointed when anyone rattled a sabre at the United States, but even he felt queasy when the adjective "nuclear" was applied. This could get out of hand. Things could escalate out of control. Mboma had the world and global harmony to be concerned about. He also had a carefully groomed stock portfolio.

Like the president of the United States, the secretary general had been huddling with his advisors, trying to figure out what could be done. François Lumiere, French ambassador to the United Nations, had stopped by, and Mboma had sent for Brunei's ambassador, Pehin Dato Hudim Incpaduka.

"I'm most sorry, sir," his secretary stammered in a quavering voice. She was a good girl. A native of Sri Lanka, she had been educated in France at the Sorbonne and in the United States at Rutgers. Nevertheless, she had the kind of Third World innocence that played so well at the secretary general's public office. At his home office, Mboma's personal secretary was icily efficient. After all, she *was* Icelandic. But at his public office, Third World charm was so much more important than efficiency.

"When I said to hold my calls, I meant to hold my calls. I don't have to tell you that there is a world crisis in the making. I am meeting with the French ambassador!"

"But sir, most distinguished sir, it's *him*. It's David Wilcox, sir."

Wilcox. The former United States president turned global reconciliator. Since leaving office he had reinvented himself as the paragon of international good guy—despite having left the United States with the legacy of double-digit interest rates and his disastrous failure to react decisively during the coal strike. The remade Wilcox became a global nice guy by touring famine-stricken world trouble spots with a videocam-toting entourage.

Thanks to the efforts of his spin doctors, Wilcox took home a Nobel Peace Prize for brokering an armistice in the Horn of Africa—despite the fact that the smiling warlord photographed with Wilcox that sunny day in Djibouti murdered the other warlord with a machete a week after the Nobel awards. This had led to a massacre that left nineteen thousand corpses floating slowly downstream in the Giuba River, but by then, the grinning Wilcox was in Guatemala, giving network interviews about an orphanage project on whose letterhead his name was featured.

Wilcox. The media loved him and followed him wherever he went. Mboma had used him, and been used by him. He was always good for pubic relations. They had shared a few photo ops when the theme was humanitarianism, or when Wilcox happened to be in New York doing the morning shows.

"What a pleasure to hear you, David," the secretary general lied amiably. "I didn't know that you were in town."

"Ah'm not, Baudouin. But I'm heading up that way," the ex-president explained in his Kentucky drawl. "I figured that we ought to talk about this Brunei thing. I figure that I might have a word or two with that gentleman over there and help get things settled down."

"That would be very good, Mr. President," Mboma lied again. "When will you be in New York? I can have my secretary put you on the schedule. Shall we meet for lunch next week?"

"Well, actually, I'm in the Gulfstream right now. How 'bout today?"

The secretary general grimaced. He hated last-minute changes to his schedule, but this could not be avoided. Better sooner than later anyway. Mboma suggested La Grenouille on East Fifty-second Street, and they agreed on 1:30. It was impossible to get the private room at La Grenouille on short notice, unless, of course, the secretary general of the United Nations was dining with an ex-president.

"Wilcox has offered to 'have a word or two' with Sultan Omar," Mboma explained to Lumiere and the others. "He believes that his personal intercession could defuse the situation."

"You seem skeptical," Lumiere said, reacting to Mboma's sarcastic tone.

"And you are *not*?"

"What could it hurt?" Lumiere shrugged. "Omar is obviously blustering to embarrass Livingstone and the United States. Wilcox has done everything possible to distance himself from Livingstone and United States policy. He has made himself the antithesis of Livingstone, no? The world hates America. The world hates Livingstone, but they love Wilcox because he is the antithesis of Livingstone. Just being seen with Wilcox will help Omar to embarrass Livingstone. It will be like rubbing his nose in shit."

"Ahhh." The secretary general smiled. "I can see how this could work."

March 6
12:27 P.M. Mountain Time

THE roads grew progressively narrower the farther north that Anne McCaine drove. It was a fast drive as she had taken Interstate 15 north from Ogden, and Interstate 90 west from Butte, but as she turned north on old U.S. 93 near Evaro, the road narrowed. As she followed Montana Route 35 around Flathead Lake, the two-lane highway became even narrower.

It was an unusually warm day for this time of year in the northern Rockies, and Anne McCaine enjoyed the drive as the landscape grew progressively more rugged. The mountains of the Mission Range seemed close enough to touch, and the steep cliffs of Badrock

Canyon reminded her of that place at St. Goarshausen on the Rhine where Lorelei lured mariners to their death.

Anne let her mind wander to what she was allowing herself to be lured into. She marveled at the madness of the impulse that had made her take this drive. Eight months ago, she had been methodical and organized, a careful and deliberate administrator. Now she was acting like an impulsive schoolgirl. She wasn't acting her age, and it was both exhilarating and frightening. Eight months ago, the idea of impetuously picking up and driving eight hundred miles to visit a man she barely knew would have been preposterous, but a great deal had changed in Anne McCaine's life in those eight months.

A sign framed against a wall of lodgepole pine trees indicated that the town of Belton, Montana, was just four miles ahead, and a lump rose in Anne's throat.

When she had phoned that number that he had given her, she knew that she was placing a call into a dark world of soldiers of fortune that few knew existed. It was a number that few could know, and that almost no one could call. Even the president of the United States could not phone this number. She knew that she was penetrating a hidden world of what they called Special Ops that was secret beyond top secret. It was a world that in a million years a person like her would never know existed, but she did because she had fallen into it and for a brief few days she had been a part of it. Anne had been there that night, with this man, as Fahrid Al-Zahir died his painful death at their feet. They had shared an experience like no other, and they shared a number that even the president of the United States could not know.

Anne had left Paris believing that she would never use this number, but that changed on the day they read the will. On that day, she knew that her old world was gone, abruptly and forever. This number became her link to what she knew was the next turn in her next life. It was like jumping into darkness, and it was terrifying.

Their conversation had been brief. She spoke her name, and he had seemed stunned to hear her voice. His reply was simply a date and time. The place, she knew, was written on the inside of the little matchbox from that tiny Paris bistro.

It was a warm and sunny day, unusually pleasant for northwestern Montana this time of year, but Anne was scared. She was driving into the dark abyss of the unknown. She started halfheartedly looking for a wide place in the lonely highway to make a U-turn as the contradictory voices in her head argued whether she should just end this capricious adventure and head back to Denver.

Suddenly, she came around a sharp bend to the right and found herself staring at the jagged and spectacular peaks of the Lewis Range of the Rockies inside Glacier National Park. The Lewis Range always takes newcomers by surprise, even those used to the Colorado Rockies. These peaks seem so much taller and steeper than their Colorado counterparts because their rise from the mean elevation of the valley floor is so much greater.

Anne was so caught up with the view that she was

distracted from her dilemma. The road dipped down into the valley, and the sign that told her that she had arrived before she could make her U-turn. She passed the junction where the road into Glacier National Park peeled off to the left, and she studied the short row of buildings on the right. She saw the gas station, and the old lodge building up ahead, and there, between them, was the Glacier View Tavern. The sign looked as though it had been old in the 1950s, and though the paint might have been touched up a time or two, neither time had been recent. The building itself made the sign look new. It had probably been constructed as a trapper's cabin at the turn of the last century, and the logs with which it was built were weathered and gray.

Anne had reached the point of no return, and the momentum pulled her forward. She parked her Mercedes in the gravel strip that separated the ancient building from the semis passing on U.S. Highway 2. She opened her purse and slid back the lid of the little matchbox. For the hundredth time, she read the cryptic note penned there that night by the man who had handed her the Hittite bronze as a memento of a shared experience like no other.

There was no doubt. Here, half a world and a million miles away, she had arrived.

Anne self-consciously checked her makeup in the rearview mirror and stepped out of the car. The Benz with its Colorado plates looked as out of place here in this small parking lot as Anne felt. She had passed the point of no return, and the momentum pulled her into the unknown.

She looked around. There was an old Chevy Malibu with red tape for taillights and two battered pickups with gun racks in their back windows. Both gun racks held the obligatory hunting rifle, and one also had a pair of fishing rods.

Parked immediately adjacent to the door of the old bar was a dark blue Ford F150. In its rack were two of the most meticulously cared-for bolt-action Winchester 30-06 rifles she had ever seen. Except for the well-worn, but well-polished, stocks, they might have been brand-new. The scopes were enormous, and it was clear to Anne that either one of them was worth more than the pickup. This, and the initials DB lettered on a pair of saddlebags draped across one of the saddles lying in the box of the truck, assured her that she was in the right place.

The lump in her throat was back.

The momentum carried her to the doorway of the tavern, and she pushed her sunglasses to the top of her head and peered into the darkness within. The jukebox was playing a song by the great Johnny Russell, and a cowboy was having a heated conversation with the pinball machine. Some guy was on a pay phone in the corner, and the neon sign on the back bar promoted a beer called Moose Drool. The woman in the tight T-shirt behind the bar could have been a runway model—except for her eyepatch.

As Anne's eyes grew accustomed to the dark, they fell upon a table in the corner and met the gaze of two men she recognized from a very different place, a very long way from here.

March 6
2:43 P.M. Eastern Time

I T seemed like déjà vu all over again. As he watched
the presentation by the director of national intelligence, President Thomas Livingstone felt as though he
had traveled back in time to October 1962, to the day
that John F. Kennedy sat in this very room and looked
at the aerial photographs of Soviet ballistic missiles in
Cuba. Back then, they were black-and-white images,
exposed on negative film in cameras carried by air-
planes at great peril to their pilots. Today, they were in
color, exposed on digital chips in cameras carried by
Keyhole satellites at no peril to anyone. But that was
where the dissimilarities ended.

"This one shows the main base of the Tentera Laut
Diraja Brunei, the Royal Brunei Navy, at Muara, up
the coast from the capital," Richard Scevoles explained.

"That's about half their navy in port," Admiral
Michael Felth said, stabbing his finger at the piers
reaching into Brunei Bay. "They've got three Waspada-
class guided-missile ships and three Nakhoda Ragam-
class offshore patrol vessels. All of them are fitted out
with Exocet surface-to-surface missiles. That's essentially their whole blue-water navy. They also have a
few Perwira-class inshore patrol boats, some armed
river craft, and about two dozen police patrol boats,
but the offshore patrol vessels and the Waspadas are
the main part of the fleet."

"I see the three larger ships," the Director of National Intelligence observed.

"That's KDB *Seteria* and KDB *Sajuang,* two of the missile ships. The third one, KDB *Pemburu,* was at sea when that picture was taken earlier today. So were KDB *Kakhoda Ragam* and KDB *Bendahare Sakam,* two of the offshore patrol vessels. KDB stands for Kapal Diraja Brunei, which means 'Ship of the Rajah of Brunei.' The other larger ship you see here is KDB *Depambak,* the newest of the Nakhoda Ragams. She was built in Scotland at BAE Systems and launched about six years ago. She displaces about fifteen hundred tons and has a top speed of thirty knots and a range of five thousand nautical miles at about half speed. She's got an Alenia Marconi Nautis II command and fire-control system, plus an AWS-9 E/F-band surveillance and target-indication radar, and a couple of 1802SW radar trackers."

"It looks like it's being repaired or something," the president said, squinting at the picture.

"She's being retrofitted to fire the damned nukes," Felth replied.

"I see."

"Yeah, normally the Nakhoda Ragams have eight MBDA MM40 Block 2 Exocet launchers. They're pulling out six of these on the KDB *Depambak* to put in three of these launchers for larger weapons."

"What weapons?" Livingstone asked.

"See these greenish things in this area next to the dark-colored building?" Richard Scevoles asked, pointing to an area below the docks.

"Yeah, I count four of them."

"These are Iranian Khomeini-6 surface-to-surface missiles. They're powered by simple jet engines and

have a range of about four hundred miles, about half
that of our BGM-109D Tomahawks."

"And these things can carry nuclear warheads?"

"Yes, Mr. President."

"Did they get them from Iran?"

"Directly or indirectly."

"Why would they have them out in the open like
this?"

"So we can see them."

"Why?"

"So that we'd know they aren't bluffing."

March 6
2:44 P.M. Mountain Time

COLONEL Dave Brannan had been up since long
before dawn had been a pinkish-purple promise in
the eastern sky. He had a neighbor that raised free-
range chickens, but free-ranging coyotes were eating
into his profits and he had asked Dave to help out. Co-
incidentally, Will Casey was at Dave's place and he
offered to pitch in. Who better to eradicate a pack of
troublesome wild dogs than the best sniper ever to
serve with the United States Special Forces?

The bait was set last night, and a few hours of
tracking and shooting this morning had removed the
coyote problem. The two men had sat down for a late
breakfast at the diner adjacent to the Conoco station
by about ten. Will had wanted to get on the road before
nightfall, but they were engrossed in conversation, so
Dave had suggested that they have a quick pint at the

tavern before parting company. It was always good to catch up with old friends, especially with men from his Special Operations days with whom he had formed the special bond of men who have shared being on the same side in exchanges of hostile gunfire.

Before they had left the service, Will had served under Colonel Brannan in the U.S. Army Special Forces. Last fall, when Fahrid Al-Zahir and his Mujahidin Al-Akbar terrorist gang had begun slaughtering Americans, President Thomas Livingstone had reached out to retired General Buck Peighton to do something. His solution had been to form an off-the-books team to track down and kill Al-Zahir. To lead such a team, Peighton had had only one choice—Dave Brannan.

Once again, Will Casey had served under Dave Brannan. Who better to eradicate a pack of troublesome wild dogs like the Mujahidin Al-Akbar than the best sniper ever to serve with American Special Forces? As with the wild dogs this morning, those wild dogs were now consigned to history.

A shadow passed in front of the doorway, blocking the sunlight, and the corner of Dave's eye glanced around instinctively to see what it was. The flash of recognition nearly caused him to drop his pint of Black Diamond Stout. It was a woman in a short mustard-colored sundress and a faded denim jacket. A pair of sunglasses was perched atop her head, and her long dark hair swept across her shoulders. The perfect shape of her legs and the flawless contours of her body were accentuated by her being silhouetted in the open door. His eyes met hers in instant mutual recognition.

"Professor, it's good to see you," Dave said, rising

to greet Anne McCaine. "When we talked, I wasn't sure that you'd come. It's *awfully* good to see you."

"Never underestimate the value of an address scribbled in a matchbox, Colonel." She smiled, giving him a slight hug.

"You remember Will, dontcha, Professor?" Dave said, introducing his companion. "You met him when we were doing that job over in Turkey."

"Of course I do," Anne said with a smile, shaking Will's hand.

Anne had crossed paths with Brannan and Casey, and the rest of the Raptor Team, in Turkey when she was out there excavating the temple of god of tempests. She fell into a tempest herself when terrorists killed half of her archaeological team. The Raptor Team came to the rescue, but she was able to return the favor by using her encyclopedic knowledge of Hittite sculpture to help track Al-Zahir. In addition to his passion for butchering infidels, the terrorist boss was an obsessive collector of antiquities. He had died in a pool of blood beneath a coffee table that contained several prized items from his collection. One of those pieces now sat on her mantel in Boulder.

"I hate to be one to run out on a conversation, but I've gotta grab my rifle outa the colonel's pickup and hit the road," Will said as Anne sat down at the table. "It was nice to see you again, Professor. I hope that you'll have a nice visit to Montana."

Casey chuckled to himself as he left the bar. The colonel hadn't taken his eyes off the professor since she walked in.

She was a small woman, about five feet five, with

dark wavy hair and dark gray eyes that cast a riveting gaze. The streak of gray in her hair and the lines around the corners of her eyes had told Dave that she was probably in her forties, close to his age, but her slender, well-toned body was that of a woman of twenty-five.

The first time that Dave Brannan had seen Anne McCaine, she was holding a rifle and wearing a scabbard with an enormous knife strapped to her thigh. Today, the hem of her dress barely covered her thigh, and she was armed only with an enormous smile that completely disarmed the ex–Special Forces commander.

March 6
3:47 P.M. Eastern Time

A light rain was falling as the big black cars lined up on East Fifty-second Street. Police were directing crosstown traffic, and a handful of people paused to see what was going on. Former President David Wilcox, surrounded by his Secret Service detail, smiled and waved at people on the street and inside the restaurant. Secretary General Baudouin Mboma and Enrique Quintara barely acknowledged the onlookers. Nobody even noticed Brunei's United Nations ambassador, Pehin Dato Hudim Incpaduka, as he scuttled across the sidewalk and into La Grenouille.

The four men and their small coterie of advisors seated themselves in the private dining room, and Mboma asserted his authority by ordering the wine. He wanted everyone to know that he was in charge, although in the back of his mind, he was unsure what turns the meeting would take.

When the wine had been served, and there had been the requisite duration of small talk, Mboma told Incpaduka—so that all could hear—that the United Nations and the world community had great respect for the sovereignty of Brunei, and its right to protect itself from any threat, real or perceived, from a bellicose superpower. Having said that, he added a checklist of other nations, including Malaysia and Indonesia—which shared the island of Borneo with Brunei—that were "gravely concerned" about a nuclear arms race in Southeast Asia.

"My nation is also concerned," Incpaduka replied. "We are a small country, and an isolated country. We are a vulnerable country. The nations with whom we share Borneo possess a military capability much greater than ours, and they have used their muscle. Remember Indonesia with Timor. And, of course, the Americans are constantly projecting their naval power into our region."

"Ah'm sure that something could be done about the American Seventh Fleet," Wilcox said in a conciliatory tone. "I could speak to President Livingstone. We could arrange a five-hundred-mile exclusion zone. Ah'm sure that he would agree to that in the interest of peace."

"Thank you, Mr. President," Incpaduka replied. "If we could make that seven hundred fifty miles, I'm confident that His Majesty would be more at ease."

"See, all it takes is a little face-to-face communication," Wilcox said, grinning his professionally polished grin. "That's the way to make the world a safer place."

Mboma winced. It could not have been that easy, he thought.

He was right.

"As I said, Negara Brunei Darussalam is an iso-lated country," Incpaduka continued, using the full name of his country for emphasis and ignoring Wilcox. "This must change. His Majesty will not accept such a gesture if it is tossed off at a meeting half a world away."

"That's no problem," Wilcox interjected. "Ah'd be happy to go out to the sultanate and sit down with him. We could announce the exclusion zone there in your capital, in Bandar Seri Begawan. Ah'm sure that some-one from the state department could come out with me. The media would be sure to cover it. My people would see to that."

"You're on the right track, Mr. President." Inc-paduka smiled. "But make sure that it's not merely 'somebody' from the state department. Make sure that you bring Secretary of State John Edredin."

The smile faded from Wilcox's face. Getting Edredin to go along with this was far easier said than done. Wilcox knew that he was despised within the Livingstone administration. He knew Livingstone and Edredin would do him no favors, but he knew that everyone had a common interest in getting Brunei's nuclear genie back into its lamp.

"I'm sure that Secretary Edredin would be delighted to join President Wilcox in a peace mission to the sultanate," Mboma said. Personally, *he* was certainly

delighted at the prospect of Edredin traveling around
the world to admit the weakness of the United States
and hand concessions to the sultan.

"Yes, this is a positive step, but it is only a step,"
Incpaduka said, turning to Mboma. "Negara Brunei
Darussalam can no longer remain a footnote in the
back corner of world affairs. The world must now accept and *respect* the sultanate as the world power that
we are."

"I don't believe that any nation, aside from perhaps
the United States, has shown Brunei any intentional
disrespect," Mboma asserted. "Certainly, all members
of the United Nations accept the sultanate as a full
member of the community of nations."

"Then I'm sure that the United Nations would not
be opposed to declaring the archaeological findings in
the vicinity of the port town of Tutong as a UNESCO
World Heritage Site. UNESCO defines such places as
sites of outstanding cultural or natural importance to
the common heritage of humankind, and I think that
we have one that meets that criteria."

"Of course, we'll arrange for an appropriate announcement befitting so important a designation," the
secretary general readily agreed. He knew nothing about
this site, but it would be extremely easy to arrange a ceremony and have a plaque made.

"And of course, that designation must come with a
UNESCO grant in the amount of one *billion* dollars to
provide suitable safeguards for the archaeological
treasures."

Now it was Mboma's turn to be speechless. He
wasn't used to being blackmailed. He had walked into

La Grenouille the world's most powerful man, and now he was being mugged by a little punk in a fez with a smirk on his face.

"A *billion* dollars?" Mboma stammered.

"That would be a very nice gesture." Incpaduka smiled. "His Majesty would feel *very* secure as a prominent head of state of a recognized world power, if you know what I mean."

Everyone did. Sultan Omar Jamalul Halauddin wanted to be bribed to put his nuke back in the box, and Mboma had no choice but to see that it was done.

"Oh, and there's one more thing," Incpaduka said, turning to Wilcox in an offhand manner. "I'm wondering if you could do His Majesty a little favor?"

"What would that be?" Wilcox asked apprehensively. The man in the fez had already extorted a billion dollars and asked to have the secretary of state come groveling. What kind of favor did he want?

"His Majesty is a very big fan of the American pop singer Caprice, who is currently on a world tour. Could you speak with whoever it would be who could arrange for Caprice to make a command performance at his Istana Nurul Iman palace in Bandar Seri Begawan?"

March 6
5:04 P.M. Mountain Time

ANNE McCaine could not believe that she had even considered making a U-turn to abandon her rendezvous with Colonel Dave Brannan. Seeing him

again and hearing his voice took her back instantly to
that night in Paris—not so much the violence of killing
Fahrid Al-Zahir and the exhilaration of avenging the
death of her husband, but the way she had abruptly left
that terrible world of savagery and death, the way that
she had walked into the dark Paris evening on the arm
of this tall man with the auburn mustache and hands as
big as trucks.

The last time that she had seen the colonel, he had
been wearing a pinstripe suit, a silk shirt, and the gold
cuff links that she had picked out for him at Dunhill.
Today, it was frayed jeans, an old flannel shirt with
grease stains on the sleeves, and a cowboy hat that
looked like it had been worn for several seasons of
cattle drives. The last time that she had seen him, he
was carrying a Heckler & Koch automatic hidden in
the small of his back. Today, his .357 Magnum revolver hung openly in the holster of his gun belt. He
told her he didn't normally carry a sidearm into town,
but that he and Will had been hunting varmints.

She smiled. The first time that she had met Will and
the colonel, they had been hunting varmints.

They had talked for hours. She had lost track of
time. So had he. He'd bought her a beer, and she had
bought the second round. She told him about Dennis,
and he instinctively took her hand when a tear started
to run down her cheek. She told him about the bronze
statue of Astarte, and he smiled. She had used this as a
cue to squeeze his huge calloused hand.

Outside, the shadows were growing long and the
early evening crowd was starting to filter into the
Glacier View Tavern when Dave asked her whether

she was getting hungry. She hadn't even thought about it, but she was. She had skipped lunch. She had been just too nervous to think about eating, but that had been a very long time ago. It seemed like a million years.

A touch of the nervousness returned when he invited her to come to dinner at his "place," which is how Montanans refer to their homes. He drove his pickup, and she followed in her Mercedes. A gravel country road turned to a rutted dirt mountain road that wound through a heavy stand of timber, climbing high into the mountains.

At last, they reached a tiny bungalow with a large semi-attached shed that doubled as a large garage. He motioned for her to park her car inside, and he backed the pickup in behind. She popped her trunk and took out a navy blue gym bag. As if it wasn't already understood, this was her way of telling him that she was planning to spend the night.

The little bungalow was hardly more than a shack, but a lamp glowed warmly from within. Anne decided that it looked cozy. As she started toward the door, he laughed and said, "This actually isn't the house."

"Oh," she said. "I was just going to say that you had a cute little 'place' here, Colonel."

"Well, Professor, technically, it's part of the 'place,' but you'll be more comfortable at the main house," he told her, nodding toward the hillside. "This humble abode just serves to confuse the random unwanted visitor."

Her sandals weren't exactly made for the next leg of the journey, so he gave her a hand. After ducking through what appeared to be an impenetrable wall of

willows, Anne found herself at the edge of a small
meadow. Ahead, at the top of a small rise, was a building that looked like a wilderness lodge out of a fairy
tale. The base of the building and the walls of the first
story were massive blocks of rough-hewn granite; the
upper part was huge cedar logs. The colonel's "main
house" was perched at the edge of a steep cliff, with a
huge porch that offered a magnificent view of the snowcapped peaks of the Lewis Range that were bathed
in the sharp white light of the rising moon.

Inside, a monumental stone fireplace dominated
the living room with its twenty-foot ceiling. With the
huge seven-point elk head above the fireplace, buffalo
robes spread across the furniture, and a well-stocked
gun cabinet, one might have taken the place for a rustic hunting lodge, but along one wall, Anne saw a feature that made the place look like a university library.

She was immediately drawn to the colonel's book-
cases. There were hundreds, perhaps even thousands
of volumes, some new, some very old. There was a lot
of fiction, but most of the books were not. She saw titles on philosophy and natural sciences. There was
one large shelf devoted to atlases, and banks of books
on history—ancient history, modern history, and the
history of the Wild West of which the colonel seemed
such a part. The books were mainly in English, but she
saw works in German, Italian, and a smattering of
other languages. In a corner of one shelf, there were
even books on archaeology!

Anne was startled when she noticed an advanced
textbook on Mogollon culture to which she had con-
tributed, and she reached for it. As she took it down,

she saw that he had bookmarked her section of the text. The notes scribbled into the margins told her that he had actually read it. She looked up. The colonel was smiling sheepishly.

March 6
10:09 P.M. Eastern Time

IT was late when former President Wilcox reached the White House. The Gulfstream had made good time from New York, but there had been a backup on the Van Wyck and getting out to Kennedy from Manhattan had eaten up a great deal of time.

Wilcox had wanted to avoid coming to the White House. He had hoped to just work out the details with Secretary of State John Edredin over the phone, but the secretary of state had insisted that President Livingstone be kept in the loop, and it was Livingstone who insisted that they meet in the West Wing, and that they do so tonight. David Wilcox felt a pang of nostalgia as the armored Lincoln Town Car wheeled into the north portico of the executive mansion that had been his home for four years. He had been so glad to leave that he didn't think he'd miss it. But he did. He was glad to have the great weight lifted from his shoulders, but he missed the aura of the place.

It was strange to sit on the *other* side of the desk, and it was strange to be in the familiar room and smell the familiar smells and to see a bitter rival like Thomas Livingstone behind the desk. Livingstone had greeted him cordially, but not warmly. There was no animosity in his voice, but no warmth. There was no pretense of asking about one another's family, or jokes about Wilcox's forced retirement at the hands of the electorate. This was a business meeting, and Livingstone got down to business.

Wilcox explained the 750-mile exclusion zone, and told Livingstone and Edredin that the United Nations would finance a UNESCO World Heritage site in the sultanate.

"That seems like a lot of money for an archaeological dig, especially for a guy who's one of the richest men on earth," Edredin observed.

"I think that the sultan sees it as symbolic," Wilcox suggested.

"I see it as extortion," Livingstone interjected. "He's blackmailing Mboma with this goddamn Heritage Site, and he's blackmailing us with this exclusion zone. That radius includes the whole South China Sea. I looked it up on a map. It's everything from Manila to Singapore. What will it look like if the Seventh Fleet can't sail between Manila and Singapore? It's international waters, and they damned well can't stop us. I won't let the United States be blackmailed on my watch."

"They have nuclear weapons," Wilcox cautioned. He'd winced slightly when Livingstone said "my watch."

"Then it's *nuclear* blackmail and I won't let the United States be nuclear-blackmailed. And we don't even know for sure that he really has nukes."

Livingstone tossed out the latter remark to mislead Wilcox. He didn't want his former rival to know that he had seen evidence of the weapons that was deemed conclusive.

"Do you want to take a chance?" Wilcox asked.

"If he dared to hit us, we could annihilate his country in three minutes."

"That would make the United States even more of a pariah than it is already."

"I don't even want to get into why this country has such an evil image," Livingstone said angrily. "With you and your pals running around the world with your peace medals second-guessing this administration. You of all people should know how damned hard it is to walk the line in this room."

"Okay, okay," Wilcox said, holding up his hands to try to calm Livingstone. "Hear me out. I like to look for ways to make these kinds of impasses into win-win situations. At this point, neither Ambassador Incpaduka nor the sultan have gone public with any of this. You could offer *him* the seven-hundred-fifty-mile exclusion zone, and it would be *your* idea."

"Win-win, my ass. That's more like lose-lose," Livingstone replied. "That would be tantamount to giving up without a fight. I really am not interested in 'winning' that way."

"I don't think that we should rule it out," Edredin interjected. "We could spin this to our advantage. It could be 'Livingstone the Peacemaker.' We could take a hard line, then offer to be conciliatory. It would make us look as though we were voluntarily taking the high road."

"I don't like it," Livingstone growled.

"What could it hurt?" Edredin replied. "We can

always fall back on the hard-line option. If we went for
that now, Mboma would stonewall our getting an International Validation and it would make us look fool-
ish. If we took an acquiescent approach and Omar
countered with belligerence, then we would be justified in applying for an International Validation."

"I *still* don't like it," Livingstone muttered. "But
you have a point. Pack your bags, John, you're going
to Brunei."

March 6
8:11 P.M. Mountain Time

THE buffalo steak with the huckleberry glaze was
sublime. Everything about that evening in the big
log building was sublime. Anne McCaine would have
had a second steak if it hadn't been for the promise of
the rhubarb pie the colonel had baked with rhubarb
from his own patch. Not only was he a reader, he was
a good cook. This man was a "keeper," Anne thought
to herself, but then she had traveled eight hundred
miles into the unknown to see him *before* she had
tasted his cooking.

By the time that dinner was finished, the fire in the
fireplace was going well, and they sat down to enjoy
it. Anne found it easy to make conversation. She just
scanned the titles of the books on his bookshelf for a
subject that interested her—and there were many. At
one point, she realized that this big man in the flannel
shirt with stubble on his chin was quoting Pliny the

Elder in Latin. You had to love a guy like this. Anne smiled to herself, and she realized that she did.

When he left the room to get some single-malt, Anne stood near the fire to warm herself. When he returned, he stood next to her and said something about it being a very enjoyable evening. She barely heard what he said. She was possessed only by an irresistible desire to kiss him. He seemed a little startled, but only a little.

Kissing passionately, they tumbled onto the buffalo robes that were gathered onto the floor before the fire. She clawed her way into his shirt and ran her fingers through the bear rug of hair across his chest. He put his hand on her leg and caressed her firm and shapely thigh. She unzipped her dress as he pulled off his shirt.

He unfastened her bra, and she pulled to unbuckle his belt as they plunged headlong into that sublime madness that exists between two people so desperately in need of being one with one another.

Her perfect breasts looked so fine in the firelight, and likewise the contour of her hip and her leg as she lay on her side smiling up at him.

His hands, hands as big as trucks, caressed her so lightly that she felt her body tingle. The big guy was bringing her back to life. It seemed like such a long, long time ago when she had felt so tired, so spent, and so lonely.

He touched her in all the right places. Suddenly, she shivered as though a cold blast of wind had blown through her body. He moved his hand slightly, and she felt her body consumed in a river of lava. She noticed that he was caressing her neck with his other hand, lightly touching places close to her spine. It was some kind of acupuncture thing.

Where had he learned this?

She didn't care, she just squirmed to get closer to him. As she did, her body convulsed in an orgasm unlike anything she could remember. Then there was another.

Where had he learned this?

Had it been in some Bangkok whorehouse from a mysterious harlot who had known a thousand men and at least that many women?

She didn't care, she just squirmed to get closer to him. He caressed her cheek, as though letting her recover from the depletion of what felt like electrocution. She kissed him as hard as she could, and felt his massive arms smother her in their embrace.

The colonel thought about the eight years since his wife had died and how he'd never expected to again feel as he did now. He had cut himself off from everybody and the world. A few women had crossed his path in those eight years, but the emptiness remained. When he first laid eyes on the professor, in that dirty back corner of Turkey, it began to change—like the sun coming out.

He felt her body, smooth and perfect, against his own, rough and scarred. It was not just the perfection of her beautiful form, but the way she moved—smoothly and sensually, like a rivulet of warm mercury. Every part of her that he touched was pure ecstasy, from her long dark hair to the soft, smooth sides of her breasts and all the points south. He loved the way she reacted to his touch. It was like the tango, but with the partners responding from instinct rather than practice.

He leaned into her and ran his left hand up her spine.

The professor gasped. The orgasms swept over her in waves like earthquakes of progressively greater magnitude, and just as she thought it was over, he kissed her deeply on the lips and it began again.

It seemed to go on for hours. Both people willed it to, and it was so. They rolled in the damp buffalo robe before the fire, moaning and gasping and toying with one another. They danced a tango that both of them were making up out of impulses that came from deep within them. For Anne, it came from a place so deep she had never been there in all her life, but here it was, and it transcended her imagination.

TWO

SECRETARY of State John Edredin caught a glimpse of the Washington Monument and the Capitol dome through a tear in the cloud cover as the Boeing VC-32A transport banked for its final approach into Andrews AFB. He was glad to be home. His trip to Bandar Seri Begawan had been like a strange dream, not a bad dream, but a very weird dream.

It had been like being in a place like North Korea after it was redecorated by somebody from Disneyland. Portraits of Sultan Omar Jamalul Halauddin were everywhere. Come to think of it, there were almost no billboards of any other kind. The man who had seized power under questionable circumstances wanted to take no chance that anyone in the world—nor in Brunei itself—would have any doubt who was now in charge.

Banners and streamers in the red, yellow, and black of the Brunei flag hung everywhere, and there were parades of schoolchildren dressed in the red, yellow, and black of the Brunei flag. It was a television event, designed to play well on the flat-screen displays of the world.

All of the networks were there, from BBC and CNN to Japan's NHK and Al-Jazeera. Everybody wanted to see the circus, and they were not disappointed. Edredin had shared the stage with former President Wilcox and a gaggle of notables from Brunei's power elite at the sultan's vast Istana Nurul Iman palace. There were several thousand people in the great hall of the world's largest palace. Aside from the media, Edredin wasn't sure who they were—or how much they had paid for their tickets. It reminded Edredin of one of those get-rich-quick seminars that are constantly being held in hotel ballrooms. Wilcox was in his element. Since turning ex-president, he'd worked a lot of those kinds of rooms.

There were speeches and speechifying. Edredin followed the script and gave Omar his exclusion zone, and he was applauded as a peacemaker. Then Wilcox spoke, recycling his carefully practiced Nobel Laureate diatribe for the cameras. At last, the lights went down and the sultan himself made a grand entrance, flanked by two-dozen children carrying palm fronds. The media had wasted more time discussing his wardrobe—a gaudy red silk robe and a big hat—than they did on his speech.

Finally, the sultan took his seat and Caprice gave
a forty-minute performance of her megahits, backed
by a thirty-two-piece orchestra and ranks of backup
singers. At least she had a good voice, and the sultan's
sound system was second to none.

"Onstage, the man is a clown," Edredin told President Thomas Livingstone. The car had taken the secretary of state directly to the White House. Livingstone
wanted to be briefed and he couldn't wait. "In private,
he is sharp and shrewd. He's not to be underestimated.
He's a manipulator of Machiavellian proportions."

"Well, he has certainly manipulated us," Livingstone
said, leaning back in his chair. "And he maneuvered
Baudouin Mboma out of a billion dollars. I guess he got
what he wanted."

"According to what Wilcox told me on the plane
going out there, a big part of what he wanted was to be
on television, and he got that. He got the news channels with us guys in suits, and posing with Caprice got
him on the entertainment shows."

"More than anything, the world has seen Sultan
Omar as a jolly fellow smiling next to a global super-
star, and not as a villain holding the world hostage to
nuclear blackmail, and that's good for us as well," the
president added.

"Instead of our having made a deal with Hitler,"
Edredin continued, "he's made it look like we made a
deal with Wayne Newton. That's how it looks on television."

"I saw the pictures of him with Caprice all over
the magazine covers in the checkout line last night,"
interjected Steve Faralaco, Livingstone's chief of staff.

"There is even talk of him appearing on her television special next month."

"You read that in the checkout line?" Livingstone asked, shaking his head.

"How else am I supposed to keep up with what's going on in the world?" Faralaco asked with a grin.

Compared to the dark mood here in the Oval Office back on March 6, the atmosphere today was almost cheerful. At the earlier meeting Edredin had predicted that the sultan's bluster would fade if he was handled correctly, and he'd been right. David Wilcox had predicted that the sultan could be bought off with a win-win deal, and *he'd* been right. The crisis had abated.

The day after the gala, Hudim Incpaduka, Brunei's ambassador to the United Nations, had let it be known through diplomatic channels that the sultanate was standing down from deploying its nuclear capability. At the same time, satellite surveillance confirmed that work had stopped on the retrofit of the gunship KDB *Depambak*. She had been buttoned up and left parked at the pier.

The world had dodged a bullet, and the global memory of the crisis was already fading. The polls recorded a four-point jump in Livingstone's approval rating, and in an election year, few things mattered more.

March 18
3:44 P.M. Pacific Time

"**A**REN'T you Reid Arthur? I thought I saw your picture in that article in the *Bay Area Protector*."

Arthur was startled. He had been sitting in a sunny corner at the coffee shop on Telegraph Avenue in Berkeley sipping his chai latte and being engrossed in a book about the ongoing war to save threatened species from capitalist greed.

"Yes, umm, I *am* Reid Arthur, and you would be?"

"My name is Bob, Bob Rashid. I'm a grad student here at Cal," the friendly man said, shaking Arthur's hand.

Good old Cal. Arthur had spent six years as an undergrad here at the University of California, but that seemed so long ago. His career as one of the founding directors of Environmental Action International had consumed so much of his time over the past three years that everything else was a blur.

Reid Arthur had come to Berkeley to walk in the footsteps of the revolutionaries of the past whom he had idolized since high school. He was too young to remember the Weather Underground, or their days of rage. He was not present to read the fresh news as they carried out bombings of police stations from Chicago to San Francisco, nor when they bombed the United States Capitol Building in March 1971. They had then beaten Al-Qaeda by nearly three decades in their bombing of the Pentagon.

Working with Environmental Action International was far tamer than doing what the Weather Underground had done—spilling paint in a corporate headquarters was not as extreme as setting off a pipe bomb in one—but Arthur imagined himself in the mold of those revolutionaries from the seventies whom he idolized.

"I read that article about what you guys at Environmental Action International are doing with Hetch Hetchy, and I would have to say that you are *right on.*"

"Thank you," Arthur said modestly, stroking his beard. "We are doing the best we can."

Since his picture had appeared in that article in the left-liberal *Bay Area Protector* entertainment weekly, a number of people had mentioned it, but this was the first complete stranger. Arthur was pleased that people were waking up to the cause.

Hetch Hetchy is a valley within Yosemite National Park that is parallel to the world-famous Yosemite Valley. Named for the native Miwok word for a grass that grows in the region, the valley is now filled with the Hetch Hetchy Reservoir, created in 1923 with the completion of the O'Shaughnessy Dam on the Tuolumne River. Since then, this reservoir has been the primary source of water for the city of San Francisco, and a supplementary source for a number of other communities. In recent years, there have been occasional proposals from environmental organizations to remove the dam and restore the valley. Unfortunately, most of those proposing such a radical change fail to realize that it would necessitate replacing the ingenious gravity-fed water system with one requiring a series of gas-guzzling pump houses. Despite this, Environmental Action International had recently added its voice to those of a myriad of other green groups in calling for the dam to be torn down.

"Your work is so important," the man named Bob told him.

"It's time for the people to wake up and do

something," Arthur said emphatically. "We believe that the time for excuses is over, and that the time for action is now. We need for the people to stand up and be part of the solution."

"I only wish that I knew how to get involved," Bob said longingly. "I wish that I could be part of the solution."

"We are having a rally on Sproul Plaza at the university tomorrow at noon. You can come by then, or phone the Environmental Action International office."

"I'm really grateful," the man said, taking Arthur's business card. "It is exciting to be in a country where the people can truly make changes."

"Where are *you* from?"

"Pakistan."

March 18
8:46 P.M. Eastern Time

STEVE Faralaco noticed the magazines on the rack in the Alexandria supermarket and chuckled. The president had really been surprised when he had mentioned them. Steve wondered how long it had been since Livingstone had stood in a checkout line. He tucked the plastic bag with his carton of milk and dishwasher detergent under his arm and pressed the button on his key ring. Out there in the parking lot, there was a happy little chirp as his BMW winked its lights at him. It was going to be a long night. There was an increasing likelihood of a token primary challenge in the Pennsylvania and Indiana primaries, and

Faralaco had to make sure that Livingstone was ready.

As he opened the door and tossed in his bag, Faralaco noticed a man standing about four cars away staring at him. Most of the time, Steve was glad that most people on the White House staff were able to go around without Secret Service protection. This was not one of those times.

"Can I help you?" Faralaco asked peevishly.

"I have a message for your boss," the man said.

He spoke with just a trace of an accent. Faralaco couldn't place it. The face was vaguely familiar, but he couldn't place that either.

"The switchboard is open twenty-four-seven," Faralaco replied impatiently, deliberately not using the term "White House" in a shouted conversation in a parking lot. "You can leave a message and it will be taken care of in the morning."

"Let me tell you a story," the man said, opening his coat to show Steve that he was not concealing a usual type of weapon in a usual place. It was obvious that this was not a casual conversation, and it had been obvious from the start. Steve just wanted it to go away.

"I really don't have time for storytelling," he said emphatically.

"As your secretary of state was told in Bandar Seri Begawan . . . as your ex-president was told in New York, Brunei is no longer a third-rate power that can be marginalized by the United Nations or the United States," the man said, ignoring Faralaco's attempts to excuse himself and get away gracefully. "Between the fourteenth and seventeenth centuries, the Brunei sultanate was a very powerful kingdom. Its territory spread far beyond present borders. It extended from Mindanao through Borneo . . . Sarawak and Sabah and all the southern Philippines. The Europeans came, and then the rajahs of Sarawak. Brunei grew smaller and smaller."

"That's the history of the world," Faralaco explained. "Sometimes countries get small."

"Sometimes they get bigger. Brunei is destined to be a world power."

"You just gained tremendous concessions that will keep the U.S. Navy out of an area a hundred times the size of your country."

"That was a start."

"A start? What more do you want, and why didn't you bring that up when the secretary of state went out to see your sultan?"

"We took those concessions as an expression of good faith, and we wanted to see that they were made in good faith."

"Were they made in good faith?"

"They were made."

"Then you should be pleased."

"We were. It was a start."

"There you go again," Faralaco replied. "What more do you want? Wait a minute, you shouldn't be talking to me about this. You need to talk to someone at the State Department."

"I told you that I have a message for your boss," the man said. "It's better that you convey my sense of urgency. But yes, the state department will become involved. Your secretary of state, who has met cordially with Sultan Omar Jamalul Halauddin, will come to the embassy of the sultanate of Brunei tomorrow at one

o'clock to meet with Ambassador Korma to discuss
the implementation of the process. We will arrange for
a joint announcement."

"Implementation of *what* process?"

"You will tell your president that he is to ask the
United Nations to arrange for the immediate transfer
to the sovereignty of Brunei all of its lost territory.
Sarawak and Sabah from Malaysia, Pelawan, Moro,
and Mindanao from the Philippines."

"The United States can't do that," Faralaco gasped.
"Those are sovereign countries."

"You will also concede to the sultanate of Brunei
the Mariana Islands, including Guam, which the
United States has occupied illegally since 1899.
Guam, with its big naval and air bases, will form the
new district of East Brunei."

"Are you joking?"

"I assure you that I'm not."

"If you think that the United States would give the
Marianas to Brunei, you're nuts," Steve Faralaco said,
climbing into his BMW.

"You forget, Mr. Faralaco, that we are a nuclear
power."

"So are we, man," Steve said as he slammed his
door. "So are we."

March 18
7:49 P.M. Central Time

"**B**OBBY Girardeau came home today," the big man
announced, standing up and raising his glass of

Abita Amber. "Bobby Girardeau came home from the hospital today, and Marcie Girardeau went *into* the hospital. Thanks to that man sitting down there at the end of the bar, she ain't a widow. Thanks to that man, Bobby Girardeau will live to see that little girl that Marcie is in labor with right now, and she is goin' to know her daddy."

"Shut up, will ya!" Greg Boyinson demanded, folding his arms on the bar and burying his face. Ever since that terrible night when he had pulled the dying man off that offshore oil rig, Boyinson had been something of a local celebrity around Cameron and southern Calcasieu Parishes. He hadn't expected the adulation and he hadn't wanted it. He'd avoided the girl from the local newspaper down around Grand Lake or somewhere until her deadline had passed and she'd stopped bothering him. He still saw her around here or there, but it was a small town where you keep running into people.

Tonight Greg was at Marie's, the local shrimp shack, with the drilling crews and some guys from the refinery. They were celebrating Bobby's homecoming—and Marcie's baby. Boyinson raised his pint glass and said he'd drink to the next phase of Bobby's life, and added that they'd all talked way too much about the previous phase.

At last, the party was winding down. Boyinson grabbed his last fistful of shrimp and told everybody that he'd see them tomorrow. If he was going to fly tomorrow, he explained, there could be no more beer tonight.

As he made his way to the head, Boyinson noticed

the girl reporter from the local newspaper down around Grand Lake. She was sitting with a friend of hers at a table in the far corner of Marie's. They were paying their tab and putting on their coats. He was glad that she had gone on to other things. He hated publicity and he had an abiding dislike for the media. She was kind of cute, but he was glad not to have her chasing him around anymore.

The air outside was clear and cool, the kind you get after a really long rain, the kind that just demands that you take a deep breath of it. As he made his way to his pickup, Boyinson saw the two girls, the reporter and her friend, getting into a small Honda in the far corner of the parking lot. He took little notice as he threw his gear into the bed of his truck and jabbed the key into the door lock. Then he heard a scream and some shouting.

There were two men hassling the girls. One guy was pulling a shoulder bag away from one of them, and the other was grabbing something out of the back-seat of their car. This was, in Boyinson's assessment, just plain *wrong*.

He sprinted toward the car, and moved toward where the guy was fighting with the girl and trying to steal her bag. The guy jerked it free and slammed her against the car with a loud thud. As he turned to move away, he felt Boyinson's hand close around his wrist. He heard a crunching sound, like the sound you make when you break a pound of uncooked spaghetti noo-dles. The purse snatcher felt an agonizing pain in his arm. It was so severe that his vision blurred and he felt like throwing up. Somewhere in the spinning darkness, a man's voice softly said, "I don't believe this belongs to you."

Boyinson shoved the recovered bag to the girl, and ran to the other side of the car to confront the other man. When he had seen Boyinson, he had pulled back from trying to untangle the strap of the girl reporter's laptop computer from the parking brake handle. Now, as Boyinson came around the car, he just stood there with a surprised look on his face and with a large bloodstain covering most of his left pants leg. The girl reporter was lying on the ground with a utility knife in her hand. She sat up and slashed at the man with the knife. She missed and he staggered backward a couple of steps, still with the surprised look on his face.

"Let's not have to file a police report," Boyinson said as he gently removed the knife from her hand.

"Are you hurt?" Boyinson asked her, and the two men limped away into the darkness. "Did you hit your head on that bumper when you fell?"

"No, I'm all right. Is Sheree okay?"

Sheree had come around the car to watch the Good Samaritan helping her friend. She acknowledged that aside from being a little shaken up, she was fine.

"You did some fast thinking there," Boyinson told her approvingly. "Good thing you clipped him before he could get that thing away from you."

"Thanks." She smiled, reaching to shake his hand. "I'm glad that you are less shy about getting involved in parking lot brawls than you are about getting inter- viewed for feature stories. I'm Julia Girod."

"Yes, I know, I have your card," he half-lied. He did

have her card—or *maybe* he still had it somewhere—but he hadn't remembered her name. "As I told you before, I didn't do your interview because you just wanted to talk about a subject that I didn't—me."

"I understand, Captain," Julia said, smiling knowingly.

"Captain? I guess you've been doing some background on me."

"You've had quite an interesting career," Julia told him. "Special Forces. Delta Team. Night Stalkers. Being written up for a Medal of Honor that was never awarded because the mission officially 'didn't happen.' I liked the one in Bosnia where you saved a platoon of British SAS commandos by flying back and forth through city streets just a few feet off the ground shooting up bad guys. As I recall, that's the same one where you shot up an entire Serbian battalion and destroyed seven T-55 tanks."

"Thanks for not using all that." Greg shrugged. "I'd rather keep a low profile."

"You seem to have a knack for saving people, Captain."

"I guess I'm just an old humanitarian at heart."

"I really would like to get out of here," Sheree interjected. "This place is, like, giving me the creeps right now."

The two women climbed into Sheree's car, and Boyinson agreed to follow as they drove to her house to make sure all was well.

Then he offered to give Julia a ride home.

She accepted.

"**W**HAT do you think, John, is this credible?"
President Livingstone asked the secretary of
state after Steve Faralaco had related the details of his
strange encounter in the parking lot the night before.

"It sounds preposterous," Edredin said, scratching
his chin. "On the face of it, I would like to agree with
Steve that it could very well be some kind of prank.
Somebody who knows that Steve works at the White
House has been reading the news and had decided to
play an early April fool joke. These demands are *peculiar,* to say the least."

"I wasn't aware that Guam was ever part of Brunei,"
Faralaco interjected.

"I don't think it ever was," the president replied.
"It's nearly a thousand miles away and part of a com-
pletely separate island group. It has no connection to
Brunei."

"On the other hand, Sultan Omar has already estab-
lished a pattern," Edredin said thoughtfully. "If this is
true, there is a consistency to his inconsistency. Two
weeks ago, he asked for an exclusion zone, which was
directly tied to his claiming to having felt threatened
by the Seventh Fleet. Then he asked to have minor . . .
but genuine . . . archaeological digs declared a World
Heritage Site. It was tenuous, but there was a connection. Then he went completely off the wall and asked
for a billion dollars."

"Just because he could."

"Exactly," the secretary agreed. "This time, the

demands were areas of Malaysia and the Philippines that once were part of Brunei, and then the Marianas, a complete non sequitur. I've looked into this man's eyes. This is a man who *is* capable of something like this."

"Then let us assume it's for real," the president said thoughtfully. "Let's arrange a meeting. Draft a letter that essentially tells him that this is a nonstarter. There is no way in hell that we will do any of these things. Tell him we will respond to any nuclear threat with overwhelming force. To hell with the International Validation Organization. Come to think of it, this sunuvabitch is also a thorn in Mboma's side. I wouldn't be surprised that he'd give us an International Validation in a heartbeat if we promised to take care of this guy."

March 19
1:11 P.M. Eastern Time

"**I**'M here from the office of the president of the United States," Steve Faralaco said, showing his identification to the receptionist at the brightly modern Brunei embassy in Washington's Cleveland Park neighborhood.

"They're expecting you," the man with the fez replied as he buzzed the White House aide into the sovereign territory of the sultanate.

The place had a vaguely sweet smell that reminded Steve of a Thai restaurant. There were large portraits of the sultan everywhere in the large entryway and the hall leading away from it. There seemed to be more of them than necessary. It was more of a Sultan Omar theme park than an embassy. He noticed with some amusement that there were copies of *People* and *Us* and several other celebrity magazines on the coffee table in the waiting room, each with the pictures of the sultan and Caprice on its cover.

A short Asian woman in an Islamic head scarf led Faralaco to a large office in the back of the building, where he was introduced to a man who was identified as the assistant to the ambassador. When the woman left, the assistant spoke to someone on the intercom in a language that Steve couldn't understand. After a moment, the door to another office opened and a short man in a dark suit came out.

"I am Pehin Dato Yayah Korma." He smiled, extending his hand. "Please come . . . step into my office."

Steve introduced himself and shook the man's hand, recognizing him as Brunei's new ambassador to the United States. Like Pehin Dato Hudim Incpaduka, Yayah Korma was one of Omar Jamalul Halauddin's cronies from his earlier days. Whether it had involved shaking down a rival "business enterprise" or making "collections," these men had long ago proven themselves on the street. When he had quietly disposed of Sultan Haji Hassanal Bolkiah, the new sultan had brought his own faithful subordinates in to fill the key positions within the government and the key diplomatic posts around the world.

"You've met my colleague," the ambassador said, nodding to the Middle-Eastern-looking man sitting in the corner. Faralaco recognized him as the man from last night. Today he was wearing a suit with no necktie.

"We met, but I wasn't introduced."

"Oh, I'm sorry, this is Abdulla Maloud. He's a consultant to His Majesty."

Eying Steve warily, the man rose to shake his hand.

"We were expecting Secretary of State Edredin," he said abruptly.

"He sends his regrets, and he also sent this. It's addressed to you, Mr. Ambassador."

Yayah Korma took the letter out of the sealed envelope and read it carefully. Twice. Then, shaking his head, he removed his reading glasses and placed them on his desk.

"This is most unfortunate, Mr. Faralaco. And most disappointing. Mr. Edredin is most emphatic and this leaves no room to negotiate."

"My understanding is that the secretary said what he had to say."

"Did he consult with President Livingstone?"

"Yes."

"Most unfortunate," the ambassador repeated. "Most unfortunate."

Yayah Korma looked genuinely disappointed that Edredin had not responded favorably to the demands. The man called Maloud stood by, saying nothing, simply watching Faralaco without expression.

"Could you please convey a message to Secretary Edredin and President Livingstone, Mr. Faralaco?" Yayah Korma asked.

"Of course."

"I'd like to ask them to seriously reconsider our

proposal. It would be a pity if things got out of hand. Please ask them to think over what we have broached and to get back in touch with me by the end of the month. We really don't want things to get out of hand. The consequences could be . . . well . . . unexpected."

March 25
9:23 P.M. Brunei Time

"**WEATHER'S** holding," Captain Roland "Roach" Rouche said, making small talk. "That will make it easier to launch the birds."

"And easier to get a fast battle damage assessment from the Tomahawk strike," replied Rear Admiral Walter Briscoe, the commander of the Seventh Fleet's Task Force 70. "If this thing goes up, we'll have to work fast."

"Aye, aye, sir."

Briscoe scanned the horizon from the bridge of the USS *Ronald Reagan* (CVN-76), one of America's newest Nimitz-class nuclear-powered supercarriers. Displacing 95,000 tons, CVN-76 was 1,092 feet long, with a beam of 134 feet, and it was a symbol of the military power that the United States still possessed after several decades of budget-pruning.

In the distance to the port side of the huge warship lay the gray hump of the Malaysian island of Banggi. To the starboard, Briscoe could see the Philippine island of Balabac and several of her sisters. Before him lay the Balabac Strait, gateway to the South China Sea. Beneath him, the 4.5-acre flight deck teemed with some of the nearly eighty aircraft aboard, and crews made ready a dozen F/A-18 Super Hornets. The strike aircraft were being fitted out with a whole host of precision weapons from JDAM smart bombs to thousand-pound AGM-158 standoff missiles.

Abeam and aft of the supercarrier were the other ships of Task Force 70—including the USS *Cowpens* (CG-63), a 9,600-ton Ticonderoga-class guided-missile cruiser, and three 8,300-ton Arleigh Burke-class destroyers, all of them armed to the teeth with offensive weapons that included BGM-109 Tomahawk cruise missiles. At one time, back in the twentieth century, when the U.S. Navy was much larger than it is today, Task Force 70 was the principal strike force of the U.S. Navy's Seventh Fleet. Today, it contained most of the surface warships that the U.S. Navy had anywhere in the Pacific.

The *Ronald Reagan*'s two nuclear reactors, driving four massive screws, had pushed the big ship south from her forward port at Yokosuka in Japan at a speed of better than thirty knots. The goal was to arrive on station today, here in the western corner of the Sulu Sea, and await orders. Hurry up and wait. They had hurried, and now they waited, just outside Sultan Omar Jamalul Halauddin's exclusion zone.

At any moment, the president might tell the secretary of defense, and the SecDef might tell the commander in chief of the Pacific Command, and CINCPAC might be on the horn to Briscoe with the go-code. If that happened, Tomahawks would roar off to predetermined coordinates, and the Super Hornets would follow them in.

It was still hurry up and wait. Hurry to the Sulu Sea. Hurry to get the offensive hardware ready. Wait for CINCPAC, who could call at any moment.

Only Briscoe and a few members of his staff knew about Omar's latest demands, but everyone knew that Brunei had nukes, and they knew that their job could very soon be to take them out. As Briscoe had been briefed, there was a veiled nuclear threat, just vague enough that the secretary of state had nothing to take to the United Nations for an International Validation. The United States would have to wait for the shoe to drop. Hurry up and wait, wait to be hit before letting the other shoe drop.

"Why would he do this when he knows we'll hit him with everything we got?" Captain Rouche asked rhetorically. "What can possibly be on his mind to try something like this when he knows we'll blow him off the map?"

"He's nuts, that's why," the admiral replied. "Who the hell knows what makes somebody like that tick?"

"The worst thing is not knowing where in the world he's gonna hit us. Will it be Sandusky or Sacramento, or some embassy somewhere?"

"We can't know that, Mr. Rouche, but we sure as hell know where he's gonna get hit *back*."

March 25
9:23 P.M. Brunei Time

"**K**APITAN, we can see them on the scope," the young ensign said. The captain looked. There they were, the ships of the U.S. Seventh Fleet, scarcely one hundred miles away. The Royal Brunei Navy's Waspada-class missile ship KDB *Sajuang* was cruising in the South China Sea, fifty miles offshore from Sikuati, a port on the coast of Malaysia's Sabah province, about 180 miles northeast of Brunei, and sixty miles southwest of the Balabac Strait.

It had been only a month ago that Adanan Vegawan had assumed command of the KDB *Sajuang*. His job, as it had been when he was a junior officer aboard the KDB *Pemburu*, was to patrol the deep water near the coastal oil installations that were the keys to Brunei's bread and butter—and its caviar. The Royal Brunei Navy bragged about its prowess. Its ships were known in official press releases as the "Guardians of the Seas," but they were essentially patrol craft. Now, they were tasked with patrolling a vast exclusion zone that encompassed an area larger than Borneo. How could this be done? What was the sultan thinking?

Normally, the navy kept a two-ship patrol deployed at sea around the clock, but that was when their radius of operation was only about three hundred kilometers. That was all that was necessary to safeguard the nation. Now, the whole fleet would have to be spending days, even weeks, on the high seas.

Until now, the Bruneian patrol craft were more than adequate to intimidate and deal with any potential threat to Brunei's economic resources. The time when they had chased the pirates away from the Champion 7 oil installations, their twin-barrelled Oerlikon 30mm gun, firing six hundred rounds per minute, had been more than adequate—it had been overkill. That was then, but this is now. Even with its Exocet missiles, what could a gunboat the size of the KDB *Sajuang* do against a U.S. Navy Carrier Battle Group?

Kapitan Adanan Vegawan stared at the radarscope. Was this some kind of joke? What was he supposed to do if it came to war with the U.S. Navy? His small ship would last exactly the length of time that it took a Harpoon antiship missile to reach it. At this range, that time would be measured in minutes. It would take them longer to simply locate a ship the size of the KDB *Sajuang*, although if he could see them on his scope, they could certainly see him. He could fire a salvo of Exocets, but the Phalanx Gatling guns aboard every American ship could chew up an Exocet even if every other method of defense failed.

It would be a one-sided battle—if or when it came to that, but Vegawan would do as ordered. He was just glad that today's orders had been to reverse course off Sikuati, and continue to patrol back toward Bandar Seri Begawan.

THREE

CALLIE Hagen blushed slightly as she passed
Richard Morgan Hollister in the corridor and
watched out of the corner of her eye as he strode purposefully and powerfully toward the bank of elevators
on the twenty-ninth floor of Embarcadero Center Four.
He had winked at her. He had never even noticed her before, but tonight, he had winked at her. She had watched
him as he made his way toward the elevator to see if he
might look back to give her another glance. He hadn't.

She walked to her cubicle and set down the armload
of file folders that she had been lugging. Even from
here, she could see a bit of the fabulous view of the
lights on the towers of the San Francisco-Oakland Bay
Bridge and the San Francisco skyline. A recent law

school graduate, she had been recruited by Roebuck,
Springer & Seigal in July. For the past four months,
Callie had put in twelve-hour days as the firm prepared
to go to trial in the Abernathy case. If Abernathy prevailed at trial, they stood to walk away with nearly *$10
million*. With Richard Morgan Hollister leading the liti-
gators, there was little doubt that Abernathy would win.
Naturally, there was big drama when the opposition attorneys came in today. The talk going around the office
postulated that they were so wary of Hollister that they
would make a $7-million offer and settle out of court.
When Hollister had reduced several members of the opposition legal team to tears and won a *$14.7-million
victory,* everyone in the firm was stunned.

Hollister is *awesome*.

It was an exciting place to work, Callie thought to
herself as she organized the files for tomorrow. Her
objective tonight, now that Abernathy was over, had
been to get out of the office by 8:00—and she had
succeeded. She took a gulp from her water bottle,
grabbed her coat, and headed for the elevator. There
had been talk that some of the junior attorneys from
the Abernathy case would be celebrating at Regine's
on Steuart Street, so she decided to stop by and join
the fun.

As Callie crossed Market Street, she wondered
whether it was a full moon. She couldn't remember
the last time that she had seen so many crazy drivers.
One taxi nearly sideswiped a bus, and another cab
driver had merely stopped in the intersection and was
laughing as he watched people on the sidewalk.

The crowd at the bar in Regine's was as boisterous as ever. Callie thought that it must have been the Roebuck, Springer & Seigal people celebrating, but it seemed as though everyone in the room was in a party mood.

"Callie!"

She heard her voice being called. It was Lotheeya, one of the young attorneys that had been hired at about the same time as Callie. She was with Jake, the guy from Sacramento who was a two-year man with the firm. They waved for her to join them.

"Can I get you a drink?" Jake asked, shouting above the din.

"Thank you, I'll have a Chardonnay."

As Jake turned to order the wine, the bartender gave him a strange look. He took a sip from his glass of water and simply stared. Jake asked him again, this time in a tone that should have been easily audible in the noisy room, but again, the man simply stared at Jake with great interest and did nothing.

Callie and Lotheeya exchanged puzzled glances. This was just plain *weird*.

Growing more frustrated, Jake pointed to the glass of white wine that Lotheeya was holding and held up two fingers.

Just as he did that, their attention was diverted to the opposite side of the room. Another young woman— Callie thought she had seen her before—had just let out a bloodcurdling shriek. Like Callie and Lotheeya, she was dressed conservatively in an expensive-looking business suit. She continued to scream. It was much too early in the evening for her to be drunk, Callie thought to herself. She was acting as though she had been injured, but they couldn't see what could have struck her. A man who was near her reached out to comfort her, and she hit him as hard as she could.

Everyone in the room gasped as the woman grabbed her own hair and ripped out two handfuls. She dropped to her knees, blood dripping from her scalp and staining her light gray blazer.

"Let's get the hell out of here," Jake suggested as a crowd moved in to surround the woman.

Both Callie and Lotheeya headed toward the door as fast as they could battle their way through the crowd. Several people were screaming now.

"What just happened in there?" Callie asked as they reached the street.

Both her companions just shook their heads.

The scene outside Regine's was like a street fair. Two men in business suits were dancing on the roof of a car. Nearby, a woman was in the final stages of disrobing.

One of the men who had been on the car fell to the pavement, smashing his head with a terrible cracking sound. His partner on the car laughed as though it was the funniest thing he had ever seen.

"Like, let's get a cab and get as far away as we can," Lotheeya said. She was starting to panic.

Callie suggested that they go to her place, because it wasn't far, and the others agreed.

There was a four-car pileup at the corner and something was on fire.

"What's going on here?" Jake asked the cab driver.

"It's like that all over town," the driver explained. "They must have turned loose a bunch of nutcases from the hospital. I just wish that it wasn't raining so hard."

The three young attorneys glanced at one another. They hadn't noticed until that moment that the cab's windshield wipers were going full speed. Nor had they noticed that it was raining. Callie looked out the window of the speeding cab. The ground was perfectly dry and it was still a cloudless evening.

"You can let us out right here," she told the driver after he ran the second red light. "This is fine."

Without a word, the driver pulled over to the curb. The meter said nine dollars, but Jake handed him a twenty-dollar bill and told him to keep the change. As they gathered on the sidewalk, they glanced back to see him examining the bill closely as though he suspected it of being counterfeit.

As they walked the four remaining blocks to Callie's flat in a two-unit Victorian building on the shoulder of Potrero Hill, they passed several people behaving strangely, but they hardly noticed. After what they had witnessed downtown, this residential neighborhood seemed tame.

They climbed the steps to Callie's front door and looked back toward the city. They could see that several large fires were burning, and the streets were filled with more flashing red and blue lights than any of them had ever seen. The air was filled with the sounds of people shouting, and with the wail of the sirens of emergency vehicles of every sort.

As Callie opened her front door, the door to the downstairs flat popped open. It was her neighbor Kristine. She lived there with her husband, a firefighter, their two little kids, and the new baby.

"Callie, thank God it's you," she said desperately. "The kids are really sick and I can't get hold of Don."

The three young downtown attorneys stepped into the narrow working-class railroad flat. The two young children were in the living room. One was sitting in the corner screaming, and the other lay on a blanket on the sofa. She was vigorously scratching herself and moaning. She was bleeding all over, and there were splotches of blood on the blanket and on the fabric of the sofa.

"I can't get her to stop," Kristine screamed hysterically.

"Did you try calling 911?" Jake asked, as though this was not something that a fireman's wife would do instinctively.

Without waiting for an answer, Jake pulled out his cell phone and dialed the emergency number. It was busy. He pushed redial and tried again, and again and again. Finally, he got a recorded message that the circuits were busy.

Callie knew the lay of the apartment, and tiptoed into the baby's room to see if he was okay. The night-light, depicting a happily smiling character from a recent animated feature film, shone brightly, illuminating the crib with a soft warm light. Inside, little Don Junior lay quietly, his little brown eyes staring up at Callie. He didn't move. He just stared at her with an expression so horrifying that it brought chills to her spine. His expression was gruesomely contorted, and his eyes bulged from his head. She reached into the crib to pick him up. He was limp and listless. He was cold, and he was not breathing.

It was not so much the fact that the tiny child was dead that had the tears streaming down Callie's cheeks, but the thought of the terrible agony that must have preceded his death.

April 5
8:29 A.M. Mountain Time

"**H**OLY Fire," Anne McCaine said in astonishment.

"That's an interesting expression," Colonel Dave Brannan said, calmly handing her a cup of coffee. "I've heard holy cow and holy shit and all sorts of holies, but never holy *fire*."

"It's not an expression, it's what happened in San Francisco last night."

Anne and the colonel had ridden into the colonel's place last night after a couple of weeks in the Montana wilderness. Anne had never been happier going without a bath for such a long period of time—but she had never been happier to finally get one.

After that night when they discovered their remarkable sexual compatibility, Brannan had not wanted her to leave and suggested that she stay around for a day or so. She'd said that maybe she would stay on for a day or so. What she really wanted was to stay indefinitely. The University of Colorado had put her on a forced sabbatical, and she really didn't want to go

back to the big executive-style mansion on the hill
with the broken pictures of Dennis McCaine all over
the floor.

They ate, slept, made love, walked in the woods,
and talked endlessly. At one point, she told him one
too many times that she really, really needed to get
away from it all, and he picked up the phone. He borrowed a horse for her, saddled up his old stallion
named Sandy, put a packsaddle on a third horse, and
they took off into the Rockies.

They crossed the Continental Divide and rode into
the Front Range country, camping as they went. They
spent a couple of nights at a snowshoe cabin up in the
Birch Creek drainage that was owned by an old
friend of Dave's who lived near Heart Butte, but
mostly, they camped out amid the aspen and under
the stars. Sometimes there were no stars, and one
morning they woke up covered with a couple of inches
of snow. After an impromptu snowball fight, Dave
made breakfast while Anne climbed up to a little
knoll to enjoy the spectacular view of the snowcapped
Rockies all around. She pointed out some tracks in
the fresh snow. Dave realized that they had been
tracked by a pack of wolves, but that the pack had
moved on. Somewhere, a sheep rancher would not be
amused.

Anne felt as though she had been transported back
into the nineteenth century—or the eighteenth, or before. There was no sense of time, except for the cycle
of the sun across the sky. They laughed and talked and
rode.

At night, they sat by the campfire and Dave told her some of the old Blackfeet ghost stories that he had learned growing up. He told her the chilling story of the Medicine Grizzly and an amusing one about Rising Wolf. Sometimes later at night, when he was asleep, she sensed that the ghosts were real. At least they were starting to seem a lot more real than the fading demons she had left behind in Colorado. Or maybe it was just the wolves.

All that she had left in Colorado and in her former world seemed distant now. She felt disconnected from that and from the twenty-first century—at least for those couple of glorious weeks.

The colonel's home, which had seemed the epitome of rustic charm when she first saw it, now seemed to Anne to be the epitome of civilization. A warm bath in a huge tub with whirlpool jets. Coffee made in a coffeemaker. An omelette made with fresh eggs from the colonel's neighbor with the free-range chickens and a selection from the veritable library of cheeses that he had in his refrigerator. And finally, Anne was reunited with her trusty laptop, which soon dragged her kicking and screaming into the twenty-first century so abruptly and efficiently that she didn't even have time to kick or scream.

Avoiding what she knew would be a cacophony of e-mails, she had opened to the news on her home page. She realized that she had neither seen nor heard any news for two weeks—and that she had forgotten to miss it.

"Tell me, Professor," he said, sitting next to her.

"What *is* a Holy Fire? What happened in San Francisco? What burned?"

"Somebody's brain. Look at this," she said in an alarmed tone of voice.

This got Brannan's attention, and he watched as she scrolled down through the lead news item. The headlines screamed and the pictures told the story. At rush hour the night before, the Golden Gate Bridge had suffered one of the biggest rush-hour pileups in California history. More than seventy-five cars were involved, but that was just the beginning.

An unprecedented rash of violent traffic accidents across the city had left a hundred dead. Meanwhile, the city seemed to have been gripped in a veritable epidemic of hysteria. People were jumping from rooftops, and hospitals were clogged with people suffering from headaches and hallucinations. Even hospital staff and first-responders were reporting symptoms. So far, nobody could figure out the cause. Absolutely no trace of chemical or biological weapons had been discovered in the air, water, or indeed, in the tox screens done at the hospitals.

"What the hell?" Brannan asked rhetorically.

"Hell is right," Anne replied. "It's St. Anthony's Fire."

"St. Anthony? As in *the* St. Anthony, the fourth-century utopian hermit monk who invented monasticism? The guy who sat in his cave and had all those visions of dervishes and demons that he decided were the devil trying to tempt him into believing that all of creation was madness? That St. Anthony?"

"So you've heard of him?"

"Yeah, it's great fun to look at all those fifteenth- and sixteenth-century paintings of the 'temptations of St. Anthony' by Peter Brueghel and Matthias Grünewald, and Hieronymus Bosch, my favorite old Dutch master. How is that related to *this*?"

"St. Anthony's Fire was a widely reported malady during the Middle Ages. The symptoms were that people started seeing weird demons and crazy monsters. It was like stepping inside a painting by your favorite old Dutch master. A lot of people who got poisoned had really scary hallucinations. Some had the sensation of being burned at the stake. They called it *ignis sacer* . . ."

"Meaning 'holy fire,'" Brannan said, finishing her sentence. "I see the meaning now. What caused it?"

"It turned out that rye bread had been contaminated with the *Claviceps purpurea* fungus, otherwise known as ergot mold. It's a sort of rare form of mold, but not *that* rare. Certainly not during the Middle Ages and the time when Bosch was painting his little monsters."

"Aha, I've heard of ergot," Brannan said. "I see where you're going with this."

"I figured you would. I'm surprised that nobody in San Francisco has figured this out yet. The active ingredient in the *Claviceps purpurea* fungus is ergotamine, a psychoactive drug which is a chemical cousin to lysergic acid diethylamide . . . LSD."

"And now they got a whole city stoned on acid," Brannan said, shaking his head. "Who could have imagined?"

"Actually, it happened a lot in the Middle Ages. It might also have had something to do with the witches in Salem, Massachusetts. There's a well-documented case of mass ergot poisoning at Pont-Saint-Esprit in France back in 1951. There were over two hundred cases. Four people died, and apparently it took weeks to calm everybody down."

"So this is the same thing, but on a much, much greater scale."

"Yup," Anne agreed. "A city of nearly a million on an involuntary acid trip. It could have been bread, or more probably, someone just spiked the water with pure LSD. Same results as in 1951, just a thousand times bigger."

"Whatever it is, I'm sure glad that *we're* not mixed up in it." Dave smiled.

April 5
1:54 P.M. Eastern Time

"**P**LEASE tell me that you're joking," President Thomas Livingstone demanded. "The entire city of San Francisco is high on LSD? Please put away your black light and tell me that we're just having some kind of a 'Summer-of-Love flashback' to the psychedelic sixties!"

"I'm afraid that it's really happening," Director of National Intelligence Richard Scevoles admitted. "Its a hellish mess because it took so long for the cause to be determined, and they still don't have a handle on who's been affected and how many. It's still out of hand."

It was around 8:30 Pacific Time the previous night

when news of a spike in traffic fatalities and of mobs of people arriving at the hospitals reached the national desks of the news channels. Over the next several hours, attempts to ascertain the extent of the situation became progressively more muddled as police communications personnel themselves fell victim to the hallucinations.

Around 10:30 Pacific Time, a reporter for the leading cable network was on a live feed when he suddenly declared that monkeys were trying to unscrew his head. The camera followed him as he ran screaming into Market Street, where he was struck by a fast-moving SUV. The SUV didn't stop until it rammed a city bus a block away.

Horrified viewers across the world watched this scene play out live, but it was only one of a myriad of similar scenes that filled all of the news channels over the ensuing hours. As the news crews gradually succumbed to the effects of the drugs, cameras were dropped, abandoned, or stolen. As this was happening, it was all being carried live.

The president was awakened at 4:30 Eastern Time. He watched about fifteen minutes of the pandemonium before convening an emergency meeting with the director of national intelligence and Secretary of Homeland Security Wally Wallingford. They assumed the worst. They assumed there had been a terrorist attack, and waited for details. And they waited, and waited. It was not until about 8:30 A.M. Pacific Time that the director of national intelligence finally was able to reach someone who confirmed that San Francisco had received the biggest dose of LSD in history.

"Why in the world did it take more than twelve hours to figure out what was going on?" Livingstone asked. "We spend billions on homeland security and millions upon millions for detection equipment. It's one thing to miss it before it happens, but another not to be able to figure it out after the fact."

"Hazmat teams were scouring the city looking for the cause within a couple of hours," Wallingford said, trying to account for this major failure by his department. "But they detected nothing. They scanned for every imaginable chemical weapon . . . phosgene . . . cyanide . . . mustard . . . sarin . . . everything. They looked for every known biotoxin from anthrax to botulism."

"How did they figure it out?"

"Actually, several hospitals figured it out separately overnight, but communications had collapsed and it wasn't until morning that the word was conveyed to us and to CDC."

"How in the hell did they miss it?" Livingstone scolded.

"I guess because they weren't looking for it," Wallingford said sheepishly, with everyone glowering at him as though looking for someone to blame.

"If I might interject, sir," Jenny Collingwood, a member of Wallingford's staff, said. "This substance is very difficult to detect."

All eyes shifted to the young woman with the pile of file folders on her lap. She was obviously nervous and unused to speaking in such a high-level conclave, but it soon became equally obvious that she had a better grasp of the facts than her boss.

"As you may know, sir, LSD is colorless, odorless,

and tasteless. Not only that, it's one of the most potent drugs of its kind known to science. Other psychoactive drugs are measured in milligrams. LSD is measured in *micro*grams. Poison gas is measured in pounds. The dosage level of LSD that will produce a threshold hallucinogenic effect in humans is generally considered to be around twenty-five micrograms. Estimates for the lethal dose begin at about two hundred micrograms per kilo of human body weight. In other words, a single ounce of LSD is capable of inducing hallucinations in 1.6 million adult males, or an average population of over three million."

"That means that an average water bottle like those on that table, if filled with something that looked smelled and tasted like water, could take down a city four times the size of San Francisco," Scevoles said. "This is a helluva lot more serious than anthrax or sarin gas."

"And it's *undetectable*," Wallingford said, excusing his department's failure to detect it. "Our best screening devices, our best sniffer dogs, our best screeners . . . none of them would have spotted this."

"If I might interject again, sir," Jenny Collingwood said, nervously adjusting her glasses. "In evaluating terrorist tactics, we understand that just the fear of imminent attack by weapons of mass destruction can cause mass hysteria. They don't have to use the weapons, but merely to convey a widespread fear and panic that their use is imminent. In this case, the perpetrators were able to go a step further."

"By doping the victims so that their fear and panic was drug induced and *real*!" Livingstone observed.

"It was more than just fear and panic," Jenny Collingwood continued. "It was fear of terrible things that were entirely unanticipated and entirely *imaginary*. It was a step beyond mass hysteria. It was mass *psychosis*. What if you could wield a weapon of mass destruction so diabolical that the victims *themselves* caused the mass destruction? That's what happened last night."

"That's certainly true," Scevoles admitted. "There were hundreds of deadly car wrecks, and the murders and suicides are still uncounted. The death toll could go into the thousands. Many were killed by other drivers, or neighbors, or panicking police."

"Furthermore, what if the cause of this mass psychosis was invisible and untraceable?" Jenny Collingwood added. "And what if you had the resources to produce not just an ounce or two, but gallons upon gallons of the odorless, colorless stuff?"

"Why did they pick San Francisco?" Livingstone asked. "Was it because they had some sick sense of irony over that city's own special psychedelic history with the odorless, colorless stuff?"

"We considered that question, sir," Jenny Collingwood replied. "And we believe that it is actually because it is one of the most densely populated major cities in the United States—nearly a million people crammed into forty-nine square miles with water on three sides."

"*Who* did it?" Livingstone asked. "Was it Jamalul Halauddin?"

"It may have been," Wallingford said tentatively.

"It *had* to have been," Scevoles said, shaking his

head in frustration. "We thought he was going to attack us with his nukes. We had prepared for that. We were on heightened alert for that, but we never anticipated . . ."

"No, we didn't, but can we connect him to this?" Livingstone asked.

"Probably not, sir," Jenny Collingwood admitted. "The source of San Francisco's water is a place called Hetch Hetchy. It's an unguarded, easily accessible reservoir high in the Sierra Nevada. It would have been incredibly easy to put several gallons or more of something that looked like water into that reservoir without being detected."

"*You know* he did it, and *I know* he did it," the director of national intelligence told the president. "But there is nothing whatsoever to associate Jamalul Halauddin with LSD. If it had been a radiological attack, everybody would assume that it was him. Even if it had been a biological or chemical attack, we could stretch it to blame him, but this . . . it's so out of left field that there's no connection."

April 6
6:05 A.M. Pacific Time

"**U**NUSUAL? Hmmmm," the young backpacker said thoughtfully. "No, I can't really think of anything."

"Are you sure?" National Park Service Ranger Jeremy Schmitt asked urgently.

The backpacker shook his head, and his girlfriend

just shrugged. More than a day had passed since San Francisco went mad, and a frantic, multi-agency search for the cause was under way. The entire water system serving the city had come under scrutiny, from the reservoirs within the city limits back through the huge pipelines to the source of the water in the High Sierra. Schmitt was at the top of the food chain, taking water samples from Hetch Hetchy Reservoir itself, and from the streams leading into it. As he hiked the wilderness trail that arched around the north side of the huge lake, he was questioning everyone he met. So far, nobody had seen anything suspicious.

"Wait a minute," the young woman said as Schmitt was bidding them good-bye and starting to head up the trail. "Like, remember that dude? Y'know, three days ago, when we were heading up to Rancheria Mountain. We stopped at Wapama Falls. Remember that dude?"

"What dude?" Schmitt asked eagerly.

"Yeah, right. The dude," the young man said as he began to recall the incident. "I thought it was really weird, y'know. He was filling his water bottles, and they were *huge*. I thought it was really weird that somebody would carry a *gallon* water bottle, much less three or four. That dude was pretty 'unusual.'"

April 6
3:09 P.M. Eastern Time

"**MR.** Secretary, you have our deepest condolences," Ambassador Pehin Dato Yayah Korma said, shaking the hand of Secretary of State John Edredin. "This has truly been a tragedy for the people of San Francisco, and of the United States."

Edredin had summoned the ambassador to the State Department for a showdown. It was simple. One question, one answer. The world needed to know. When the first stories of San Francisco, the epicenter of the psychedelic sixties, being high on LSD came through, many people around the United States had reacted with a chuckle. However, as the death and destruction became apparent, and it was obvious that a terrorist attack had occurred, there was a groundswell of empathy for the victims and anger at the perpetrators. The trouble was, the identity of those perpetrators was unknown. No group had yet claimed responsibility, and a frenzy of speculation ran rampant.

Amid this speculation, few people and fewer media pundits considered the rascal Sultan Omar as a possible culprit. The demands and scarcely veiled threats made to Steve Faralaco two weeks ago by Abdulla Maloud and Yayah Korma himself had not been made public. So, the possibility of his involvement seemed far more remote to the general public than it did to the people huddled in the Oval Office on the morning after.

"I have one question for you, Mr. Ambassador," Edredin said sternly when all of the aides to the two men had left the room, and diplomatic niceties had concluded. "Was your government involved in this attack?"

"Mr. Secretary, I'm surprised and insulted that you would ask such a thing," Yayah Korma replied indignantly. "Your park rangers recovered the bottles containing this dreaded chemical, did they not? It was on the news this morning. Is such an attack not the work of ecoterrorists? Are not such criminals a product of your own culture?"

"To date, no ecoterrorists have made any threats on the scale that you have," Edredin said.

"Threats?" Yayah Korma asked.

"What do you mean asking me that? You threatened us. You told Steve Faralaco that there would be 'consequences' if all that territory from Sarawak to Mindanao and Guam didn't become part of Brunei."

"That is another issue," the ambassador said calmly. "The consequences that must be paid are those that must be paid by decaying colonial powers everywhere who stand in the way of the people who want to emerge from the shadows to become the major nations of the world in the twenty-first century."

"As I told you in the memorandum that I sent to you in the care of Mr. Faralaco, the United States will never give Guam to Brunei. I seriously doubt that you'll find Malaysia handing over Sarawak and Sabah without a fight. I believe that they have your armed forces outnumbered a hundred to one?"

"Blessed are the peacemakers, Mr. Secretary." The ambassador smiled. "You reacted antagonistically to my proposal, but you should have looked at it as an opportunity."

"What in the world do you mean by that?"

"It is an opportunity to go to the United Nations and offer the concessions that would recast the global image of the United States as a peacemaker and a decolonizer. We have not made our proposal public. We are completely willing to allow you to claim credit for it."

"Your proposal is nothing but a threat."

"You keep talking about 'threats,' Mr. Secretary, but who is threatening who? We are well aware that your Seventh Fleet is right at this moment hovering in the Sulu Sea with the sole purpose of threatening *my* country."

"They are there in response to the threats that you made on March 19th."

"We give you a golden opportunity to alter your global image, and you threaten us with warships. The world hates the United States because of its bellicosity. Apparently, even the ecoterrorists within your own country hate you so much that they are willing to kill hundreds of people in a major city. Your true threat comes not from His Majesty, but from the winds of history. It would be a shame if this were to happen again. You have the opportunity to prevent that, Mr. Secretary, and I truly hope that you do."

April 6
12:10 P.M. Pacific Time

"**I**'M not asking you, man, I'm telling you," Reid Arthur screamed at the two FBI agents. "Leave these premises immediately. We know our rights."

Rod Llewellan and Erik Vasquez were part of the flotilla of agents that the bureau had flooded into the

San Francisco area after the attack. What the park
ranger learned from the backpackers led to the discovery of the gallon bottles with traces of LSD at Wapama
Falls, upstream from Hetch Hetchy, and a look at the
most militant of the groups advocating the demolishing
of the O'Shaughnessy Dam led the FBI to Environmental Action International. This, in turn, brought Llewellan
and Vasquez to this seedy storefront just north of Telegraph Avenue in Berkeley.

Though they are within sight of San Francisco,
Berkeley and most neighboring cities, including Oakland, get their water from different sources, so they
were generally unaffected by either the disaster or the
subsequent quarantine.

"I don't have to tell you a damned thing," Arthur
asserted.

"This is a Gestapo-free zone," added a short woman
with a tattoo on her neck and rivets in her nostrils.
"Agents of that pig Livingstone aren't welcome here!"

"Aren't you just a little bit concerned about what happened across the Bay the night before last?" Llewellan
asked sarcastically.

"We don't know who did it," Arthur said.

"Neither do we," Llewellan told him. "But it's our
job to find out. That's why we're here."

"You're blaming Environmental Action International, aren't you?"

I didn't say that, but I could certainly *infer* that
from things that your outfit has done in the past."

"We never poisoned anybody."

"But you've been very outspoken about tearing
down the O'Shaughnessy Dam, and you splattered

about thirty gallons of green paint all over the inside of that office building over in San Ramon about three weeks ago."

"That was an *oil* company!" Arthur shouted, justifying the vandalism. "That was a capitalist exploiter of the 'people.'"

"I guess you showed a thing or two to the 'people' who had to clean up that mess," Erik Vasquez interjected.

Arthur said nothing. He just stared at the Hispanic agent, imagining for a moment the crew that indeed had to clean up thirty gallons of oil-based paint spattered on the walls and floor of an office building reception area. Most of them were probably Hispanic.

"Look, man, we don't want to be here any more than you want us here," Llewellan told the bearded environmentalist. "If you don't stop giving us rhetoric and start giving us some straight answers, we're going to come back here with a warrant and make your life *really* miserable. After what happened over in San Francisco the other day, we can get a warrant so fast it'll make your head spin."

"I told you, we don't know anything."

"What about your membership? Assuming for the moment that you wouldn't *officially* want to poison anybody, do you have any members inside your organization who might be a little more zealous?"

"I can't think of anybody."

Llewellan and Vasquez hit a brick wall with Arthur, and left the storefront with the caveat that they would be back if they turned up anything that led them back—and next time they wouldn't be so nice. They stepped out into the sunshine. The stench of stale incense wafted down the side street from Telegraph Avenue, and up on the corner, a panhandler with one shoe was obscenely demanding that a woman give him an additional dollar.

"I noticed that the chick with all the face piercings got pretty nervous when we started asking the guy about his membership," Vasquez observed.

"Yeah, nervous as hell," Llewellan agreed. "She was smoking like a fiend and trying not to make eye contact with us. She knows something. They both do."

With their similar windbreakers, wingtip shoes, and wire-rimmed sunglasses, the two agents could not have looked more out of place. As they turned the corner, the people lounging on the sidewalks selling used clothes stared at them suspiciously, and a man with his hair tied in little knots shoved something in the pocket of his leather coat and quickly skittered across the street.

"Should we have them watched?" Vasquez asked.

"Not a bad idea," Llewellan agreed. "Somebody within that organization knows something, or at the very least, somebody knows somebody."

April 6
5:59 P.M. Eastern Time

"**H**E said it would be a shame if this happened again," John Edredin explained to the small group of men gathered in the Oval Office.

"What the hell does that mean?" President Thomas Livingstone said angrily. "It's diplomatic language for, 'It will be done again if you don't do what I tell you.' That's it and exactly it."

"Then I'll order CINCPAC to blow Sultan Omar to kingdom come," Admiral Felth interjected.

"Well, actually we don't really have that option," Edredin cautioned.

"Why the hell not? It's a plain-and-simple case of retaliation. We don't even need a goddamn International Validation. We were attacked."

"Not as far as the world is concerned," Edredin said. "Nobody knows about the March 19th conversation. That threat was never made public and there is no record that it happened. The only evidence that exists so far points to ecoterrorism. The only ecoterrorists that we have had to deal with are homegrown."

"Are you saying that we can't retaliate?" Livingstone asked.

"Mr. President, you'd be seen as barking up the wrong tree. I can contact Mboma and ask him for an International Validation, but that won't do a bit of good. I can tell you what he'll say. He'll accuse us of blaming Sultan Omar for domestic terrorism. I don't have to tell you how that will play on the global stage."

"He's a shrewd bastard, I'll grant him that," Livingstone growled. "There has to be *something* that we can do."

"No, Mr. President, we've been outmaneuvered. He saw how easy it was to get his exclusion zone."

"Like a shark goes after raw meat," Felth said tersely.

"I was sure that he could be placated," Edredin admitted. "I was sure that if we gave him that he'd be satisfied."

"It's like Chamberlain and Deladier in 1938," Livingstone reminded his secretary of state. "They met Hitler in Munich and let him take the Sudentenland part of Czechoslovakia. They gave away part of somebody else's country and called it 'peace in our time.'"

"Then Hitler came back in March 1939 and swallowed the rest of Czechoslovakia," Edredin added, continuing the analogy.

"And they let him get away with it," Livingstone snarled. "When nobody stopped him in the spring of 1939, he went on and invaded Poland in September. Again, in 1994, Jimmy Carter and Bill Clinton gave Kim Jong Il millions to shut down his nuke plants. He just pocketed the money, became the world's single largest consumer of Hennessy Cognac, and did nothing about the nukes. This time, it's even worse."

"How's that?"

"In this case, our little Hitler wannabe is blackmailing us into giving away Czechoslovakia, and making it *our* idea."

"Yes, Mr. President," Edredin said sadly. "And the other thing that he's telling us with this colorless tasteless stuff . . ."

"What's that?"

"He's telling us that he can do it again, and again . . . until you give him exactly what he wants!"

April 8
6:16 A.M. Brunei Time

"**MESSAGE** from CINCPAC, sir," Captain Roland "Roach" Rouche told the admiral, handing him a scrap of paper.

Rear Admiral Walter Briscoe could have read it off his BlackBerry, but he didn't have a BlackBerry. He was old-fashioned that way. He was bred in an old Navy. He came of age as the skipper of a destroyer in the six-hundred-ship Navy that Ronald Reagan built in the 1980s, the same six-hundred-ship Navy that helped to bring down the Soviet Union without firing a shot. Those were the days. Now he commanded a task force that centered on a supercarrier that bore Reagan's name, though it was part of a Navy that was less than a third the size of Reagan's Navy.

They were armed and ready. The Navy might be just a ghost of its former self, but Task Force 70 still had the hitting power to bring almost any foe to heel, and certainly the power to annihilate Sultan Omar Jamalul Halauddin the moment he crossed the line.

The crew of USS *Ronald Reagan* and the crews of the guided-missile cruiser, the destroyers, and the support vessels who sailed with her had all heard the news of what had happened in San Francisco. As improbable as it seemed, many people were sure that Omar had had something to do with it, but that was just scuttlebutt.

Everyone—from the squids in the ready room who were itching to strap on their Super Hornets to the sailors who would plot the trajectories of the Tomahawks—was ready to go to war, ready to strike back. They saw the sultan as just another punk dictator in a world with way too many punk dictators.

The sailors and the pilots were ready to go to war. That was their job. Mainly, though, they were ready to do *something*. Task Force 70 had been steaming back and forth across the Sulu Sea for two weeks. Hurry up and wait. They had been on edge and ready to move at a moment's notice, but after two weeks of constant hurrying up and waiting, they were itching to do *something*.

The sailors at least had the constant drills to fill their hours of hurrying up and waiting. For the four embedded reporters who had shipped out from Yokosuka aboard the USS *Ronald Reagan,* the time passed slowly. In the beginning, there was a demand on all the cable channels for the latest news of Task Force 70, but since the San Francisco debacle, the news channels had different fish to fry. San Francisco was far more ominous, and far more riveting than small-screen views of Super Hornets taking off and landing. The viewing public forgot about Task Force 70. The embeds had interviewed nearly everyone aboard to whom Briscoe permitted them access, and they had almost resorted to interviewing each other.

Briscoe had reluctantly agreed to permit the embeds to come aboard, but this was the new Navy. Napoleon once said that an army travels on its stomach. Briscoe had been told that the new Navy runs on sound-bite visibility. The more that people back home saw their new Navy, the more their congressmen would be inclined to keep the new Navy well funded.

Even as Rouche approached with the teletype, Briscoe sensed that a climax was near, that the hurry-up-and-waiting would soon reach the turning point. The sailors would have their action, and the embeds would have their magic bites of digital video.

Briscoe fully expected that CINCPAC would be giving him the go-code. He glanced at the USS *Cowpens,* barely a quarter mile off the *Reagan*'s bow, and fully expected that within moments, he'd be watching plumes of straw-colored missile contrails arching upward and outward from its deck. He glanced at the F/A-18s parked on the flight deck beneath him, and knew that soon pilots would be scrambling aboard and he'd hear the powerful din of the catapult and the shriek of the twin F404 turbofans, a sound like no other.

Briscoe couldn't believe his eyes as he glanced at the message.

"Stand down, Mr. Rouche," he said after a brief pause. "Transmit orders to the Task Force to stand down and stand by for further orders. We will *not* be going to war today."

April 8
6:46 A.M. Eastern Time

"**Y**OU'RE moping," Joyce Livingstone said.

"I am not," the president told his wife defensively. "I'm thinking. I'm thinking about those people who did that to San Francisco, and how they could do it again, and there's nothing we can do about it."

The ripple of nervousness about the attack on San Francisco had become a temblor. The paranoia was spreading, ironically aided by the uncoordinated efforts made by local municipalities to protect their people. Contradictory warnings were being issued. In some places people were being told not to drink bottled water, although the evidence showed that people in San Francisco who had drunk bottled water rather than tap water had been unaffected. People were uncertain what to do, and the conflicting suggestions only added to the problem. If people couldn't drink the water, what could they do?

Livingstone and Faralaco had crafted a public statement in which the president had assured the people that it was an isolated incident, and that the FBI would soon round up the perpetrators. The statement was misleading on both counts, but many people wanted to believe it, and this calmed the hysteria. Livingstone had bought some time, but even he did not know how much.

"Was it that sultan character?" Joyce asked, spreading a dollop of jam on her toast. The president had already skimmed his morning papers, and he and the First Lady were having a quiet breakfast before going their separate ways for a busy day of appearances and meetings.

"We don't know."

"I'll bet you do," she contradicted. Nobody else argued with the president of the United States or put him in his place like the First Lady. "I know that you don't tell me everything. I'll bet you do know that he's mixed up in this, and he's one of the things you aren't telling me."

"Well, maybe," Livingstone said defensively. "But we *really* don't know for sure."

"Then you should do something about it. He's a twerp and he shouldn't be allowed to get away with this. You're the president. You can do *something*."

"We're evaluating our options, but we really don't have any. We can't use military force without an International Validation, and with what we have . . . or *don't* have . . . to connect the sultan to San Francisco, we can't get one."

"Don't use words like 'evaluating our options' with *me,* Tom Livingstone. Save that for your press releases," Joyce Livingstone scolded. "I know that you have more 'options' than you talk about. I know that last year when that Al-Zahir person was running around killing people, you were beside yourself. Then suddenly that other guy, that guy Badr, killed him and you suddenly got all smug . . . like you had something to do with it. I saw you with Buck Peighton. I know that you guys cooked something up. I'm not going to ask what it was, because I don't really want to know, but whatever it was, it got you over feeling like you do right now."

Livingstone smiled. She had him figured out. He had indeed cooked something up with Buck Peighton last year, and the terrorist mastermind Fahrid Al-Zahir was dead because of it. Even Livingstone himself did not know exactly how it had worked out, but it had. Fahrid Al-Zahir was dead, and the world was a better place for it.

"Are you?" Joyce asked.

"Am I what?"

"Are you going to call Buck Peighton and get this thing taken care of."

"It's a complex geopolitical problem," Livingstone replied. "I'm not sure that you can just call up someone like calling a plumber."

"Don't give me this 'complex geopolitical problem' stuff, Thomas." She glowered. "I'm not some cub reporter at one of your press conferences, and you're not some bureaucrat trying to weasel out of taking charge and getting something done. You're the man who goes to work every day in that office where Harry Truman said the buck stopped. Stop making excuses. Call the plumber."

As Joyce went back to eating her fruit salad and reading the paper, Livingstone leaned back and thought about it. Should he call Peighton? What would Peighton do?

Livingstone had called Peighton when Fahrid Al-Zahir's terrorists had struck the United States, when Livingstone couldn't strike back with conventional military forces.

Livingstone had asked Peighton to build him an American Volunteer Group like Chennault had built in China, and terrorists had died. Hundreds of them, culminating in Al-Zahir himself. Livingstone had never asked Peighton how it was done, nor who did it. He knew his American Volunteer Group only as the mysterious "Raptor Team." Somehow, Peighton and his Raptors had done it. Livingstone just watched from the sidelines, maintaining his plausible deniability.

There was nobody inside the military establishment that he could trust as he trusted Buckley Peighton. Indeed, there was nobody anywhere in the government whom he could trust as he trusted Peighton. They had gone to school together at Penn a long, long time ago. Afterward, they went their separate ways. Livingstone went into politics. Peighton became a soldier. Peighton retired with four stars. Livingstone became President.

In that terrible week when Al-Zahir had first struck the United States, they had met again in an aircraft hangar in Denver. The two men had greeted one another with a mix of joy and guilt, as old friends that have been too busy to stay in touch often do. Peighton had been to Livingstone's inauguration party, but they had not had a chance for more than a few minutes of conversation.

Once again they were close friends, sharing a secret known only to a handful of people.

April 8
6:46 A.M. Eastern Time

"WE can't wait," Abdulla Maloud insisted. "They must get the message."

"They *have* the message," Ambassador Pehin Dato Yayah Korma insisted. "I spoke with Edredin. He understands that the United States has no choice. Believe me, they are backed into a corner."

"His Majesty has ordered me to keep up the pressure."

"They *feel* the pressure."

"I see no evidence of that." The sultan's Iranian "advisor" scowled. "I see only intransigence."

"I see the secretary of state like the captain of a very large ship. Very large ships are difficult to turn. They are very unwieldy. I learned that as a young man working aboard barges in the Malacca Strait. He will turn. The United States will turn. We have given them no choice."

"They must be trained," Maloud argued. "The whelp is trained by the laying on of the whip, not through compassion."

"I wouldn't compare this to whipping a dog."

"You may recall in history when the Great Satan used its atomic bombs against Japan in 1945."

"Of course."

"One bomb fell, and the Emperor of Japan was paralyzed with indecision," Maloud hissed in a conspiratorial tone. "Three days later, another bomb fell. He 'turned his ship' promptly after that."

"It has been nearly four days since San Francisco. Does this mean that you want to attack another city now?"

"Perhaps it is time?"

"What does His Majesty have in mind?" Yayah Korma parried. He was getting nervous. He wasn't sure where the line between the wishes of Sultan and the zeal of Iranian lay.

"One more week." Maloud shrugged. "We'll give them one more week to show evidence that they are turning their ship. I like that metaphor . . . turning their ship. In one week, we will discuss this matter again."

Yayah Korma watched from his office window as Maloud swaggered across the street toward his car. So far, the sultan's plan had worked better than anyone could have imagined. When Hudim Incpaduka had phoned him on the secure line from New York to tell him that the secretary general had so promptly paid a billion-dollar ransom, he had been astounded. Cheers had echoed through the embassy. When Edredin had gone to Brunei to agree to the exclusion zone, there were more cheers.

Yayah Korma felt a little bit like a young boy involved in a youthful prank. It had worked so well thus far, but how long and how far could they push this powerful and unwieldy barge that was the United States?

April 10
10:45 A.M. Eastern Time

THE president acknowledged the applause with a wave, and turned to shake hands with the leadership of the National Association of Certified Underwriters who had invited him to appear at their national convention. As he passed the end of the line, several of the organization's bigwigs pressed closer to have his influential ear for a moment longer, but at last, he pulled free and moved toward the subterranean passage to the parking garage at the Washington Hilton.

There, a nondescript man in a nondescript suit with an American flag pin stepped forward and smiled. As he shook hands with the president, the phalanx of Secret Service men spread out to form a perimeter so that the two men could have a private conversation.

"We'll have to stop meeting like this, Tom," the man said.

"Buck, I really long for the day when we won't be meeting for these kinds of reasons. I wish that someday we could just go fishing."

The only times that Livingstone had crossed paths with General Buckley Peighton since his inaugural were when they had met to coordinate the actions of the Raptor Team. Tom Livingstone had told him "who and what." Peighton had handled the "when, where, and how."

"I take it that we're not planning that fishing trip today?" Buck Peighton smiled.

"I only wish. Actually, I need to reactivate our American Volunteer Group, our Raptors."

"I guessed as much from the half-dozen words you said on the phone when you called. I'm also guessing that it may have something to do with what happened in San Francisco."

"Is it that obvious?"

"What do you need, Tom?"

"It's Sultan Omar Jamalul Halauddin. Thanks to Wilcox and Mboma, and my own willingness to appease the sunuvabitch, he's back with more demands. He wants us to ask the United Nations to restore Brunei to its sixteenth-century borders, at the expense of the Philippines and Malaysia, and he wants Guam."

"Is that *all*? I assume you told him to shove it," Peighton said.

"Of course. But then this thing in San Francisco happened," Livingstone replied.

"That was *him*? I heard some conspiracy theorist mention it on television somewhere, but most people think it was the Wood Nazis, the ecoterrorists."

"So did we, but Edredin's talked to their ambassador and he's sure that it's the sultan."

"What can I do?"

"Get rid of the sultan."

"Is that *all*?"

"We can't let this happen again. LSD is undetectable. We have to cut off the head of the snake. I need to have you get the Raptors in there, and get rid of him, and his nukes and whoever he's got helping him."

"I thought you had the Seventh Fleet on station," Peighton said. "It's all over TV. I've watched the stories that the embedded reporters have filed from the Sulu Sea. Have you thought of just taking him out that way?"

"We can't because of the damned United Nations and the damned International Validation Organization. Especially not with the embedded reporters there for the whole world to see. And besides, I don't relish the idea of killing a lot of Bruneians. They didn't elect this guy. They aren't getting any of that dough that he extorted from Mboma last month. They're not the bad guys."

"So what's the first step? Where do we get our intel?"

"Your guy in the FBI, this guy Llewellan. He's out in San Francisco. I learned that in a briefing from the director of national intelligence. He's out in San Francisco, and he's been following up on some environmentalist outfit that may be involved. Get with him. See what you can shake loose. When it comes to interviews, the Raptors may have powers of persuasion that aren't available to the FBI."

"Okay," Peighton said thoughtfully. "We'll take it from there. Oh, and there's just one more thing. . . ."

"Buck, I have already taken the liberty of reactivating your bank account. You should find everything you need."

April 10
3:16 P.M. Mountain Time

"I thought you were on an indefinite sabbatical," Dave Brannan said as Anne McCaine folded up her cell phone.

"I am. That's part of what makes this so unusual."

Anne had gotten an e-mail from Asa Henderson, the chairman of the archaeology department at the university. He wanted her to come in to talk about a special project. She had phoned to ask him what it was, and he'd said that he needed to discuss it with her in person.

"He thinks I'm in Colorado," she said. "I didn't want to disabuse him of that notion."

"Aren't you curious?"

"I'm not there. I'm here . . . and for the moment, I can't get enough of your 'hospitality,' Colonel. Are you trying to get rid of me?"

"Why don't you go?" Brannan suggested. "I'll go with you. I haven't been on a road trip for a while. It would be an excuse to get out of the house."

April 10
2:17 P.M. Pacific Time

R OD Llewellan had been watching for an out-of-place rental car to turn onto the street for fifteen minutes, but General Buckley Peighton was a no-show. The general had called last night at the motel with a fast cryptic message. He just asked about Rod's ailing aunt, named a location in GPS coordinates as though it were an address, and said he'd see Rod today.

Rod got rid of Erik Vasquez by suggesting that they tail separate members of Environmental Action International, and dashed over to this bumpy side street in the industrial area on the west side of Berkeley near Emeryville. It was a good place for a meeting. There was lots of activity, but it was entirely truckers, factory employees, and people who worked here or had business here. There were no casual onlookers or panhandlers as there were across town near the university.

As he waited, Llewellan wondered. He wondered where Peighton was, and whether he had gotten the location right. He also wondered what this was all about. Was it about the Raptor Team? Had the president and Peighton decided to reactivate Dave Brannan's band of commandos? Was it about the San Francisco debacle? How and why would the Raptors be involved in that? Was it really domestic ecoterrorism, or was it something else?

Llewellan lived a double life. Not actually "double" in the sense of his being a double agent, but a schizophrenic life nonetheless. Nobody within the FBI knew that he operated in the same shadow world as the Raptor Team, but unlike them, he operated mostly alone.

The first time he had met Peighton, the general took him aside and said, "The president needs you." The rest had been the strangest trip of Llewellan's life—his double life. Everything that he did for Peighton and the Raptor Team would have been illegal, had the orders not come from the president himself. When the Raptors had secretly gone to war against the Mujahidin Al-Akbar, Llewellan's job had been nothing short of stealing top-secret intelligence documents from the director of national intelligence. If he had been caught pilfering intel for Peighton and the Raptors, he could have been executed. He *was* working for the president, but the president would have had to disavow him. He'd been glad when that war was over, and his stomach had turned when Peighton had called him last night.

As Llewellan carefully scrutinized everyone who came and went on the street, a man in an Oakland Raiders cap carrying a clipboard bumped into him. It was Buck Peighton.

"How are things, Rod?" Peighton said, pulling him aside and pretending to discuss a bill of lading that was on his clipboard.

"We're looking at Environmental Action International for possible links to the LSD incident," Llewellan told him, assuming that the general already knew about his investigation. "How are things with you, General?"

"Basically, I'm on the same case. The bigwigs in DC have figured out who's behind all this and we need your help in setting up to take him down."

"I'm just a foot soldier out here, General. Who *is* behind the LSD thing?"

"The Sultan of Brunei."

"The Sultan of *Brunei*? *Why?*"

"Why? Because he wants territorial concessions from the Philippines and Malaysia and he wants Guam from us."

"Wait a minute, General," Llewellan cautioned. "We're following a completely different track here. The attack on San Francisco has all the earmarks of ecoterrorism. The FBI is already developing some good leads. There was some Environmental Action International documentation found up there in Yosemite that the media doesn't know about."

"We're sure that the sultan's people are using Environmental Action International."

"How come the sultan is using LSD? I thought he had nuclear weapons."

"Think about it," the general explained. "If he used nukes to get what he wanted, everybody would know it. Everybody would see it. The United Nations would have no choice but to give us an International Validation to blow him off the map. This way, all eyes are on the nukes. Nobody thinks to connect him to some other weapon of mass destruction."

"But why LSD? Why not anthrax or ricin or something?"

"He's using the acid because it's virtually undetectable and untractable. And because nobody, not
even you, had thought to connect him to it."

"So you figure that he somehow got Environmental Action International involved in planting the
LSD?"

"Either that or he framed them." Peighton shrugged.
"That's my question to *you*. What do you think? You've
investigated them."

"We've talked to several. They know more than
they're letting on. We've been tailing them, trying to
get enough to bring one of them in for questioning."

"Why don't you just grab hold of an ear and drag
them in and give them the third degree?" General
Peighton growled.

· "We can't do that anymore," Llewellan cautioned.
"We have procedures we have to follow."

"But we're at *war* with these bastards."

"Procedures are procedures. As an agent, I have to
follow strict guidelines."

"But civilians don't have to follow guidelines?"

"No."

"I seem to recall an incident last year when you
were having some trouble in your interrogation of a
Mujahidin Al-Akbar hijacker, and you turned to a former Special Forces man named Jack Rodgers to help
you out."

By a twist of fate, Llewellan had been in the right
place at the right time—or vice versa, depending on
how you look at it—to have been picked by Peighton as
the intelligence conduit for the Raptor Team. He had

been on the ground, debriefing passengers after Captain
Jack Rodgers killed three Mujahidin Al-Akbar terrorists and saved everyone onboard the hijacked airliner.
Later, he'd discovered that Rodgers was a key member
of Brannan's Raptors.

"I did," Llewellan admitted. He knew exactly
where Peighton was going with this. "I was frustrated
by the 'guidelines' and I turned to Rodgers because he
was a civilian."

"And did he get the intel that led to a takedown of
the Mujahidin Al-Akbar in Mexico?"

"And eventually the whole Mujahidin Al-Akbar
operation up to Al-Zahir," Llewellan said, nodding his
head. A wry grin creased his lips as he recalled how
Rodgers had reduced the last defiant terrorist to tears
without visibly touching him.

"I think Jack Rodgers is due for a trip to the Bay
Area very soon." Peighton smiled.

April 13
12:04 P.M. Mountain Time

"**THANKS** for coming in, Anne." Chairman Henderson smiled. "You're looking well. Your sabbatical seems to be treating you kindly."

Indeed, she did look well, and it was not just the
way that the apricot-colored suit with the slightly ruf-
fled skirt accented her figure and her skin tone. It was
her relaxed, almost nonchalant, manner. Her hair was
longer than he remembered it, and she was wearing it

down, rather than tied back into a bun as she usually did. The sense of urgency that possessed his faculty members was absent. He began to wish that he could send himself on a sabbatical.

"You were very mysterious on the phone," she said. "You piqued my curiosity."

"The department was in the running to undertake a special project. There were a lot of upper-level negotiations going on and I wasn't really able to discuss it then. I am now," the chairman explained. "I really wanted us to get our hands on this. Both Columbia and Duke were in the running. We got it. The trouble is, with Anderson recovering from his coronary, and all the doubling up of the workload, I don't have anyone to spare. I was wondering if you'd consider taking this on."

"What exactly is it?"

"What do you know about the archaeology of Borneo?"

"Borneo? That's pretty far afield."

"Yes, Borneo," Henderson said, lighting his pipe and leaning back in his chair in a chairmanlike way. "I realize that not much work has been done out there, and that's because the jungle is so heavy it generally swallows things up and it's hard to get in. As you know, we've suspected that there are prehistoric archaeological sites in the interior, and even along the coastline, that are untouched."

"Well, I have heard about the human remains they found in the Niah Caves in Sarawak that date back thirty-five thousand years or so," Anne said.

"There are more sites on the Malaysia mainland,

such as the Bujang Valley site, where they unearthed
that Hindu temple complex from about twenty-five
hundred years ago," the chairman continued. "But
very little on Borneo. Then came an interesting opportunity."

"From who? Who gave you the grant?"

"The United Nations, specifically UNESCO."

"Whoa," Anne said, surprised to hear that the United
Nations was funding archaeology in a remote area
largely devoid of the sort of high-profile "important"
sites generally favored by UNESCO. "Where exactly is
the site?"

"It's in Brunei," the chairman replied. "UNESCO
is funding the exploration of a site near the town of
Tutong in Brunei. Eventually, most of the work will
probably be done by a UNESCO team, but the United
Nations wanted someone from a major American university to go over there to do the initial site survey.
Just a few weeks and then you can go back to your sabbatical."

"This is a political boondoggle," Anne said, a
frown wrinkling her forehead. "This is part of that
payoff that Mboma and Wilcox arranged to get the
sultan to put his nuclear weapons program on ice."

"Technically, yes," the chairman admitted apolo-
getically. "But it's an excellent opportunity for the university to do some work in an area where not much
has been done. Actually, since 2005, it's easier to meet
the criteria now than it once was. Up through the end
of 2004, UNESCO had six stringent measures for cultural heritage sites. Now, there is only one set of ten

criteria and nominated sites only have to be of 'out-standing universal value,' which is a matter of opinion and thus easily fulfilled. Plus you only have to meet *just one* on the list of ten."

"What *are* on the list of ten?"

"Oh, things like representing a 'masterpiece of human creative genius,' or being 'a testimony to a cultural tradition or civilization.' "

"That's really vague," Anne said, shaking her head. "In short, that's just about anything."

"All you have to do is go over there and call it 'important' or 'significant.' "

"Is it even a legitimate site?"

"Well, that would be part of your survey."

"You want me to go over there and put my stamp of approval on this site so that the university can get a grant?" Anne said, shaking her head again.

"I'd like to have you go over there and do the preliminary site survey. Yes, the grant money is useful, and so is the prestige that the university would derive from being involved in something that is liable to get some favorable publicity. I can also see this developing into an important site."

"I really don't know. . . ."

"Anne, if you're worried about the nuclear issue, you really shouldn't be. That whole episode is behind us, and I'm told that the sultan is really a charming man."

"No, I really don't think I'll do it," Anne said after a long pause. "I think I'll stay on sabbatical. You shouldn't have any trouble finding someone else."

April 13
12:07 P.M. Mountain Time

"**H**OW soon can you come to Denver?"
"Actually, I'm there. I mean *here*."
"How fortuitous! When can we meet?"

General Buckley Peighton had waited until he left the Denver airport before picking up the phone to dial the number that he had memorized for the man who had led the president's American Volunteer Group against the terrorist Al-Zahir. He was startled to discover that Colonel Dave Brannan was in Denver. He had expected him to be halfway around the world or in the middle of nowhere, hundreds of miles from cell reception. A week ago, Peighton would have been right.

The general asked Brannan to meet him at an out-of-the-way coffee shop. It was the spot they referred to as the place where the Mormon missionary had converted the hooker, or at the least he had gotten her to come to church. Anyone eavesdropping on the call, had anyone been doing so, would have had no idea what they were talking about.

Peighton had *asked* Brannan to meet him. He did not "order" him. In the service, Peighton's four stars put him far up the food chain from a mere colonel's birds, but both men had retired, and they had entered a completely different service. They both knew their place. Peighton had the ear of the president. Brannan was the legendary Special Forces commander who had accomplished missions in the field that few, if any, men with four stars could even imagine.

"What brings you to the Mile-High City?" Peighton asked when they had each ordered a sandwich.

"Visiting a friend." The colonel smiled.

Brannan had decided to spend the day poking around Denver while the professor went to her meeting at the archaeology department over in Boulder. "What's up with you? You sounded like you've got something a little bit more pressing than a lunch date on your mind."

With that, the general spun out the whole sordid story of global extortion, and the involvement of Sultan Omar Jamalul Halauddin in the San Francisco acid trip.

"Your mission—that is, if you're still on board to put your Raptor Team back into action—is to take this guy out."

"What other options does the president have?" Brannan asked thoughtfully. He was really not anxious to head out halfway across the world just now. Anne had been talking about driving down to Mesa Verde for a few days. She knew of a couple of undisturbed archaeological sites that might interest him, and they had developed a mutual affinity for the primal joys of spending the night together with nothing above them but the Milky Way.

"None," Peighton said succinctly. "The political and diplomatic downsides of launching a full-fledged 'shock and awe' on the guy are too numerous to mention."

"Not to mention messy and imprecise," Brannan agreed.

"Yet something has to be done," Peighton stressed.

"The consequences of inaction are staggering and unacceptable. There's no other way. The president called me, and I called you. If anyone can do this, you can."

"Not to mention the plausible deniability of sending a bunch of civilians rather than Delta Force." Dave smiled.

"Civilians that know what the hell they're doing," the general replied, choosing to let the obvious issue of plausible deniability slide. "Can you do it?"

"Anything's possible. We'd have to get a look at the lay of the land. It would be tricky, but anything's possible."

"Will you do it?"

"I don't know," the colonel said. "I have to talk to some people, but I'm inclined to pass on this one."

Brannan found himself facing a familiar quandary that he never imagined he would face again. Many years ago, he had gone into the violent dark side of the world to do the job that was required of the uniform he had worn. More often than not, it was a job for which his own extraordinary skill was uniquely suited. His country had needed him, and he had answered the call.

In doing so while he was still in uniform, he all too frequently had to tear himself away from a wife to whom he owed an allegiance of a different kind. Now she was gone and the uniform had long since been hung away in the back of a closet. He had been freed from a paradox and placed in a world with neither commitment.

The last time that Buck Peighton had come calling,

Brannan had seen it as an opportunity for the adventure that he had come to miss. His country had needed him, and he had answered the call. This time, a new presence had blossomed to fill that other void in his life, and he loathed the idea of being back in the position of having to make a difficult choice.

April 13
4:58 P.M. Mountain Time

"**H**OW'D your meeting go?" Brannan asked as the professor got into the car.

"It was really interesting," Anne said, shaking her head. "It didn't take very long, so I spent some time catching up with some of my friends in the department. The chairman had a pretty curious special project that he wanted me to take on. I told him no, thanks. I'm enjoying my sabbatical too much."

As he turned to look at her, she put her hand on his thigh and kissed him on the lips. He could feel her tongue stroking his upper lip as he turned away to watch traffic. It was, after all, her Mercedes and he felt he should pay attention.

"I'm enjoying your sabbatical too." He laughed. "What sort of special project was it?"

"He wanted to have me work on some deal for the United Nations. Of all the places in the world, he wanted me to go over to Brunei."

"Why don't you go?" Brannan asked, looking back at her. She still had her hand on his thigh. "I'll go with

you. I haven't had a road trip for a while. It would be
an excuse to get out of the house."

"*What?*"

"I just got offered a job in Brunei myself. Let's go.
It could be exciting."

April 14
7:11 P.M. Central Time

GREG Boyinson maneuvered the Jet Ranger onto
the pad, clicked his way through the engine-
shutdown procedure, and pulled off his helmet. Subconsciously, he looked at his reflection in the Plexiglas
and pawed his messy hair into what could pass for pre-
sentable.

He hadn't started doing that until he started doing
Julia Girod. He sort of disliked the fact that she had this
civilizing effect on him, but only *sort of*. He let that dislike fade when he thought of all of the other effects that
Julia Girod had on him.

A few days after that night when he drove her home,
she called to invite him over for jambalaya. He told her
that he had no interest in being interviewed, and she
promised she wouldn't. He enjoyed the meal and she
didn't try to interview him. She hadn't scrimped on the
tabasco, but it wasn't nearly as hot as the jambalaya
they wound up making in the bedroom later that night.
He had seen her a time or two after that, and he was
planning to see her again later tonight.

Boyinson signed out and was walking toward his

pickup when he noticed a man with a salt-and-pepper beard and a pale yellow sport shirt watching him.

"Rodgers! You sunuvabitch, what the fuck you doin' here in Looz-iana?" Boyinson shouted as he grabbed the man's hand in his viselike grip.

"I see you're gainfully employed down here." Jack Rodgers smiled. "I even heard in town that you're some kind of hero."

"Ahh, it wasn't nothing. The boss was ready to let the poor kid die out there, and I just went and picked him up. The doctors made him well. Funny thing was, after givin' me so much shit about it, the boss got made into almost as big a hero for *lettin'* me do it. Hey, I'm meeting a friend of mine for a drink. Lemme call her and see if she's got any horny friends she can bring along."

"Before we do that and I get to drinking, I gotta talk with you about a job," Rodgers admitted.

"Is this gonna be another one of those out-of-country experiences?"

"Yep." Rodgers nodded as he began to give Boyinson an overview of the situation, and their ultimate destination. "We'll leave first thing in the morning. The gang is getting together near Denver. I'll drop you there before heading out to the coast to visit our old buddy Rod Llewellan."

"Cool. Let's go kick us some Third World ass."

"Can you get a leave from your job here for a couple of weeks?"

"Damn well better." Boyinson grinned. "I'm a fuckin' hero *and* I made the boss look good."

April 15
9:55 A.M. Eastern Time

I T was tax day, and throughout the United States,
people were lining up at post offices for an annual rit-
ual that nobody liked and many dreaded. The taxpayers
were paying. Unlike that day this coming November,
today they had no choice—or few choices. President
Thomas Livingstone was alone in the Oval Office and it
was strangely quiet. It had been a frantic morning. His
10:00 appointment would arrive shortly, but for this rare
moment, he was alone with his thoughts.

Livingstone thought about those taxpayers who
would be voting in the fall and about the kind of job that
he had done. All presidents think about such things. He
knew that. He had read a shelf-load of presidential bi-
ographies. His predecessors had fussed and fidgeted.
They had sat in this room, wondering and worrying.

Often, presidents did things that the taxpayers and
voters could never be told, and not infrequently, presidents did these things because they thought that the
lives of those Americans would be better for it. Livingstone had had some grave doubts when he and
Buck Peighton had secretly sent the Raptor Team off
to hunt those who had plotted the deaths of Americans
on American soil. But it had worked.

Buck Peighton had gently scolded him, quoting
Theodore Roosevelt, who might have been speaking
about the Raptors when he wrote in 1910 about the
man of action "who spends himself in a worthy cause;
who at the best knows in the end the triumph of high

achievement, and who at the worst, if he fails, at least fails while daring greatly, so that his place shall never be with those cold and timid souls who neither know victory nor defeat."

Now Livingstone was calling upon these mysterious men of the shadows who he would never meet. He had crossed the line again, and had called the genie forth from the lamp.

Even he was part of the lie. He had lied to Edredin when he took him aside at a cabinet meeting this morning to tell him that the United States was at a historic impasse, and that the secretary of state should begin secret discussions with Malaysia and the Philippines. The president had lied to Edredin when he said that this was the only way. In fact, he knew that leaks would occur, and word of his entreaties would reach Sultan Omar Jamalul Halauddin and he would taste victory at the same time that Peighton's secret army was doing whatever it was that they would do. He'd lied because he thought that the lives of those Americans out there at the post offices would be better for it.

"Mr. President?"

"Um, yes," Livingstone said, startled to be awakened from his thoughts.

"Your ten o'clock appointment is here, sir. Shall I show them in?"

April 16
9:55 A.M. Mountain Time

"**A**DRENALINE is a strange drug."

Those were the words that the professor had

used as she had told the colonel what she thought about the prospect of being a part of another escapade with his band of miscreants.

Those long months ago, she had been numb with fear when her grad students were attacked at that remote camp in the Anatolian wilderness of Turkey. She had reacted coolly, but beneath the surface, she had been gripped with terror—until that moment when that strange band of armed men who rescued her had turned out to be Americans. As silly as it seemed, the danger did not seem dangerous after she met this tall man with the auburn mustache. Blood, carnage, and large-caliber rounds fired from automatic weapons seemed inconsequential when he was near. She had found herself captivated both by the thrill of the action, and by this man.

Adrenaline was an addictive drug.

Sure, she'd go to Brunei with him. She'd go anywhere with him. Life with him was an adventure, and she had discovered that she craved the adventure nearly as much as she craved the big man with the auburn mustache.

They took a circuitous route to get to General Buck Peighton's summer place, heading east out of Denver before cutting south and west on Highway 470 to U.S. Highway 295. It was improbable that anyone would be following them, but Brannan knew that you often don't get a second chance when you make a potentially fatal choice.

At last they reached the small cluster of buildings in the foothills of the Rockies to which Peighton retreated in the warm summer months. Most of the

homes on this narrow dirt road were summer homes
and most of them were deserted. It was a quiet and
out-of-the-way place to meet.

The colonel and the professor were the last to arrive
at Peighton's safe house. The other members of the
Raptor Team, all former Special Forces men who had
a long history with Brannan, had filtered in over the
past few hours. Brad Townsend, Jason Houn, and Ray
Couper had all arrived together from New Mexico
in Couper's Camaro. Will Casey had driven in from
Idaho, and was unpacking some new state-of-the-art
gear on the living room floor. Jack Rodgers and Greg
Boyinson had arrived from Louisiana after spending a
very pleasant night with Julia Girod and one of her
friends.

Buck Peighton watched as Brannan parked the
Mercedes and headed up the stone walkway toward
the main house. Brannan had said that he was bringing
an archaeology professor who would be useful, but
Peighton had expected a short balding man in a tweed
jacket, not a tall, shapely young woman in a long
denim skirt. When they reached the front door, he noticed the streak of gray in her hair, and realized that
she was probably not as young as she looked.

"General Peighton, this is Professor McCaine from
the University of Colorado. The rest of the men have
met the professor."

"Pleased to meet you, General." Anne smiled,
shaking Peighton's hand. "The colonel speaks highly
of you."

"The pleasure is mine," Peighton said. He could
sense what Brannan saw in this woman. She had an

electrifying presence. "The colonel speaks way too little of you."

"The professor has been invited to Brunei by the United Nations, and she'll need an entourage," Brannan explained. "We can help."

"That'll make getting into the country pretty damned easy." Ray Couper grinned.

"What exactly are you going to be doing for the United Nations in Brunei, Professor?" Peighton asked.

"As you probably know, a few weeks ago, when Sultan Jamalul Halauddin was threatening the region with his nuclear weapons, the United Nations cut a deal to placate him so that he would back off and be nice," Anne explained. "Part of the arrangement was for an archaeological site near a place called Tutong to be declared as a UNESCO World Heritage Site. This week, the University of Colorado received a grant to survey the site."

"It sounded like a scam when I heard about that on the radio, and it still sounds like a scam," Greg Boyinson said.

"It sounded like a scam to me when the university asked me to do the survey of the place, which is why I told the university to find somebody else," Anne replied. "But when the colonel told me about the 'project' that you boys have got going, I decided that it would be useful if I changed my mind."

"What will we need to know about Bruneian archaeology in order to be part of your 'entourage,' Professor," asked Jason Houn, the Lebanese-American commando in the group.

"Not very much, because there is not a lot to know,"

Anne told the men. "The archaeology of this part of the world is relatively undeveloped because there are relatively few sites that have been excavated to date. Unless it's hacked at constantly, the heavy, fast-growing vegetation covers and envelops most things that have been built in or near it. Most archaeological excavations around the world follow from discoveries made on the surface, and in this case, the surfaces are covered with thick jungle. As for what you should know, like Captain Boyinson pointed out, this is mainly a scam, a political boondoggle, so there really isn't much to know. I'll give you a crash course in the archaeology of the region as a whole, and if you boys pay attention in my class, you'll come out knowing more than 99 percent of the people that you will likely come in contact with."

"Besides taking out the sultan, what exactly are the objectives once we're on the ground?" Will Casey asked the general. As the team's lead sniper, he knew that he'd be playing a key role.

"The president characterized the mission as one of cutting off the head of a snake, so that's obviously the first priority," Peighton explained. "But a close and obvious second is getting the nukes out of there. The sultan also has a bunch of henchmen around him, and these characters will also have to be terminated."

"Do we know who these guys are?" Brad Townsend asked.

"Since he's been shopping for arms in the Middle East he's got a ring of Iranians around him. 'Technical advisors,' I guess you'd call them. When he sacked the former sultan's government, he mostly replaced

them with people that aren't connected with his rack-
eteering days in Europe. They're mainly expatriates
that were living in Singapore or Australia or some-
place outside the country, people who had no particular
attachment to any of the internal factions. However, he
did bring in his two top lieutenants from the old
days. They're both in this country as ambassadors.
Hudim Incpaduka at the UN, and Yayah Korma in
Washington."

"Both of whom are now running around with diplomatic immunity," Brannan cautioned.

"The great thing about diplomatic immunity, just
like an International Validation, is that it only applies
to *countries*." Rodgers smiled. "None of *us* are in the
Army anymore."

The general proceeded to pass out dossiers on the
Bruneian leadership, as well as photographs for the men
to review. There were KH-12 Keyhole satellite photos
of various points of interest in Brunei, and there were
photographs of people who had been killed in the San
Francisco attack. One such picture, more than any of
the others, brought silence to the room. They could now
see in graphic detail the handiwork of the gruesome
monsters that they were being sent to eradicate. Even
the iron-assed Greg Boyinson could be seen choking
back a sob. The image was that of a small baby, about
six or seven months old. His little brown eyes stared,
bulging from his head. The rest of his face was contorted into a ghastly, silent scream.

Anne took one look and walked away, her hands on
her face. After a few moments, Dave Brannan picked up
the terrible photo and slipped it into his shirt pocket.

A moment later, someone broke the icy silence, and the Raptors went back to work, studying the Keyhole images, including those of the port of Muara with detailed highlights of the area where the Khomeini-6 missiles had been. The missiles were no longer to be seen. They had been moved somewhere else when the sultan had agreed to stop his offensive nuclear program. This section of the base seemed to be a compound within a compound, a fact that was duly noted. Gaining access would be an important part of their planning.

After the intel materials had been reviewed, and procedural questions were addressed, the general stood to make his exit.

"I've outlined the strategic overview," he told them. "That's where my part of this ends and yours begins. It's up to you to develop your own tactical plan, and your own schedule, and to implement the plan. I have no desire to know or meddle in any of that because I know that there's nobody anywhere who is better capable of carrying out this mission. I'm proud of you and so is the president. If you need anything that either he or I can provide, you know where to reach me. Good luck."

With that, the men stood and came to attention to return his salute.

On his way out, Peighton took Brannan aside.

"The professor there," he said, nodding at the woman standing near the window sipping a diet cola. "I know that she helped you on that last mission in Turkey and France, but are you sure that she's up to being on a mission like this?"

"Don't worry, General." Brannan laughed. "She was essential to our success last time, and I have every reason to believe that she will be this time as well. Hell, she more than proved herself over there, and these guys watched her do it. She can outride most of these men, and can probably outshoot nearly any man *except* these guys. After all, *she's* the one who killed Fahrid Al-Zahir."

FOUR

REID Arthur was enjoying himself. He was sitting in his favorite corner at the coffee shop on Telegraph Avenue sipping his chai latte. He had been reading, but he stopped to listen to the man in the corner who was playing a guitar and singing old folk songs. Today they call it "roots music," but this man called them "folk songs." As Reid knew, that was what they had called them back in the sixties at the time of Pete Seeger and Eric von Schmidt.

Despite his scraggly salt-and-pepper beard, the man was too young for that, but he sang with the timeless spirit of a man who might even have ridden the rails with Cisco Houston and Woody Guthrie. In fact, he was singing one of Guthrie's old songs, the one about the Ludlow Mine massacre, when he really got Arthur's attention.

"I'm impressed with your passion, man," Arthur said when the man finished with the line about hanging his head and crying.

"Anything that keeps people's mind on how loathsome these corporations could be and still are."

That struck a chord with Reid Arthur and they began talking. The man explained that he was an out-of-work fishing boat captain who had last shipped out from Newport, Oregon. But the fish weren't running, and he had caught a ride to California. Arthur could tell by the calluses on his fingers that he worked with his hands, and he could tell by the number of knots in the man's mismatched shoelaces that he was probably pretty deep into the abyss between paychecks.

"Have you got a job down here?" Arthur asked him.

"Well, not exactly yet."

"You look like a man that knows his way around manual labor. Personally, I don't know one end of a wrench from the other. We got a bunch of things that need fixing over at the office. Damned landlord won't do a thing. Maybe you could help out and we could give you a little spending money."

The guitar player agreed, and they strolled back over to the Environmental Action International office. Arthur introduced him to Karla, the short woman with a tattoo on her neck and the rivets in her nostrils, and they went into the back room to discuss what Rodgers would do. As they were talking about his duties, another man walked in.

"Oh, hi, Bob." Arthur smiled. "Bob, this is Jack Rodgers. Jack, meet Bob Rashid."

April 18
11:21 A.M. Eastern Time

"**TAKE** your time and be sure," Jenny Collingwood said, pushing her glasses up the ridge of her nose.

"I think I'm sure," Steve Faralaco said cautiously. "I'm sure I'm sure."

Faralaco was staring at mug shots of dozens of faces from the Terrorist Watch List, trying to point out the man who had identified himself as Abdulla Maloud.

Steve was not having a good day. He had not been having a good week. He was feeling powerless in the task at hand. One ugly face was like another ugly face—almost.

The wave of hysteria that came to a head a few days after San Francisco had subsided somewhat. There were no further incidents, and many people began to believe subconsciously that this meant there would be none. The administration knew that it meant no such thing, but they also knew it would be useless and counterproductive to admit that the next attack could come at any time, and that the only possible preventative measure was to appease Sultan Omar Jamalul Halauddin.

Only a handful of people in the White House and the national intelligence community knew that the president was trying to meet the ransom demands. Only that same select few knew that meeting the sultan's demands was easier said than done. Reached on a back channel to be sounded out regarding ceding Mindanao to Brunei, the Philippine government had refused. Malaysia, when asked to consider cession of Sarawak and Sabah, had said it would declare war rather than do such a thing.

Fortunately for the Livingstone administration, these diplomatic disasters had yet to be leaked to the media.

Unfortunately, the clock was ticking on a second attack.

"I'm sure," Faralaco said at last, after staring at one mug shot for several minutes. "That's the guy. That's the one who called himself Maloud."

"I see," Collingwood said, pressing the intercom button to summon the director of national intelligence.

"So, you have a match?" Richard Scevoles said as he came into the room. He was curious to see who Faralaco had picked, although he seemed a bit perturbed at having been interrupted to view just another mug shot.

"I'm sorry to bother you with this, sir," Jenny explained. "But the one he picked, well, I thought you ought to know right away."

"That's Jahar Abiddijab!" Scevoles exclaimed, picking up the photo. Steve thought he was going to come unglued.

"Who's Jahar Abiddijab?" Faralaco asked. He had obviously picked someone who was higher on the intelligence chief's radar than most of the bearded thugs on the watch list.

"He was picked up several years ago in Afghanistan with blueprints of several key landmarks in the United Kingdom," Jenny Collingwood explained. "The Tower of London was one of them. I think that Buckingham Palace was also there."

"What happened to him?" Faralaco queried.

"He was a British citizen—" Jenny began.

"We had him at Gitmo for a year and a half," Scevoles interrupted. "Because he was a British citizen, we got petitioned to turn him loose. We sent him home. He stepped off a plane at Heathrow and faded into the night. Never saw him again . . . until now."

April 20
11:30 P.M. Brunei Time

THE young woman in the ultra-low-cut, skintight latex catsuit knelt and placed the large burnished brass tray on the low table and bowed slightly before stepping away.

Sultan Omar Jamalul Halauddin barely noticed. He grabbed a fistful of chocolate-covered cashews and changed the channel on his immense plasma-screen television. He shouted at another young woman, ordering her to pour him a drink from the chilled margarita pitcher. Wiggling uncomfortably in a fringed and sequined dress that barely covered her hips, she obliged and bowed slightly.

The sultan was bored. More than a month had passed since Caprice had given her command performance

here at the Istana Nurul Iman palace. At first, the idea of
dressing a hundred or so teenage girls in replicas of the
costumes that Caprice had worn onstage had seemed
like a marvelous idea, but now he was bored.

Slowly, Omar Jamalul Halauddin lifted his 322-
pound body from the silk cushions and lumbered from
his bedroom into the vast dressing room with the gold-
plated fountain. He could hardly believe that it had
been just six months since his cousin had suffered his
unfortunate demise through "natural causes." He could
hardly believe that it had been just six months since he
had transformed himself from a mere "businessman"
into a world leader whom everyone took seriously.

As he waddled from the dressing room to the shower
stall larger than most bedrooms, he glanced down the
hallway, marveling at the vast scale of his new home.
He had been living here in this 1,788-room palace for
six months, and he guessed that he had actually set foot
in fewer than a quarter of those rooms.

He had been waiting for a table at Cannes the night
that he had the idea. It was the week leading up to the
film festival. There he was, Omar Jamalul Halauddin,
the cousin to the sultan, and he was *waiting* for a table.
Then there was a bustling sound and a Hollywood star,
a *minor* Hollywood star, was quickly rushed to a table at
a window overlooking the sun-splashed Mediterranean.

He was indignant.

What could he do?

He decided then and there that he would remake
himself as a world leader that *everyone* took seriously.

Omar had surrounded himself with bodyguards

who made sure that he was never trifled with, and he could be quite firm in his many business dealings. Indeed, there were several men and one woman who had died trying to cross him. He had the reputation of a man who should not be angered, but his public persona was merely that of a jolly knave.

He remembered that when Kim Jong Il took over North Korea, the world laughed. He had killed those people in Rangoon in 1983, and on that airliner in 1987, but still they laughed. Like Omar, he was merely a jolly knave. They called Kim "Dear Leader" to his face, but they snickered at him behind his back and called him "Baby Kim," a play on "Baby Doc" Duvalier, the inept son of Haiti's feared "Papa Doc."

Then Kim blew their minds by shaking down Clinton and Carter for millions. Nobody was laughing then. Poor Clinton had laughed at first, but he later admitted that Kim *scared* him. Omar Jamalul Halauddin decided that this was for him. He had wanted to be feared by the president of the United States.

The nuclear threat was an obvious first step. It was Omar's homage to Kim, who had been his inspiration. The LSD was Omar's *own* idea. It was a brilliant idea—if he did say so himself. It was his way of taking global extortion to a whole new level.

It had actually come to him on one of his occasional visits to the United States. He was at the Hollywood Hills home of a rap star. He couldn't remember which one. Was it "Dog Something," or "Something Dog"? Omar couldn't remember because he had done quite a lot of cocaine at the club before they went up to the Hills.

The important thing was that he remembered those people talking about "dropping acid." He had been around LSD users once or twice before, but he had never had occasion to know much about it. Everyone he knew smoked weed, and cocaine was everywhere, but Omar had no direct experience with LSD.

What intrigued him most was how compact it was. These people spoke of amazing and intricate hallucinations that were derived from a quantity of drugs that could be balanced on the head of a pin. In the following days, as he researched the drug, he became even more intrigued with its immense possibilities. Then he came across an old book by a man named John Grant Fuller that told about the relationship between LSD and ergot poisoning. It told the story about Pont-Saint-Esprit, the little town in France where two hundred people went insane in 1951. If that happened there, what could be wrought if it were done on a larger scale?

Sultan Omar had wanted to be feared by the president of the United States, and now his wish had come *true*!

April 21
11:32 A.M. Mountain Time

"**Y**ES sir, Mr. Ambassador, my team will be in Brunei in forty-eight hours," Asa Henderson said into the phone. "Professor McCaine is one of our best . . . no, is *the* best we've got for this job. Knows her stuff. Very thorough. She's been on sites all over the world."

"I'm delighted, Mr. Chairman," Pehin Dato Hudim Incpaduka replied. "Brunei is anxious to have this Heritage Site be an important monument to the culture of our country, not only as it is today, but as it was at the apogee of our past glory, and as it may well be in the future."

"You will not be disappointed," Henderson promised the Bruneian ambassador to the United Nations.

"I look forward to meeting the professor and her team. I'm flying out there myself in a few days."

Henderson was proud of himself. He had debated whether or not to phone Anne McCaine to ask her one more time, but it had been the right thing to do. Something that he said in that second conversation had convinced her to reconsider, and she had plunged into the project with her usual thoroughness and attention to detail. This was a good thing too, because with the end of the term coming up and graduation just around the corner, he had absolutely no time to oversee the project, but he had no need to. Professor McCaine was a good manager.

She was taking care of all the details too. To help her, she was bringing in a team of people that she had met abroad. He hadn't even glanced at their resumes. If they were good enough for her, then they were the best people for the job.

She had even lined up a helicopter crew from down in Texas or New Mexico somewhere who were willing to donate their services to the project. That Anne McCaine! She thought of everything. When she returned from her sabbatical, he would have to look into a little bump in her salary.

April 21
10:32 A.M. Pacific Time

BASIM "Bob" Rashid became an open book. Jack Rodgers had that effect on people. He could always get them talking about themselves and saying far more than they otherwise would have, and far more than they probably wanted to.

Rashid told him that at the madrasa in Pakistan, he had learned to like American hip-hop, but to hate America. He had come to the University of California to learn computer science and adopted an easy American nickname. As he immersed himself in life around Berkeley, he easily fell into line with the anti-American sentiment that was de rigueur in many social circles around town.

Rodgers baited the impressionable Rashid, and he took the bait.

Rashid told of the man he knew as Abdulla Maloud, who had shown up around campus a few months back. Were the Islamic students truly sincere in their anti-Americanism, or was it merely an affectation? Maloud had asked.

Rashid smiled proudly. He had convinced Maloud that he unquestionably hated what the United States stood for. Over a nice meal at a tandoori place on University Avenue, he'd convinced Maloud that he would be happy to do what he could to whip America like a small dog.

Rodgers said that he would like to meet this man. Any enemy of Livingstone was a friend of his. Rashid promised that this could be arranged.

April 23
11:09 A.M. Sydney Time

"**O**OOH, you're with the UNESCO people," the
woman in the cream-colored head scarf said
with a smile as she perused Anne McCaine's travel
documents at the Royal Brunei Airlines check-in
counter in the terminal at Sydney International Airport. "There has been much news about this in our
country."

"You must be pleased that your sultan made this
possible." Anne smiled.

"Yes, of course, His Majesty is celebrated for what
he has done since coming to the throne," the woman
said, wrinkling her nose. The smile had disappeared
from her face. Apparently, the celebrated sultan was
not as popular with his subjects as he would like to
pretend.

Anne and the colonel, as well as Jason Houn and
Ray Couper, had arrived in Sydney with plenty of time
to transfer to Royal Brunei Flight 194 with its 12:50
departure for Bandar Seri Begawan. Boyinson, along
with Will Casey and Brad Townsend, would be coming in late tomorrow on an Apex Air cargo flight that
was also bringing in the helicopter. Jack Rodgers was
making other travel arrangements. He had met "Abdulla Maloud," who was returning to Brunei himself.
The Iranian had invited Rodgers to join him. He'd said
that he needed a boat captain. Any enemy of Thomas
Livingstone was a friend of his. They were kindred
spirits.

"I had an idea as I was half-asleep back out there

over the Pacific somewhere," Anne told the colonel as they sat down in the airport lounge to await their boarding call.

"Oh-oh," Brannan replied in mock trepidation.

"Have you ever heard of Suvarnadvipa?" Anne asked.

"No, I guess I haven't," Brannan replied tentatively. He didn't like to be stumped when it came to trivia.

"Almost nobody has," she said, gently taking him off the hook. "Have you ever heard of Cibola?"

"Of course. The seven cities of gold that Cabeza de Vaca claimed that he found in New Mexico after he got separated from the Narvaez expedition in the 1520s. People hunted for that place for years. It was the motivation for Francisco de Coronado's 1540 trip into the Southwest when his guys discovered the Grand Canyon. Cibola was to the Southwest what El Dorado was to South America."

"Well"—Anne smiled—"Suvarnadvipa is the Southeast Asian version of Cibola or El Dorado. It's a mythical island or city of gold, with an emphasis on 'myth.' They were writing about it in India more than half a millennium before the Spanish set foot in the Americas, or Cabeza de Vaca staggered out of the Sonoran Desert, but it's never been pinpointed. The stories just say that it's somewhere in the lands to the east. Some people think that it might be on the Malay mainland, and others say it may even be on Java, but nobody knows."

"I think I see what you have in mind." The colonel laughed.

"I thought you would. As long as the sultan and

UNESCO are buying into the spurious fabrication of a World Heritage Site where really nothing exists, I think that it would be only right for us to embellish it," Anne said with a wink. "And to sting the con men."

April 23
1:09 P.M. Brunei Time

"**A**LL clear, Kapitan, nothing to report."

Kapitan Adanan Vegawan nodded as he squinted through his binoculars. No vessels other than the usual barge traffic were visible between here and the coastline, and farther out to sea, there were no ships to be seen, either visually or on radar. This was good news. The men were exhausted. Vegawan didn't know what they could do if they were called upon to deal with a serious threat.

The Waspada-class missile ship KDB *Sajuang* had been on almost continuous patrol since the middle of March when the exclusion zone was declared. The U.S. Navy had backed off, but there was a fear, voiced at headquarters in Muara, that the Americans might try something. It was imagined that a SEAL Team might be inserted from the South China Sea, either by a surface craft or submarine, but that had not happened—yet.

At first, the idea of challenging the U.S. Navy had been overwhelming, but Vegawan had begun to warm up to the idea. The idea of fighting a true naval battle with the world's most powerful navy excited him.

Most of the men were excited too. They had all expected to go through their naval careers as glorified traffic cops, but here was the opportunity to fight a real navy.

Clearly, the KDB *Sajuang* could not take on a Ticonderoga-class cruiser, but they certainly had the firepower to destroy the type of vessel that might be used by the SEALs. Vegawan even fantasized about getting off a lucky shot and piercing the hull of a submarine.

The U.S. Navy had the power to annihilate the Bruneian Navy, but the Americans were timid. They were cautious and tended to *fear* using their own power. They seemed to fight wars as though they feared making their enemies unhappy. Their politicians would not allow their navy to fight to overwhelm Brunei. They would fight an even fight, and one that Vegawan could win. When he survived his real naval battle, Vegawan would be a hero.

In the meantime, however, there was the tedious process of patrol. The Royal Brunei Navy had the resources to keep track of the coast. The Perwira-class inshore patrol boats could monitor the nooks and crannies of the jungled coastline, while the larger vessels patrolled farther out to sea. However, Brunei's small blue-water navy was not at full strength, and there was no indication when it would be again. KDB *Depambak*, the newest of the Nakhoda Ragam-class offshore patrol vessels, had been stuck in port since the end of February. It had been undergoing retrofit work, but that had been suspended and she just sat, while the other ships worked continually.

KDB *Depambak* was supposed to be outfitted with
the longer-range Khomeini-6 missiles. They were supposed to be equipped with the nuclear warheads that
Sultan Omar Jamalul Halauddin had acquired, and
they were supposed to ship out aboard KDB *Depambak*, but that project had been halted on the authority
of the high command after the exclusion zone was announced.

It didn't make sense, Vegawan thought, that just as
the blue-water responsibility of the navy was expanded
by an enormous factor, their newest blue-water warship
was taken off line. There was no word as to when the
ship might be back, but officers of Vegawan's pay grade
were not privy to knowing about those decisions until
they had been made.

April 23
6:18 P.M. Brunei Time

THE three-and-a-half-hour flight through two time
zones reached the Bruneian capital as the late afternoon sun was tinting the city below in its intense
light. As the white-and-gold Airbus A320 banked for
its final approach, the golden dome of the Omar Ali
Saifuddin Mosque, the city's most prominent landmark, glistened like fire. Located in the concave side
of a bend in the lazy Brunei River, the sultan's sprawling Istana Nurul Iman palace complex looked from the
air like a very large shopping mall.

Bandar Seri Begawan is located at the neck of a
fifteen-mile peninsula extending southwest to northeast

into the South China Sea, with the Brunei River feeding Brunei Bay to the south. The port and the Jalan Tanjong Pelumpong naval base at Muara are located at the tip of the peninsula, with the airport roughly halfway between Muara and the capital.

The Americans were met by a low-level delegation from the Ministry of Heritage, who offered to drive them to their hotel, but Anne insisted that they would rent a car using the American Express Platinum card set up by the University of Colorado with their generous UNESCO grant. This made the two men a little nervous, but they were unaccustomed to arguing with women, so they acquiesced.

The main road leading into the city was still festooned with the decorations that had been installed a month ago when the American secretary of state had come to sign the historic deal that committed the United States to the exclusion zone.

"I reckon that there's no chance that people here will forget what their sultan looks like," Brannan chuckled, looking at the numerous billboards bearing the portrait of Jamalul Halauddin.

"I've lost count, not that I was counting," Anne added. "At least we'll have no trouble recognizing him when we have lunch with him at the palace tomorrow."

April 22
9:55 P.M. Pacific Time

"**W**HO was that you were talking to?" Reid Arthur asked suspiciously. He had just walked into the back room of the Environmental Action International office as Bob Rashid was ending a call on his cell phone.

"Just a friend down in Santa Cruz," Rashid replied, nervously closing up his cell phone.

"I heard something about milligrams. You're not dealing drugs, are you?"

"Oh, no, not at all."

"Good. I don't have to tell you that we've had the FBI coming around. The last thing Environmental Action International needs is for them to bust somebody here for dealing."

"There's no problem with that," Rashid assured him.

"You didn't strike me as someone who does drugs," Arthur said, more in the interest of making conversation than probing secrets that Rashid might not wish to reveal.

"I am Muslim," Rashid said, starting to explain. "We don't take drugs."

That doesn't make sense, Arthur thought. *If he doesn't take drugs, why is he talking about milligrams of something, and why does he seem to be so reticent to talk to me about it?*

Suddenly, it dawned on Arthur in a tidal wave of paranoia—Rashid's eagerness to associate himself with Environmental Action International, the gallon jugs at Hetch Hetchy that were mentioned on the news, the visits by the FBI, and now the surreptitious chatter about milligrams.

"You weren't mixed up in putting the acid into Hetch Hetchy, were you?" Arthur asked pointedly.

Rashid did not answer.

Could it be true? Arthur was taken aback. How could Rashid have duped him? Had he deliberately incriminated Environmental Action International, or had he just been that stupid?

Arthur was angry and he was nervous. A month ago, when he had met Bob Rashid, the two of them had hit it off from the start. They were both from well-to-do families, and they were both angry about the rape of the environment. They were, Arthur felt, like kindred spirits. Arthur had been pleased by the skill and the enthusiasm that Rashid had brought to the work of Environmental Action International, especially around the Hetch Hetchy campaign. How wrong he had been!

"Why?" Arthur asked as Rashid stood there silently. "Why did you do something so fucking insane? Environmental Action International is being blamed for this. People were killed."

Rashid caught himself thinking that suddenly the sultan's whole elaborate scheme had been laid bare, but he quickly realized that it had not. Arthur had no inkling of the sultan's involvement. He couldn't see the big picture, but only a tiny portion of it. He hadn't guessed *why* Rashid had poisoned Hetch Hetchy, only that he had. Things had started to spin out of control, but Rashid realized that he could regain control and spin them back.

"Didn't you tell me that extreme measures were often necessary to make a point?" Rashid parried. "You spoke of burning that lake resort in Idaho. You bragged that you personally planted the bomb in that van at the biotech company."

"But those were intended to destroy capitalist property, not to kill random people. I knew that nobody would be in the van."

"But Karla told me that when you were young, you pounded many hundreds of ten-inch spikes into trees in the Klamath National Forest when you knew there would be logging. Was not that potentially lethal?"

Reid Arthur paused. The spikes in the lumber had cost one life and had maimed at least seven millworkers that he knew about. In one case, the sawmill blade had splintered when it hit the spike, sending a shard of broken blade cartwheeling across the face of a twenty-four-year-old father of two. It shredded his flesh horribly, while blinding him and causing minor brain damage. Arthur still justified his actions, because the net result was the closing of the sawmill.

"What I did was no different," Rashid said. It was now his turn to scold. "My act of defiance was simply on a much grander scale than *yours*. Thanks to Environmental Action International, the people know of the issue. They know that Hetch Hetchy must be destroyed, and the pressure will now be on them to follow through!"

"But you could be arrested," Arthur groaned. "*We* could be arrested!"

"Don't be a coward, my friend," Rashid counseled. "The corporations that you despise . . . that we all despise . . . will not respond to the cautious acts of cowards, but to the *bold actions* of revolutionaries."

April 24
12:55 P.M. Brunei Time

"**T**HE palace is well guarded, but it's not impregnable," Ray Couper observed as they drove into the largest palace complex in the world in which royalty actually resides. They had driven from the hotel, escorted by the same two men from the Ministry of Heritage that had met them at the airport. "I count only three heavy machine guns, plus these guys with the assault rifles."

"It's probably more for show than anything," Brannan added. "They're not expecting a frontal assault from the ground. Hopefully, they're not expecting any kind of assault from any direction."

"They're still in the euphoria phase," Houn interjected. "They're still so used to getting what they want that they haven't paused to realize that they need to keep up their guard regardless."

"This place reminds me of a cross between a casino and an office park," Anne commented as they were directed to a parking place near a half circle of banyan trees that shaded the driveway.

As the Americans walked toward the Istana Nurul Iman Palace, a film crew from Bruneian State Television approached them, or more correctly, they approached Anne. The young reporter seemed eager to speak with the woman archaeologist from the United States. It was as though she was a celebrity. In a sense, she was. She was coming to Brunei from a country that was not on the best of terms with Brunei, and she was coming to draw world attention to Brunei's cultural heritage.

"I am absolutely delighted to be in your beautiful country," Anne said with a smile when asked for a comment. "I am anxiously looking forward to meeting with the sultan, and to getting a firsthand look at Brunei's cultural treasures."

As the Americans were ushered into the air-conditioned foyer, it was obvious to them that the decorators hadn't scrimped on amenities. However, it still reminded Anne of a casino.

This being technically a Muslim country, she had dressed conservatively in a black dress with an ankle-length skirt. Despite the tropical mugginess, she had even draped a shawl around her shoulders. Entering the palace, she realized that such constraint was unnecessary as she saw a couple of the sultan's young friends passing in the hall dressed in skimpy costumes such as those worn in this very building a month earlier by Caprice.

The Americans were shown into a huge dining room illuminated by a half-dozen of the building's 564 chandeliers. Here, they were greeted by Ambassador Pehin Dato Yayah Korma as well as by Dr. Awang Uhtaud, the minister of heritage himself. The niceties out of the way, the door at the back of the room opened, and His Majesty made his grand entrance, flowing into the room draped with a red-and-gold silk robe festooned with designs similar to those found on the Bruneian flag.

The three Raptors glanced at one another. Each knew that they were all thinking the same thing: Let's whack the sunuvabitch here and now and get out of here. Nevertheless, they grinned and played along.

The immense monarch seated himself at the head of the table, with Anne at his left and Uhtaud at his right. They had been told that they would be meeting the sultan at a "simple working lunch," but after several courses of starters, the word "simple" went out the window, and it took a while for the term "working" to work its way into the agenda.

In the beginning, the big sultan did most of the talking. Having been educated in England, and having spent virtually his entire life in either Europe or the United States, he spoke flawless English. The theme of his monologue came down to how happy he was to have academics from the United States—of all places—coming to him to validate the importance of his kingdom as a world power. Blah, blah, blah. He made several references to his expectations that his country would once again be as large as it had been in the sixteenth century. Anne pretended to be surprised by this. Brannan interpreted his smugness as complacency.

As the sultan paused to swallow a glass of cabernet, the head waiter identified the main course as Udang Sambal Serai Bersantan, which turned out to be prawns cooked in a coconut-based red curry, with the distinguishing flavor of *asam jawa*, or tamarind.

"Tell me, Professor McCaine, are you not looking forward to going out to visit the site at Tutong tomorrow?" Jamalul Halauddin asked as curry was being served. He had pontificated as much as he felt necessary and was ready for conversation.

"Oh, very much." She smiled. "There's always an excitement of anticipation on the eve of visiting a new site, especially one that promises to be as important as this one."

"Well, of course it's important," he said. He was almost startled to have an archaeologist with international credentials refer to the site as "important." Clearly, he had demanded that UNESCO treat it as such, but he'd had a gun to their heads. Everything that he had read about the Tutong site had described it as a minor Hindu temple complex, scarcely older than the fourteenth century. He was surprised to hear it considered truly significant.

"Well, it may be more important than we thought," Anne said earnestly, taking a sip of red wine.

"Really?" Sultan Omar said, putting down his fork and concentrating his attention on the woman. She was quite an attractive woman, but at the same time, she was someone with whom a man could have a conversation. Had his taste in women not focused on the fourteen-to-seventeen age group, he might even have been tempted. "Please tell me more."

"Have you ever heard of Suvarnadvipa?" Anne asked.

"Suvarnadvipa? No, that is not familiar to me."

"It's a fabled golden kingdom referred to in ancient Hindu texts, Your Majesty," interjected the minister of heritage.

"It's the Southeast Asia equivalent of El Dorado," Brannan interjected, showing off his newly acquired knowledge and underscoring his credibility as part of the professor's team of archaeologists. "It's legendary."

"What does this have to do with Tutong?" the sultan asked.

"We think that the Tutong site might actually *be* Suvarnadvipa," Anne told him.

"*Really?*"

"Obviously, we won't know until we get out there, and we may not know until there has been quite a lot of excavation, but I've done some preliminary calculations based on the descriptions of distances and travel routes in the old texts and . . ."

"I can see it now," the sultan gushed. "We'll build a huge museum and a hotel. People will come from all over the world. It will be as great as Angkor Wat, or the Taj Mahal."

April 24
5:18 P.M. Pacific Time

"**H**E'S coming out of the building now," Erik Vasquez whispered. "He's getting into a car. The guy is definitely on the move."

A block away, Rod Llewellan started the car and put it into gear. He hoped he was right. Vasquez didn't think so. Vasquez had insisted that Reid Arthur, rather than Basim Rashid, was the man who should be deserving of the primary attention of the two FBI agents.

Vasquez had said that he "had a feeling." Llewellan had countered that he too "had a feeling," and that as the senior agent, his "feeling" trumped that of the younger man. What Llewellan could not—and would not—tell him was that it was not his feeling, but that of Captain Jack Rodgers. Vasquez had never met Rodgers, but he had seen his dossier. The retired Special Forces captain's portfolio was filed in that murky corner of the FBI files where the FBI lumped mercenaries, vigilantes, loose cannons, and double agents.

When Rodgers called three nights ago to tell him to keep a close watch on Rashid, Llewellan agreed. Rodgers was on the inside. He ought to know. In the past, Rodgers had been right, even though Llewellan had often sweated bullets, never completely sure that the Raptors *weren't* mercenaries, vigilantes, loose cannons, or double agents.

When Rodgers had arrived in Berkeley, tasked by Buck Peighton with figuring out exactly how the San Francisco attack was linked to Sultan Omar Jamalul Halauddin and his palace guard, Llewellan had had little contact with him. When Vasquez was otherwise engaged, they had taken a short walk. Llewellan gave him a briefing on what the FBI had learned about Environmental Action International. He pointed out Rashid and Arthur. To Llewellan's surprise, Rodgers simply bought a used guitar from a secondhand store and told him to stand by.

Llewellan had once watched Jack Rodgers turn a Mujahidin Al-Akbar hijacker into a sobbing wreck, and he expected to see him repeat that tactic with the persons of interest that had been identified within Environmental Action International. Instead, Rodgers had worked himself into their organization, and had disappeared into it like a submarine dipping beneath the waves.

As Llewellan stood by as directed, Rodgers had contacted him only once. He had called late the other night to tell Llewellan that he was going out of the country for a few days, and that it was imperative for Llewellan to keep an eye on Rashid. This, to the consternation of Erik Vasquez, was exactly what they were doing.

As Llewellan made a hard left onto Dwight Way, Vasquez was walking quickly toward him. The younger agent leapt into the Volvo as Llewellan braked.

"He just turned left onto Sacramento Street," Vasquez said, slightly out of breath. "He's in that blue Honda Accord."

"Did you get a chance to stick on the tracking device?" Llewellan asked.

"No, I couldn't get close enough," Vasquez admitted, patting the GPS tracker that was still in the pocket of his windbreaker.

The other thing that Rodgers had told Llewellan was to get rid of the rented Ford Taurus and get a car that was less conspicuous in a rearview mirror. Hence the ten-year-old tan Volvo that they'd picked up at a used-car lot. That, Vasquez had approved. He had told Llewellan that he thought it was a stroke of brilliance. Indeed, it had allowed them to stay close to Rashid, and it was allowing them to follow him now, even without the GPS tracker attached.

Just short of Ashby Avenue, one of the main streets in Berkeley that connects with a freeway on-ramp, they saw the brake lights of the blue Accord flash on in the middle of the block. Llewellan slowed and they watched as the trunk sprang open. Reid Arthur put two backpacks into the trunk, slammed down the lid, and hopped into the car.

"I told you so." Llewellan smiled. "Arthur and Rashid . . . together again. I wish I'd taken you up on that five-dollar bet."

"The next coffee shop stop is on me," the younger agent promised. "I wonder where they're planning to go hiking."

The brake lights on the Accord flickered again at Ashby, and Rashid signaled for a right turn. Moments later, the two cars merged onto Interstate 80.

April 25
8:18 A.M. Brunei Time

THE big Boeing 747-200F aerial freighter taxied off the main runway at the Bandar Seri Begawan airport, lumbering onto the taxiway on the far side from the main terminal. It passed a long row of metal-skinned warehouses and hangars, including the one that contained the Gulfstream V executive jet that had belonged to Omar Jamalul Halauddin since before he had become Brunei's monarch.

"We may have trouble," Greg Boyinson said, looking down from the flight deck of the big freighter. When the aircraft had taxied to a stop, everything had looked good. It wasn't until the Pratt & Whitney JT9D turbofans started to wind down that three Bruneian army vehicles appeared on the flight line.

"I thought you were expecting some sort of welcoming committee," the pilot said cautiously. Apex Air flight crews were used to the unforeseen. They expected the unexpected, but nobody liked to get shot at.

Apex Air was the "quiet company" of the air cargo business. They had a good reputation for meeting tight schedules with high-value, high-priority freight shipments. They carried everything from fresh fruit to fresh flowers, and from racehorses to race cars. Apex had also long ago earned a reputation for its discretion, meeting tight schedules and asking few questions. Among their clients around the world was the United States Special Operations community. Buck Peighton had known the owner of Apex Air since they had served in the Army together long ago, and Apex had made several flights to support his secret army. Today, however, Apex was flying above the radar. Unlike the last time they carried the Raptors, the Little Bird was scheduled to be off-loaded in broad daylight.

"Yeah, we *are* supposed to have an official welcome," Boyinson confirmed. "I just wasn't expecting their fuckin' *army*."

Will Casey and Brad Townsend sized up the three army vehicles, counting between eight and ten men, plus two officers. They were lightly armed. The odds were actually quite good. If push came to shove, three Raptors with Heckler & Koch MP5 submachine guns could probably take down this bunch in about two minutes. Of course the 747-200F would then have to get itself airborne in about the same amount of time, and the whole damned mission would go down the tubes.

A pickup with a set of APS60 air stairs attached to its bed approached the aircraft, and the loadmaster opened the side door. Boyinson hurried down to head off the welcoming committee before any of them decided to come aboard.

"Welcome to Brunei," said an officer in a white dress uniform. "I am Kapitan Mohammed Haji. My men and I are here to facilitate the arrival of the University of Colorado helicopter and its personnel."

"Well, I'm Greg Brown," Boyinson said, shaking the man's hand. "I'm the pilot. I'm here to be facilitated."

The nose of the 747-200F tilted up to reveal the items strapped into the cargo hold. First and most evident was a McDonnell Douglas MH-6 Little Bird, painted in bright red and blue to emulate a civilian Model 530 helicopter. Behind it were containers strapped to pallets.

Deceptively small, the Model 500-series choppers are capable of carrying sizable loads, including eight or nine people if external platforms are installed, and of operating nearly anywhere. Part of the advantage of its size is its ability to function from small pads and in tight situations. These durable helicopters are widely used by commercial operators around the world, as well as by military operators. In the U.S. Army, MH-6s, AH-6s, OH-6s, and other Little Bird variants are used for Special Operations, especially by Boyinson's former outfit, the 160th Special Operations Aviation Regiment, better known as the Night Stalkers.

Today, Boyinson's Little Bird was equipped with its forward-looking infrared turret, but for the prying eyes that would watch it being unloaded in Bandar

Seri Begawan, it had been stripped of its launch tubes for AGM-114 Hellfire missiles and its pair of M134 7.62mm six-barrel Gatling-type machine guns. This equipment was packed separately, along with other items that Professor McCaine's "University of Colorado team" might need in the field.

Kapitan Haji ordered his ten-man contingent to assist the University of Colorado team in unloading their gear, but they were mainly in the way. Though they were clearly superfluous to the process of unloading the aircraft equipment, Boyinson decided to give them as big a part in the activity as possible. After all, they were here to scrutinize the helicopter crew as much as to help them, and Boyinson wanted them to go away believing that they had seen everything. While the Raptors and the Apex loadmaster removed the Little Bird, the Bruneian soldiers and two airport ground handlers hauled out the crates of gear.

As the air freighter prepared for departure, the Bruneian officers directed the Americans to an unused hangar that would be their base of operations. It would be their home away from home, as their archaeological project unfolded over what was expected to be several weeks.

The Raptors had a shorter stay in mind.

April 24
5:25 P.M. Pacific Time

AS Bob Rashid and Reid Arthur headed southward on Interstate 80, the skyline of the city of San

Francisco was clearly visible in the distance, and the huge flashing "Do not enter" signs on the entrances to the Bay Bridge were a reminder of what had happened over there. Essentially, the city was still under quarantine. The Bay Bridge was still closed to all but essential traffic, and the signs directed everyone else south through Oakland on either Interstate 580 or 880.

Reid Arthur stared at the skyline, then glanced over at Rashid. It was numbing to be sitting here almost casually with the man who had apparently been single-handedly responsible for one of the biggest acts of terrorism in American history. It was probably the biggest ever to have been successfully carried out solo. This strange young man from Pakistan had a streak of audacity that put everyone else in the environmental-defense movement to shame. While people in Arthur's circle were spilling blood on old hags in mink coats or spiking redwoods, this man had had the gall to send an entire major city—along with a handful of minor cities—on an acid trip.

Arthur had reacted with colliding roller coasters of conflicting sentiments. At first, he was stunned, then he was fearful. What would happen if the FBI had blamed *him*? Then there was anger, anger at Rashid for making Environmental Action International vulnerable. But when Arthur had admonished him, Rashid had barked back, and he had made Arthur feel guilty. Arthur had been made to feel almost ashamed of himself for his faintheartedness.

Now, to be sitting next to someone so brazen made Arthur almost numb with conflicting emotions that ranged from trepidation to elation. Rashid had made him the proverbial offer that he could not refuse. If he was serious about conveying a firm message against Livingstone, and against the corporations and their lackeys, he should be willing to embrace a full spectrum of revolutionary action.

It was Arthur's opportunity—handed to him on a platter—to truly live out his Weather Underground fantasy. *They* hadn't been afraid to injure or kill to make Nixon hear the message. That pig Livingstone, and all the pigs, they must all hear the message. It was time, Arthur decided, to take his own place beside the heroes of his youth. Rashid was going to strike again, and Arthur would be there in solidarity with him.

The blue Accord followed Interstate 880 south around San Francisco Bay, through San Jose to its intersection with Interstate 280, where it became State Highway 17. They continued on Highway 17 as it wound its way up into the steep and heavily wooded Santa Cruz Mountains. In Rashid's mirror, but still unseen, was an old tan Volvo.

April 25
8:25 A.M. Brunei Time

"**H**OME sweet Suvarnadvipa." Brannan chuckled as they contemplated the random piles of hewn stone lying in the brush at the edge of the jungle.

"Our little charade shows some promise," Anne replied. "The stone bases of these structures in what is probably a temple complex are larger than I had expected."

The University of Colorado professor and her entourage had arrived at the newly designated UNESCO World Heritage Site, and were beginning to walk the perimeter of the place. They were five miles inland from Tutong, which was about twenty-five miles southwest of the center of Bandar Seri Begawan. As they walked, the Raptors had used the outdoor time as an opportunity to speak freely and make plans. This they could not do in their rooms at the hotel, which they presumed to be bugged.

"I hear a chopper," Jason Houn said, looking up. The whup-whup of rotors could now be heard above the murmur of jungle fauna rustling in the treetops.

"If that's Boyinson, he's about two hours early," Brannan said, looking at his watch. They had made contact with the helicopter crew, and had made plans to view the would-be Suvarnadvipa from the air. In so doing, it would also afford them the opportunity for an aerial survey of locations between Bandar Seri Begawan and Tutong, and of the Jalan Tanjong Pelumpong naval base at Muara where the nukes had been.

The helicopter came in low over the treetops, banked, and circled. It was not Boyinson in the Little Bird, but a Bell 214 in the markings of the Tentera Udara Diraja Brunei, the Royal Brunei Air Force. The pilot located a level spot and set the large aircraft down in a cloud of loose leaves and debris. The side door popped open and out hopped Awang Uhtaud, the heritage minister.

"His Majesty is quite interested in what you've found," he said eagerly as he approached the Americans.

"We've only been here for about an hour," Anne told him. "It's really too early to tell, but I was just saying that it looks very promising."

"Promising? Wonderful. He has asked me to keep track. He wants daily briefings while you're here."

The Suvarnadvipa ploy had apparently worked better than even Anne had hoped. The sultan's interest in the project had definitely been whetted. It had been evident when they met him at lunch yesterday that Omar had originally seen the archaeological site only as another element in his manipulation of the world community. However, the more they had discussed the mythical Suvarnadvipa, the more he had become interested in the site's potential, and in using it to further his long-range scheme of making his tiny country into a major player in the world. For the Americans, however, his new infatuation meant that they would have him where they wanted him. They had, in Anne's words, conned a con man.

April 25
8:25 A.M. Brunei Time

"I'LL be returning early in the afternoon," the man called Abdulla Maloud told the American. "When I come back, we'll talk. I'll show you the vessel that you'll be operating, and your cargo."

"Aye, aye, sir." The American smiled.

The Iranian and the American had arrived at the Jalan Tanjong Pelumpong naval base in the dark of night, having changed from a United flight to Royal Brunei in Singapore. Rodgers feigned exhaustion, and seemed to be dozing off. In fact, he was carefully studying the lay of the land within the base.

What had appeared on the satellite photos as a compound within a compound was exactly that. Surrounded by a razor-wire fence were two reinforced concrete buildings, one half again larger than the other. Between them was a paved open courtyard area about the size of a basketball court. It was here that the satellite photos had showed the Khomeini-6 missiles. About thirty yards of open pavement separated the compound's perimeter fence from the dock area.

Maloud—who had been Jahar Abiddijab until he slipped his chain at Guantanamo—felt quite pleased with his find. Actually, the American was Basim Rashid's find, but Rashid worked for Abiddijab, so he was Abiddijab's. He was everything that Abiddijab wanted.

Rodgers was an American veteran who hated America. He had even been arrested in an antiglobalization protest. He had an eagerness to strike a blow against the United States war machine, and this excited Abiddijab. But *how* could he channel that hatred usefully? What was the best application?

Just as he had done when he was in middle-level management in his family's construction business in Iran, Abiddijab matched skills and qualifications to the tasks at hand. Basim Rashid had been radicalized to the point where bloodlust was the passion of his life—yet he was from a rich and cultivated family, and

he could charm his way into a situation where he
could do the maximum damage. The people of Environmental Action International had been the ideal pat-
sies to take the blame for the San Francisco attack.
Their past actions were an ideal framework with which
Abiddijab could work. They were such obvious suspects in the poisoning of Hetch Hetchy that even the
Americans themselves were convinced of their culpa-
bility.

And now, this American who hated America and
who was also familiar with the operation of oceangoing vessels. How could these skills best be put to use?

The idea had come to him as he was dining with
Rashid and the American at that tandoori place on University Avenue. The American spoke of having operated tugs, fishing boats, and barges. As he mentioned
barges, Abiddijab recalled his earlier conversation with
Yayah Korma at the embassy in Washington. The ambassador had used an unwieldy barge as an analogy for
the ponderous ship of the American state. It was an
easy metaphor to visualize. When the American was
talking about ships, Abiddijab mentally compared their
size to that of warships—the little Bruneian warships
and the immense American warships.

As he studied his new surroundings, Rodgers had
observed that there were about a dozen men within the
compound, but they didn't seem to be doing very
much. Six of them were sitting around a table just inside a metal roll-up door in the larger building playing
cards.

As he was watching the card game, there was a

thundering sound, and the building's other metal door was rolled up. Inside were another half-dozen men working around two large wheeled carts, each with a pair of long metal tubes about eighteen inches in diameter. These were the Khomeini-6 missiles. The stabilizing fins and most of the tubelike fuselages were painted a dark gray-green. The forward sections of each missile were bare metal, with brightly colored flush screws, evidence that these forward sections had been recently fitted to the missiles. This confirmed that they now carried a different payload than that for which they were originally configured.

Pretending to ignore the missiles, Rodgers ambled off in the other direction and bought his way into the card game. The men readily welcomed the friendly stranger. They would be more than happy to have some American dollars in the pot.

From this vantage point, Rodgers could blend into the social scene in the compound within a compound, while watching the missiles that he pretended to ignore. As he played, one of the four missiles was removed from its cart, and the other three were wheeled out of the concrete building and through the gate in the compound's perimeter fence.

As they were moved slowly across the thirty yards of open space toward the docks, Rodgers understood that he would not need to wait for Abiddijab's return to be briefed on the cargo that he would be asked to transport.

After about an hour, as the players were taking a break, he asked to borrow the cell phone of one of them. He wanted to phone his sister in the States, and the young man had an unlimited calling plan. After all, he had just beaten the poor American with a royal flush. It was the least he could do—and Jack Rodgers had a notorious knack for talking people into things.

FIVE

April 25
11:01 A.M. Brunei Time

"**WHAT** in the world is Suvarnadvipa?" Pehin Dato Hudim Incpaduka asked.

"It's a mythical golden city," Sultan Omar Jamalul Halauddin explained. "Uhtaud had heard of it. I hadn't. Apparently, they've been writing about it for hundreds of years, but no one knows where it is."

The two longtime associates were lounging on cushions in one of the sultan's many large sitting rooms at the Istana Nurul Iman palace, waiting for Jahar Abiddijab, who was scheduled to join them for lunch.

"And this American archaeologist thinks that this golden city is *here*?"

"That's what she said. They're down there today, looking at it."

"This is a remarkable coincidence, Your Majesty," the United Nations ambassador said, shaking his head. "I had no idea when I presented our demands to Mboma to have this declared a UNESCO site that it was anything more than a few old rocks in a line."

"Neither did I, of course, but it looks as though we have gotten more than we bargained for. It must be real. This woman has no reason to make it up."

"Even if she is wrong about the site, we will have her expert opinion attached to it." Incpaduka shrugged. "Even if other archaeologists question her work, the burden of proof will be on them to provide conclusive evidence that this is *not* this place called Suvarnadvipa."

"If nobody else has been able to find this place in two thousand years of looking, I don't think they'll be able to prove that she is wrong."

"To Suvarnadvipa, whatever it is," Incpaduka said, raising his tumbler of rum and cola.

"Here, here," said Sultan Omar with a laugh. "To Suvarnadvipa, and to the *American* archaeologist who has given it to us."

Having toasted Suvarnadvipa, the men turned to the more serious issue at hand. Suvarnadvipa was, of course, merely a sideshow to the overarching objective of humiliating the United States and projecting the sultanate as a world power.

"The Americans are afraid and I think they actually *want* to comply with our demands," Incpaduka told the sultan. "Before San Francisco, they were defiant. Now they're afraid. Yayah Korma had meetings with Edredin. Our demands have been presented, and the Americans have made overtures to the Philippine and Malaysian governments."

"What did they say?" Sultan Omar asked eagerly.

"They refused, of course."

"Then we are at an impasse?"

"Yayah Korma feels that it will be just a matter of time, Your Majesty, but Abiddijab feels that they need additional urging."

"And you?"

"I believe that we should ask Abiddijab. He has spoken with the man called Faralaco, who is Livingstone's chief of staff."

One of the scantily dressed teenage girls who had been darting about the room bringing beverages and snacks came up to the sultan, bowed, and whispered to him that Abiddijab had arrived.

"My friend, please come in and join us," Sultan Omar said, moving his large mass slightly and graciously gesturing for the stern Iranian to pick a cushion and have a seat. Being less encumbered by enormous girth, the ambassador stood to greet Abiddijab.

They were an odd group. A year ago, if someone had said that today they would be running a country on the threshold of becoming a major player on the world stage, you'd not have believed them. Just that long ago, the two hard-drinking native Bruneians had been running rackets and import-export scams in Europe, while carousing with prostitutes in and around Marseilles. The third man, a former guest of the United States government at Guantanamo Bay, was a teetotaling serial killer who had solicited suicide bombers from Tunis to

Ankara. He had been captured in Afghanistan with a duffel bag full of blueprints for British landmarks. Fortunately for him, he had applied for a British passport in the 1990s, and was among the Gitmo inmates released under pressure from a group in Britain who promoted the freedom of people like him.

As white-jacketed waiters served the Serondeng Padang—chicken with garlic, onion, and coconut milk—the sultan took great delight in explaining Suvarnadvipa to Abiddijab. They laughed when they realized the delicious irony of having an *American* archaeologist confirm the immense importance of a site that they had considered to be worthless. It was too good to be real. What started out as a barely refined hoax might possibly be genuine. Even if it was not, simply having the imprimatur of an American archaeologist gave it a level of credibility that served their purposes immensely.

"Ambassador Incpaduka tells me that you and Ambassador Yayah Korma have a tactical disagreement," Sultan Omar observed casually, looking at Abiddijab.

"Your Majesty," Abiddijab began. "The ambassador feels that in due time the Americans will relent and we will have our way. I believe that an unruly dog, like an impudent woman, is better trained with lashing than with leniency."

"Do you suggest we attack another city with the LSD?" Hudim Incpaduka asked.

"To keep up the pressure, they must know that San Francisco was not an anomaly," Abiddijab insisted. "They must think . . . they must *know* . . . that we have the capability of striking them again and again. There is only one way to do this, and that is to strike them again!"

"We must not lose sight of our goal, which is to humiliate and emasculate the Americans," Sultan Omar reminded them.

"The LSD attacks *will* continue to humiliate them, and especially Livingstone, because they will continue to appear to have been carried out by *Americans*." Abiddijab beamed. "As with the Oklahoma City bombing in 1995, the Americans will feel the disgrace of being attacked within their own borders by their own people."

"This is good," agreed the sultan. "It seems to be working."

"Not only this, but soon we will have an American snubbing his nose at the U.S. Navy's Seventh Fleet with nuclear weapons." Abiddijab smiled.

"What?" Sultan Omar gasped, lurching forward.

"Without knowing it, Ambassador Yayah Korma gave me a very intriguing idea," Abiddijab said, leaning back and relishing the fact of his having startled the sultan. "He told me of what he had learned as a young man working on barges in the Malacca Strait. We were discussing Edredin and he was saying how difficult it is to change directions with a very large ship. He used that as a metaphor in discussing how a large country such as the United States changes course. I pictured in my mind a barge loaded with nuclear weapons attacking the Seventh Fleet."

"I absolutely oppose attacking the Americans with nuclear weapons!" Sultan Omar said in a reproachful tone.

"So do I," said Abiddijab with a smile. "If that happened, they would sink the barge, and they would never find my American. I only want them to *see* the barge and to *see* what an American who hates America can do."

April 25
11:01 A.M. Brunei Time

"**M**y brother wants to speak with you," Anne said, handing Dave Brannan her cell phone. Rodgers had called her phone rather than the colonel's in order that the young enlisted man from whom he borrowed the phone would overhear a female voice answering. Now that the man was distracted and no longer paying attention, Jack asked to speak with Brannan. He quickly outlined where he was, who he was with, and reported on the missiles—describing them as "dogs" for the benefit of anyone who might be eavesdropping—and the probability that they would soon be going to sea.

Brannan had mixed feelings about the missiles leaving the country. On the down side, they were in play in a possible showdown with the Seventh Fleet—but on the other hand, they were leaving Brunei, Rodgers was going with them, *and* he had promised Brannan that they would not be used. If anyone could pull this off solo, it would be Rodgers.

The colonel was glad that the three elements of the Raptor Team were now in a position to cover all their objectives—although a comparison to Custer at the

Little Bighorn had crossed his mind. In that infamous calamity, the cocky "Boy General" (who was actually a lieutenant colonel) had divided his command into three detachments against overwhelming odds. Brannan's command was likewise divided into three, but he still had two advantages that Custer had not. He was not underestimating his enemy, and unlike Custer's 7th U.S. Cavalry Regiment back in 1876, the Raptors still maintained the element of surprise. So far at least, they were still undetected, and hiding in plain sight.

Thanks to the professor, Brannan's own team had access to the sultan and could choose their time and place. They just needed to ascertain the who's who of his inner circle. Rodgers alone was with the nukes, but Rodgers alone was worth a platoon of most any other troops. Boyinson and the Little Bird would give them air cover when the time was right.

The problem was still one of coordinating their attacks and of withdrawing while leaving as little trace as possible of their work.

April 24
8:01 P.M. Pacific Time

BOB Rashid barely slowed as he made a tight right turn off California Highway 17, and Reid Arthur felt the sudden jerk in his neck. He didn't complain. They were on their way to buy the weapon that had the potential to kill thousands, so griping about a sore neck seemed pathetically out of place.

It was very dark as they followed the twisting country lane though the dense redwood forest that blankets the steep slopes of the Santa Cruz Mountains. There were a fair number of cars on the road. It was the tail end of the Silicon Valley rush hour, and these were mainly the executives who could afford secluded plots in these hills on which to construct their large and imposing mansions.

Because of their proximity to the San Francisco Bay Area, these mountains had at one time been one of northern California's most important sources of the old-growth redwood that was so favored by builders because of its resistance to decay. However, the logging activity had slacked to nearly nothing long before organizations such as Environmental Action International declared their jihad against the loggers and lumbering. In the sixties, counterculture refugees from California's cities moved here looking for seclusion and privacy, much as the Silicon Valley executives would a generation later. Today, both demographics lived side by side here, sharing the dark hillsides and occasional meadow with a few small family farms that predated both.

Arthur's neck continued to take a beating as Rashid whipped the blue Accord around the tight turns faster than he should have. At last, he noticed Arthur grimacing and slowed down.

"It won't be long now," Rashid said reassuringly. "Just about one mile."

A few minutes later, he turned into a gravel driveway and stopped about four car lengths up the road to remove a single chain that was stretched across. After he had driven through, Reid volunteered to step out to reattach the chain. As he did so, he caught sight of a surveillance camera hidden in the thick foliage. It looked down silently on anyone and everyone who passed this way.

A short distance later, they reached a heavy metal gate.

"We'll have to walk from here," Rashid told him.

They hiked upward for about fifty feet to a seventies-vintage cinder-block ranch house. The absence of lights in the windows made the place appear deserted, but the door clicked open as they neared it. Obviously, their approach had been watched. Inside, a heavy black curtain separated the entryway from the rest of the house.

When they passed through the curtain, they were greeted by a bald man with an unkempt gray beard whom Rashid introduced as "Harry." Rashid had said that they were going to meet his dealer and procure the LSD for the next attack. Based on the fact that Harry's house resembled a college chemistry lab—including the irreverent posters on the walls—Harry was evidently the source.

"I told you, man, I'm not going to sell you any more acid until you can promise me that you weren't mixed up in that thing up in San Francisco," Harry told him.

"Of course not, Harry," Rashid lied. "The media say that it was ecoterrorism. Clearly, I am not involved."

"That was a terrible fuckin' mess up there," Harry

observed. "I feel sorry for those people. Lots of little kids too."

Harry offered a joint from his stash as much to top off his own buzz as to be hospitable. Arthur readily accepted a toke, but Rashid declined. They sat down to discuss the transaction, which, in Harry's mental state, took much longer than it would have without the marijuana.

In the haze of the especially good weed, Arthur thought that he heard the men discussing *nine gallons* of acid. He did the math in his head, a process that was not easy under the influence, but at last he formed a mental picture of what this meant. The most potent acid that he had taken during his undergraduate years at Cal had been alleged to be about 150 mikes. He was stoned for two days. A gallon of a liquid such as water weighs 8.3 pounds, so nine gallons would be the equivalent of more than thirty-three million micrograms!

April 25
11:48 A.M. Brunei Time

LEAVING Will Casey and Brad Townsend to tend the gear at the airport—and shoo away the riffraff—Greg Boyinson headed southwest toward Tutong. Because the airport was located between the capital and Muara, he was able to get a pretty good look at the Jalan Tanjong Pelumpong naval base as he climbed out steeply from the airport. Boyinson took the Little Bird up to five thousand feet. He wanted to get a

good sense of the lay of the land between Muara and
Tutong, and especially of the roads leading in and out of
Bandar Seri Begawan. He could see the sprawling Istana Nurul Iman palace, and made a mental note of
places around it where he could set down a helicopter.

For the twenty-five-mile flight to Tutong, he followed the same main coastal highway that Brannan and
others had driven earlier in the day. From the air, Tutong looked a lot like a medium-sized Hawaiian coastal
town such as Lihue or Kahului, with larger buildings
clustering around the crossroads and fewer structures
on the periphery as small fenced fields blended into
deep jungle. He backed southward here and within
about a minute, he could see the Heritage Site. It con-
sisted of a series of what looked like stone foundations.
Some were in the open, while others were partially or
mostly overgrown with trees.

There was a group of people clustered around a
Bell 214 with Bruneian markings, and Boyinson set
the red-and-blue Little Bird down nearby.

"Greg, this is Awang Uhtaud. He's the minister of
heritage here in Brunei," Dave Brannan said as Boyinson walked over to the group.

Introduced as "Mr. Brown," Boyinson shook hands
with the jolly little man in the fez. Dressed in shorts,
flip-flops, and a brightly colored Hawaiian shirt, Boyinson was probably as far from looking like an American
Special Forces operator as possible.

"Welcome to Suvarnadvipa." The minister smiled.
"We have been discussing great plans for this area.
What do you think of positioning the casino in that area
over there by those trees? I think that the revolving

restaurant would have an excellent view of the diggings, don't you?"

"I guess so," Boyinson said, squinting in the direction that the little man was gesturing. "Where do most World Heritage Sites put their casinos?"

"That's a good question," Uhtaud said earnestly. He turned to the two aides that had accompanied him, instructing them to find out where the casinos were located at other UNESCO World Heritage Sites.

Boyinson noticed that Professor McCaine was rolling her eyes. She had probably never been to an archaeological site where the whereabouts of the future casino was a topic of conversation on the first day.

"I'm sure that your capable staff will find a perfect location," Anne said diplomatically. "Now that Mr. Brown is here with our helicopter, I'd like to get a look at this place from the air."

"That's a very good idea," Uhtaud agreed. "May I accompany you?"

Boyinson glanced at Brannan with a worried look on his face. They were supposed to be working on planning and operation, and this was the first opportunity for the two men to talk face-to-face since they had all arrived in-country. Obviously, they couldn't speak freely with the minister of heritage aboard.

"Well, actually, we were planning to fly directly back to Bandar Seri Begawan with Mr. Brown," Anne interjected.

"That's fine, you can drop me at the ministry." Uhtaud grinned. "We have a helipad there."

"Sure, please join us," Dave said. Sure, it complicated things, but it was more important to maintain friendly relations and the element of surprise. "You can ride in the back with me. "We'll let the professor sit up front with the pilot."

Arranging for Couper and Houn to take the car back to town, the four people squeezed into the Little Bird, and Boyinson handed out the headsets so that they could communicate.

Anne then directed Boyinson to spend a good deal of time circling over the site and probing the jungle behind it as she snapped pictures with her digital camera. Finally, when she had decided that they had spent enough time to convince the minister of their legitimate intentions, she said she was ready to return to the capital.

On the way, she continued to take pictures, remarking at how beautiful the beaches looked. This naturally sucked Uhtaud into a conversation. He was a thorough booster of his country, and explained that he had been a travel agent in Singapore for many years. As they neared Bandar Seri Begawan, he started showing off landmarks. Over the capital, he pointed out the golden-domed Omar Ali Saifuddin Mosque, the government ministries, and other locations as Anne took more pictures.

Brannan couldn't believe that he was hearing correctly when Uhtaud eagerly pointed out the Royal Brunei Ground Forces Headquarters at Berakas Garrison. He had started the flight as an unwanted guest, but the minister had become their personal guide on what had become a thorough photoreconnaissance flight. The former travel agent was too interested in promoting the sights and sites of Brunei to think for a moment that these people were here to assassinate its sultan.

As Greg Boyinson banked the Little Bird to descend to the helipad at the Ministry of Heritage, their host insisted that they fly all the way to the tip of the peninsula so that he could show them the sites around Muara.

As the helicopter came over Muara, both Brannan and Boyinson craned their necks to look at the Jalan Tanjong Pelumpong naval base. This morning Greg had seen it from five thousand feet and a distance of about four miles. Now they were below a thousand feet and nearly at the perimeter. Uhtaud cautioned Boyinson not to fly directly *over* the base, but he didn't stop Anne from grabbing several shots as they cruised near it.

In the satellite photographs that Buck Peighton had showed them there were several larger ships, but today, they were all out on patrol. Aside from the KDB *Depambak,* which was still tied up with construction scaffolding over it, the only vessels in port were smaller vessels and a couple of barges.

As Boyinson banked to keep from overflying the base, Brannan caught sight for a split second of at least two long tube-shaped objects on a cart being wheeled across a large open area adjacent to the docks. The Khomeini-6 missiles were on the move.

April 25
1:04 P.M. Brunei Time

JACK Rodgers heard the sound of a familiar helicopter flying nearby, and glanced up to see the Little Bird just past the perimeter of the naval base. He didn't know how Boyinson had managed to get so close, but he was glad that he had. He just hoped that Greg had seen the missiles as they were being moved toward the docks.

The card game was going well. At one point, he had been down by $400, but he was only down by about $50 when Jahar Abiddijab returned. He could have done much better, but he was more interested in keeping the game going until the Iranian got back.

"I'm anxious to get to work," Rodgers said as he folded his cards and joined the Iranian. "I'm tired of losing money in a card game. Let's go see this ship and the cargo."

"The Tentera Laut Diraja Brunei, the Brunei Navy, will be staging a show of force for the Seventh Fleet tomorrow," Abiddijab explained, gesturing for Rodgers to follow him toward the docks.

"What kind of force are you showing?" Rodgers asked with a laugh, nodding at the KDB *Depambak,* which was tied up at a nearby pier. "A bucket like that won't even get their attention."

"Possibly not," Abiddijab admitted. "But those weapons *will.*"

"What's that?" Rodgers asked, pretending not to recognize the missiles when Abiddijab nodded toward them.

"With those, you'll taunt the American fleet from within the exclusion zone," the Iranian said. "Their helicopters have been watching the Bruneian Navy in the waters west of Balabac Strait for weeks. They will send their helicopters again. They will see you, but they will be unable to touch you because you'll stay within the exclusion zone. You'll be rattling nuclear weapons at the U.S. Navy. Best of all, the Americans have embedded reporters with them, and the television cameras of those reporters will show these missiles to the world. The Americans will be able to do nothing, and their impotence will embarrass them in the eyes of the world!"

"Isn't this kinda dangerous?"

"They can't touch you, you'll be within the exclusion zone. Brunei is a sovereign nation. If the U.S. Navy can carry nuclear weapons across the oceans and waterways of the world, certainly Brunei has the right to carry whatever it wants in its own territorial waters. And thanks to the American television cameras, the whole world will see that the weapons are in its territorial waters."

"They know what those missiles are all about. If they think that we're about to launch, they blow me to kingdom come."

"They wouldn't *dare* blow up an American in Bruneian waters. The world will see your face. You are not Bruneian. You are not Iranian. Who are you? The Bruneian embassy in Washington will issue a press release describing this scruffy American veteran as the face of domestic opposition to Livingstone and the United States government. The *world* will see your face, and they will see that you are an American mocking America."

April 24
10:04 P.M. Pacific Time

THE two FBI agents had managed to follow the blue Honda Accord as it made the tight turn off

Highway 17 and slithered into the Santa Cruz Mountains on the snakelike mountain road. Rod Llewellan and Erik Vasquez maintained their distance, carefully watching the brake lights for any indication that Rashid might turn off.

Llewellan hoped that Rashid hadn't noticed him. On a road like this, and at the speed that he was traveling, there was a good chance that Rashid would be inclined to keep his eyes forward. There had also been plenty of cars on the road, so this would have made Llewellan's Volvo just another set of headlights in his mirror.

As they had followed the car around San Francisco Bay and into the mountains, Llewellan and Vasquez had theorized about the destination of Reid Arthur and Basim Rashid. Where were they going? Why were they traveling together? As soon as the blue Accord had left the highway and headed into the mountains, the pool of possibilities narrowed abruptly.

"I think I know where they're headed," Llewellan said.

"Me too," Vasquez agreed. "These hills are alive with drug labs and marijuana plantations."

Indeed, the Santa Cruz Mountains, with hundreds of square miles of steep, fenced terrain not visible from public roads, had a well-developed reputation as a source for illicit pharmaceuticals that dated back to the first arrival of the counterculture in the sixties.

When the Accord finally did turn off the narrow road, Llewellan ignored it and maintained his speed until the Volvo was around the next corner. At that point, he braked just long enough to allow Vasquez time to tumble out and sneak back on foot. Making a U-turn on this road would have been dangerous, and it greatly increased their chance of being seen.

"There was a chain across the road near where they stopped, but they moved it and went through. There were cameras in the tree," Vasquez whispered. He had phoned Llewellan from his hiding place in the brush. "It's just a narrow, dirt road. I'm going to circle around on foot so that I won't get seen by the cameras."

"Okay," Llewellan replied. He had turned off and parked about a quarter of a mile away. "I'm headed back in your direction."

Vasquez weighed the pros and cons of following through the brush or on the road, and decided on the latter. There was a chance that they might see him on the road, even in the dark, but there was a lot more of a chance that they would *hear* him as he stumbled through the dense brush.

He caught sight of Rashid and Arthur just as they reached a large gate and left the car and made their way toward a house that was fifty feet beyond the gate. As they knocked on the door, exchanged pleasantries with someone named "Harry," and went into the house, Vasquez studied the area around the gate, looking for another surveillance camera. At last he saw it, hidden in some bushes nearby. As he crept forward, screening himself from the camera with the bulk of the Accord, he felt the weight of the miniature GPS tracker in his pocket.

At last, he had his chance.

Activating the tracking device, he carefully reached up under the rear bumper and secured it.

With this accomplished, Vasquez considered his next move. Should he try to get closer to the house to ascertain what was going on? If he moved closer, he ran the risk of being spotted by a CCD camera. He had located one, but there might be others. These things were so small these days. Not so very long ago, all-weather cameras were the size of a box of crackers, but now there were wireless ones that were the size of your thumb. They were hard to see in daylight, impossible in moonlight.

Vasquez talked himself out of getting closer to the building. To do so meant the risk of being seen by another camera. If there was, in fact, a drug lab here, it wasn't going anywhere. It had a known location. Tracking the car undetected was a much higher priority.

He crept back down the dirt driveway and retraced his steps to the road. There, he reconnected with Llewellan for a long night of waiting for Arthur and Rashid to resume their journey to wherever they were headed next.

April 25
8:54 P.M. Brunei Time

"**P**LEASE tell us more, Professor," the sultan said. He had become thoroughly entranced with the legend of Suvarnadvipa. His heritage minister, Awang Uhtaud, had been extolling the tourism possibilities, but Sultan Omar Jamalul Halauddin saw the prestige value of the place as going far beyond mai-tai bars and baccarat tables.

The sultan was excited by his newfound asset, and commanded that there be an impromptu dinner at the Istana Nurul Iman palace to celebrate. All of his cabinet ministers were present and enjoying a meal of Daging Masak Lada Hitam. The fiery beef curry was heavily spiced with peppers and fragrant with seasonings known locally as *ketumbar, jintan putih,* and *jintan manis*—but better known to Americans as fennel, coriander, and cumin.

"If this site really is Suvarnadvipa, as I am encouraged by the evidence to believe," Anne began, "then it is arguably the most important archaeological find since King Tut, and possibly since Heinrich Schliemann found Troy in the 1870s."

"Certainly King Tut was more important than Troy," Hudim Incpaduka, the United Nations ambassador, asserted. As had been the case at lunch the preceding day, he was seated at the sultan's right hand.

"Troy was more important for a lot of reasons," Dave Brannan interjected, jumping into the conversation. He didn't know much about Suvarnadvipa, but he certainly knew about the historical importance of Schliemann's Trojan discoveries, and he saw this as a good opportunity to underscore his bona fides as a part of the professor's entourage.

"The discovery of Troy substantiated a major element of Western literature," Brannan continued. "Homer wrote about it in the Iliad and the Odyssey three thousand years ago. Then Virgil wrote about it eight hundred years later. It was a huge part of Western myth and legend for centuries, but generally assumed to be fictitious. Then suddenly, Schliemann digs it up and it's *real*. That same thing is about to happen out there by Tutong. It's time to start reprinting the world atlases."

"If the professor does dig up Suvarnadvipa at Tutong, and it is *real*, then that will indeed change much more than world atlases," Incpaduka said, nodding both to Brannan and to the sultan.

"The ancient Hindu texts that speak of Suvarnadvipa are as important to South Asia literature as the Iliad is to the West," Anne continued. "Especially in the tenth and eleventh centuries, Suvarnadvipa is written about in a very matter-of-fact way. It is just as real as places like Malabar. There's the Jatakamala narrative about a mariner called Suparaga who traveled to Suvarnadvipa. In the second decade of the eleventh century, the Buddhist intellectual Atisa Dipamkara Shrijnana went to Suvarnadvipa with a group of jewelry traders, and wrote extensively about the experience."

"What did he have to say?" Sultan Omar asked eagerly.

"He had a great deal to say," Anne confirmed. "After all, he actually *lived* in Suvarnadvipa for a dozen years, studying with a guru called Dharmarakshita, who was regarded as one of the most prominent teachers of the age. Atisa is also remembered as later being the master who reintroduced Buddhism into Tibet, when the king had nearly obliterated it. I think that this makes him a historical figure on par with Homer, don't you?"

"Of course." The sultan nodded with a smile. Just as he followed the previous day's seating arrangements by placing Incpaduka on his right, he had seated the archaeology professor next to him again tonight as well. He was fascinated with her stories, and he was captivated by her. Though his lusts gravitated toward teenage bodies, he found something indescribably fascinating about this lovely woman with her timeless beauty and her personal charm. He was glad that she had chosen to wear a dress that was a bit more low-cut than the one that she had worn to lunch yesterday.

Anne returned the smile, and continued her story.

"One of the things I find most fascinating about Atisa's account of Suvarnadvipa is the apparent importance of Suvarnadvipa to the eleventh-century commerce in precious stones."

Anne let that statement hang in midair as she took another sip of wine. Dave Brannan almost burst out laughing as he saw the dollar signs flickering in the eyes of Incpaduka and the sultan.

"Could there still be jewels at the site?" Dr. Awang Uhtaud, the heritage minister, asked eagerly. He was beginning to see wealth coming from more than simply his casino.

As Anne began to speculate about the remote possibility that there could be buried treasure at the mythical Suvarnadvipa, Brannan looked around the room, profiling the men—except for Anne, they were *all* men—who were seated around the table. The mission was to decapitate the snake and his henchmen. The snake was identified, as was Incpaduka, Omar's former gangster crony who was literally and figuratively his right-hand man.

As Buck Peighton had briefed the Raptors, the majority of the sultan's cabinet, like Heritage Minister

Uhtaud, were not participants in the sultan's previous "business" interests, but merely young political appointees who were along for the ride of their lives. Their road was about to get a bit bumpy.

Also at the table were two large men who had been introduced with bureaucratic titles, but who had the refinement and bearing of nightclub bouncers. They simply sat there and said nothing. The way that they were positioned at the table convinced Brannan they were the sultan's bodyguards. In his mind, Brannan had nicknamed them "Tweedledum" and "Tweedledumber."

And then there were the Iranians. There was this guy called Abdulla Maloud, who Brannan knew to be Jahar Abiddijab, and *his* two bodyguards. What a contrast between them and the Bruneian cabinet. The Bruneians grinned often and conversed among themselves in an animated way. The Iranians sat together and never cracked a smile. Being Shi'ite, they considered the Hindus and Buddhists who had created Suvarnadvipa and its folklore to be infidels. Therefore, they were decidedly unworthy of the sort of admiration that the sultan and his circle were heaping on this mythical land of gold.

As Anne carried on her congenial conversation with the immense monarch, her thoughts continued to return to those photographs of the dead people in San Francisco, especially of that little boy with the dreadful expression on his face. She thought about all those pictures that she had seen of a smiling Adolf Hitler patting small children on the heads, and how this contrasted so starkly with the stark images of the dead children stacked in death camps awaiting incineration.

Why?

It was, she supposed, part of a bizarre lust for power and glory that overwhelms all other emotions in dictators and demagogues. But why then could such people appear so affable, while ordering such indiscriminate atrocities? The thought of this chilled her to the bone, but she carried on, smiling cordially and playing the role in which she had been cast by her addiction to adrenaline.

The official dinner concluded; the guests paid their respects to His Majesty and broke off into small groups to continue their conversations. Anne noticed that the Iranians had been the first to leave, and that the colonel was speaking with the United Nations ambassador.

The sultan suggested that she might like to see some of the artifacts that he had in his private study. They were, he told her, not from the region, but were things that had been collected by his predecessors. He really didn't have a clue what they were, and he hoped that she might be able to tell him.

Anne smiled. This was apparently the royal equivalent of being invited back to his apartment to see his etchings.

The sultan's office was a large room, nearly forty feet on each side. Everything was in disarray. Tables and shelves were jumbled with haphazard piles of papers and junk. It was a veritable monument to disorganization. It looked like an apartment that someone had moved into without the previous tenant moving out, and where the new tenant preferred to live out of boxes to avoid unpacking. Of course, this was exactly the case.

Along one wall there were glass museum cases filled with a random assortment of artifacts. They were an eclectic lot, but many were actually quite nice, and she told him so. There were some Chinese ivory carvings from the early Manchu Dynasty that were exquisite, and an eighteenth-century cinnabar-red lacquer box. He also had some first-century Greek pottery and a Roman dagger.

Soon, he grew weary of standing, and suggested that they sit for a moment in some big leather chairs near his cluttered desk.

He poured them each a cognac and sighed as he lowered his 322 pounds into his chair.

"Just as we are an emerging political power, we are an emerging cultural center," he told her after they had toasted Suvarnadvipa. It was about the fifth such toast that evening. "As you know, even without gemstones, the discovery of Suvarnadvipa will alter the course of cultural history. I can make a place for *you*. I could build an institute. In the United States, you are a professor, one of many I suppose. Here, you could be the director, the executive director of the institute. You choose your own title. You would be the one associated with Suvarnadvipa. As you traveled to conferences around the world, or whatever archaeologists do, you would be a woman of eminent importance."

"Sultan, are you making a proposition?" Anne smiled, flirting slightly with the massive potentate.

"You could make an important contribution. I *will*

be creating an important center here, and *you* could be part of this. You could have a place here. I encourage you to consider this."

Anne smiled thoughtfully as though she was giving it some consideration, but her mind wandered as he droned on and on about his plans for his institute. She hadn't noticed whether he had mentioned whether Uh-taud's casino would be located close to the museum.

Eventually, his generous portion of cognac was gone and his mind turned to other items that he wanted to show to the woman he now imagined as his future institute director. She remained seated near his desk nursing her drink as he lumbered about the huge room picking up various artifacts and baubles to show her. He was like a small child seeking approval for the magnificence of his stamp collection.

Because of his enormous bulk, he moved slowly and sluggishly, giving her ample time to look around. Numerous FedEx and DHL cartons and envelopes with diplomatic seals were scattered about on the desk and on the floor. Each time he turned his back, she peeked into another one.

She didn't actually know what she was looking for until she found it. Swaddled in a cloud of bubble wrap within one of the cartons was an open box. In that box were transparent plastic tubes containing some sort of clear liquid.

Could it be? Could it be that this was some of the LSD?

Anne looked at the return address. It was a mail drop on Shattuck Avenue in Berkeley, California. Somebody was sharing samples with the boss, and the boss had simply tossed them aside in an apparently offhand way. The tubes were taped together in groups of three or four. There were at least a half-dozen groups. Impulsively, she grabbed one of the clusters and slipped it into her purse. She hoped that in this mess, he wouldn't notice it missing.

She strolled across the room to where he was and admired some of the baubles that he was arranging on a shelf.

"Professor, we must very soon embrace the notion that the United States is no longer an important world power," the sultan said in a serious and almost ominous tone. "I encourage you to think of the world outside the borders of the land of your birth. I encourage you to think of your own place in the world. Brunei is one of the fresh, new nations that will emerge in the twenty-first century as the bones of the old colonial powers rot on the garbage heap of history. In a very few days, the United States will suffer defeat and humiliation unlike anything that has gone before. And just as America plummets toward its nadir, we will be rising like the morning sun over the Banjaran."

"I realize that many countries and many factions in the world are anxiously awaiting the downfall of America." Anne smiled. "But it hasn't happened yet. I don't know what sort of humiliation you're talking about. Can you be a little more specific?"

"I was speaking *metaphorically,* of course," Sultan Omar said. He had been drinking a bit too much and his tongue had slipped.

"Of course." Anne smiled as she examined a little Javanese vase.

"I want to go out to Suvarnadvipa tomorrow to see it for myself," he said, changing the subject. "We can have lunch at my bungalow."

"I didn't know you had a house at Tutong," Anne said to this man who seemed to live his life as a succession of rich meals.

"Neither did I until last week." He laughed, gently touching her arm. "But I'm the sultan. Apparently, I have houses everywhere."

April 25
8:54 P.M. Brunei Time

THERE was only a thin sliver of light on the western horizon, but the piers at the Jalan Tanjong Pelumpong naval base near Muara were a beehive of activity. At least two of the three Waspada-class missile ships had been at sea at any given moment since mid-March, and the round-the-clock operations were beginning to wear on crews that were used to a more leisurely schedule.

Tonight, things were busier than usual as the KDB *Sajuang* was being made ready for long-range escort operations. The missile ship would be steaming far to the northeast in the vicinity of the Balabac Strait, escorting the large oceangoing barge that was being prepared at the adjacent pier. There were rumors flying at Muara this morning. They whispered that the barge and the KDB *Sajuang* would actually enter the strait sometime over the next several days, and that they would actually confront the U.S. Navy's Seventh Fleet.

Normally, the idea of a barge escorted by a ship the size of the KDB *Sajuang* would be taken as a ludicrous joke. Today, that was not the case, because the three Khomeini-6 missiles that were aboard the barge were an enormous force-multiplier.

At the helm of the KDB *Sajuang,* Kapitan Adanan Vegawan watched the Iranians stringing cables on the barge, preparing the launch systems. Vegawan thought it a testament to disorganization that a barge was being used for this mission when the KDB *Depambak* was sitting idle just fifty meters away. This ship, the newest of the Brunei Navy's Nakhoda Ragam-class offshore patrol vessels, was clearly the appropriate choice to be the first ship in the fleet to be armed with nuclear weapons. Now it lay tied up to the pier, merely a quiet witness to history in the making.

Vegawan didn't like the Iranians being involved in Brunei naval operations, and he disliked taking orders from the man called Abdulla Maloud, but what could he say? This self-important, sour-faced man was getting his own orders directly from the sultan, so there was nothing to say. At least Vegawan and his crew were going to finally have an opportunity to thumb their noses at the American Seventh Fleet. And the whole world would *see* him thumbing his nose at them, thanks to the Americans' own embedded reporters. Vegawan wondered for a moment what it would be like to have embedded reporters aboard his ship. He couldn't imagine. Why did they do it?

Strange people, these Americans.

Finally, the majority of the Iranians stepped ashore, gathered up their gear, and began heading back to their compound. There were two that remained aboard, along with the mysterious American that people were whispering about. Vegawan wondered why an American would want to be involved in a show of force against the ships of his own country.

Strange people, these Americans.

SIX

April 25
5:54 A.M. Pacific Time

"**THEY'RE** coming out," Erik Vasquez said, jabbing Rod Llewellan in the ribs.

"Arrraugh," Llewellan replied as he awoke from a deep sleep in the seat of the old Volvo. "I'm dreaming."

"Nope," Vasquez said. "They're coming. I can see the car on the GPS screen and they're heading back out of there."

The two FBI agents had spent a fitful night on stakeout deep in the Santa Cruz Mountains. They had followed Reid Arthur and Basim Rashid to a secluded drug lab high on a steep hillside off a winding mountain road, and had slept in their car as their quarry had apparently rested in real beds, courtesy of a man named "Harry."

Llewellan looked out into the gloomy stillness of

the redwood forest. Except for the sound of Vasquez fumbling with the keys, the only sound was the *plung-plung* of drops of condensation dripping onto the roof from the fog-shrouded branches high above.

He really liked this little GPS tracker. The data contained in the system didn't show the driveway on its map display, but it showed the mountain road where the agents had spent the night, and thanks to Vasquez's reconnaissance last night, their suspects' car could be seen clearly as it moved slowly toward the road. As the dot on the LCD screen representing the car reached the line representing the road, both FBI agents looked up. There, in the distance, a real blue Honda Accord emerged onto a real mountain road.

"They're on the move," Llewellan said, having dialed his boss. Since yesterday, he had been in touch periodically with the bureau's San Francisco field office, which had been temporarily relocated to San Jose after the April 4 attack.

"Keep them in sight and let us know where they're headed."

"The good news is that Erik managed to get a GPS tracker onto their bumper last night."

"That's certainly useful."

"You bet it is," Llewellan agreed. "Have you made contact with local authorities yet about this drug lab?"

"They're getting the proper paperwork together. It should be later today, but we don't want to do anything until your suspects make a move."

"If they do, you'll be the second to know," Llewellan promised.

The Accord retraced the route followed the previous

night, heading down off the mountain toward California Highway 17. As Rashid and Arthur hesitated, waiting for traffic to clear so that they could make a left turn onto Highway 17, the agents paused out of sight.

Llewellan really liked this little GPS tracker.

"They're headed back into the Bay Area," Vasquez observed as they made their way into the mass of freeway loops and interchanges around San Jose. "I can't believe that they'll strike again in the same place."

"Expect the unexpected," Llewellan said. With every quarter mile of San Francisco's water system—from the city's own reservoirs to Hetch Hetchy—now under surveillance, it seemed improbable that they would do it again, but who could have predicted what they had already done?

However, they did not stop. The Accord, and the dot on the map that represented it, passed through the Bay Area freeway grid, across Altamont Pass, and into California's broad San Joaquin Valley. Here, they turned south toward Interstate 5.

As the FBI agents followed their quarry, they passed under the big green sign that indicated the direction toward Los Angeles. Llewellan and Vasquez just looked at one another. Nothing needed to be said.

April 25
8:54 A.M. Eastern Time

THE director of national intelligence handed the satellite surveillance photos directly to the president, who spread them on the table so that Admiral

Michael J. Felth, the chief of naval operations, could view them as well.

"They left port three hours ago and are heading northwest toward the Balabac Strait," Richard Scevoles explained. "I wouldn't have come rushing over here and screwing up your schedules with these but for the barge. You can see that they've got three of their Khomeini-6 missiles on the deck."

"Why don't they have them covered?" Thomas Livingstone asked.

"The bastards want us to see 'em," Felth growled. "They know we're watching and they want us to see that they're carting those damned things off toward our ships."

"The barge is being escorted by this other ship and they're traveling at about seven knots," Scevoles added.

"That's one of their Waspada-class missile ships," Felth said. "It's capable of cruising comfortably at twenty knots or so, but a self-propelled, oceangoing barge like this is pretty well maxed out at around seven."

"Why are they using a barge instead of one of their faster warships?" Livingstone asked.

"Converting a warship takes time, because missile launchers have to be fitted in alongside other equipment on deck," Felth said. "With a barge, they have a large flat area to work with, and they can fabricate a simple launch platform rather quickly. They had the KDB *Depambek* undergoing conversion, but they deliberately stopped last month when the United Nations paid them off and they agreed to stand down their nukes. Apparently, they just shifted the work to this barge."

"Why didn't we see this?" Livingstone asked Scevoles.

"It was a barge, there was work being done, but there was no way of knowing that the work being done was to build something to launch missiles."

"How long before they reach our Seventh Fleet?"

"At this rate, they could be in the Sulu Sea in about twenty-four hours. It could take longer if they can't maintain their seven knots," Felth told the president.

"That's assuming they don't turn back," Scevoles added. "We've been watching their patrols in this area for weeks. They run up as far as the vicinity of Sikuati, Malaysia, then they come about and head for home."

"What's the range of the missiles?" Livingstone asked.

"About fifty miles."

"Meaning that they could launch from near Sikuati and hit one of our ships?"

"Theoretically," Felth said tentatively. "We have countermeasures that could almost certainly take them out, but I would sure as hell want to preempt them if they don't turn back near Sikuati . . . if not *before*."

"How much before?" Livingstone asked.

"Permission to attack *immediately,* sir?" the admiral asked the commander in chief.

"No, Admiral," Livingstone said cautiously. "I'd like to keep that option on the table, but not immediately. We are still walking the line of avoiding an international incident. I also want to avoid the risk of detonating those warheads and creating a nuclear explosion a dozen or so miles off the Malaysian coast. They might just be taunting us. As the director said, they could still come about near Sikuati. Have your reconnaissance aircraft keep an eye on them without getting too close, and let's monitor this thing very closely."

"May I remind the president that the ships of Task Force 70 represent 86 percent of the U.S. Navy's surface combat strength in the Pacific," Felth said pointedly. "That's a larger proportion of the Pacific Fleet than was at Pearl Harbor on December 7, 1941. With three nuclear weapons of any size hitting anywhere near our ships, Task Force 70 could be annihilated."

"Order the ships to disperse as much as possible and await further instructions, Admiral," Livingstone told him. "I don't want to have another Pearl Harbor on my watch, but I also want to avoid a disastrous incident that may yet be avoidable."

"What if they launch in the meantime, sir?" Felth asked.

"*If* that happens, have Briscoe defend himself," the president replied. He paused for a moment before continuing. "And launch the immediate full-scale attack on Brunei. Take out the whole damned place."

When the director of national intelligence and the admiral had left the Oval Office, Livingstone paused to contemplate the enormity of the situation. Naturally, his thoughts turned to those famous black-and-white photos that had been taken in this room in 1962 as John F. Kennedy agonized over the Cuban Missile Crisis. This time the missiles weren't targeting the United States homeland, but if the admiral's worst-case scenario played out, thousands of Americans could die, and over half a century of American naval superiority in the Pacific would come to an end.

Livingstone wondered about Buck Peighton and his American Volunteer Group, his Raptor force. Where were they? Where would they be when the full-scale retaliation came? Had they ever made it to Brunei?

April 26
11:35 A.M. Brunei Time

THE day had dawned picture-postcard lovely. The deep blue sky was dotted with just a handful of puffy white clouds. The sun shone warmly on the palm trees swaying gently in the tropical breeze.

It was a beautiful day for a helicopter flight, thought Sultan Omar Jamalul Halauddin as the Bell 214 carrying him and Hudim Incpaduka dashed from Bandar Seri Begawan to Tutong barely two hundred feet above the sandy beaches along the coastline of the South China Sea.

For the sultan, today was to be a big day.

He was making his first visit to a formerly anonymous patch of jungle that was about to become the crown jewel in his newfound global prestige. How easily, and how fluidly, the word Suvarnadvipa rolled off the tongue. He smiled and enjoyed the view as he whispered it over and over to himself.

For the Raptor Team, today was to be D-Day.

Dave Brannan, along with Jason Houn, Ray Couper, and Professor Anne McCaine, were driving south along the coast road when they glimpsed the sultan's helicopter zipping past. If everything went according to their plan, this would be the last time the sultan would make this flight. If not, then none of the Raptors were likely ever to see this stretch of road—or any other stretch of road—again.

Having made their earlier trip to Tutong unarmed, each of the Raptors now carried a Heckler & Koch Mk.23 automatic with a twelve-round clip. Houn carried an AN/PRC-148 multiband intra-team radio, and the professor had another one in her large canvas tote bag.

Instead of turning inland from Tutong, they turned seaward from the main highway about a mile short of the city. Twelve yards from the highway, there was a large gate guarded by two men in Bruneian army uniforms carrying British-made L64 assault rifles. Developed in the 1970s, these 5.56mm weapons dated back to the days when British military advisors were still active in this former British colony.

The guards had been alerted to their arrival, and were ready to let them pass after a cursory glance inside the trunk of their rental car. They also recognized Anne from her brief appearance on Bruneian television, taped as she had visited the palace for lunch. One of the soldiers noticed the canvas bag on Anne's lap and asked to look inside. He pulled out the AN/PRC-148 and examined it quizzically.

Fortunately, the Raptors had planned ahead, disguising their radios to look like MP3 players. In normal combat situations, having a black radio was better camouflage. Today, the pink plastic case was perfect camouflage. Anne smiled broadly, and the guard smiled back, handing her the AN/PRC-148.

The sultan's house in Tutong was a far cry from the Istana Nurul Iman palace, but still a very substantial building and not a modest bungalow. It was a low structure nestled among the palm trees and completely ringed by an open, wooden lanai.

They parked near the sultan's Bell 214 and walked up the large staircase. A small number of soldiers were standing around outside, armed with L64s. Inside, Brannan counted six of the sultan's palace guard, but just two of them were carrying rifles. Both were the more up-to-date Royal Ordnance L85A1s with twenty-round magazines. The guards had their weapons slung. They weren't expecting any trouble. They probably also still had the safeties on.

Brannan noticed that "Tweedledum" and "Tweedledumber," the two big, pudgy tough guys from last night, were on the job again. Each was carrying a sidearm, which bulged beneath his jacket.

The smell of curry wafted from a large room from which the South China Sea was visible in the distance. It was a very idyllic setting for their third meeting with this huge sovereign for whom it was impossible to have a meeting without copious amounts of food and drink.

April 26
11:35 A.M. Brunei Time

A S the self-propelled, oceangoing barge chugged out into the South China Sea, Jack Rodgers set a northeasterly course toward the Balabac Strait. He had plenty of time to ponder the situation. He was nominally in charge of the 150-foot, flat-bottomed vessel, but the two Iranians on board probably wouldn't be inclined to take anything but the most operational of orders. Neither of them seemed as though he had ever been to sea before, so they were pretty useless in the operational category. When it had come to cast off, the dock crew had had to step in to help.

There wasn't much to do but steer. The throttle was wide open, and the 150-foot barge was doing about seven knots. As long as the seas remained relatively calm, they would be close enough to the Balabac Strait to warrant the attention of the Seventh Fleet's LAMPS helicopters by the end of the day.

Then what?

Jahar Abiddijab's great idea was to cruise out to the Balabac Strait where an American would be observed playing chicken with the Seventh Fleet. Jack Rodgers would become the poster boy for domestic anti-Americanism. Or at least that was the idea as Abiddijab had explained it. If his plan also involved some sort of scheme to actually launch the three Khomeini-6 missiles, Rodgers was sure that he could stop it.

Just as Abiddijab had his great idea, so too did Jack Rodgers. He went along with the part of Abiddijab's plan where the missiles left Brunei, but this is where the ideas diverged. Rodgers had no intention of thumbing his nose at the U.S. Navy. In fact, his plan was to *give* the three missiles to the U.S. Navy. He still wasn't exactly sure what he going to do about the KDB *Sajuang*, which was still shadowing the barge, but he was sure that he would think of something. At just seven knots, he had plenty of time.

The missile ship was lumbering along about a hundred yards astern, and about the same distance to the starboard of his wake. He imagined that the skipper of a vessel capable of thirty knots must not be too happy to be having to keep pace with a garbage scow doing seven. He also wondered what the skipper must think of having to escort a boatload of nukes.

Aboard the KDB *Sajuang,* Kapitan Adanan Vegawan was indeed pondering that question. However, any apprehension that he might have felt was submerged beneath the exhilaration of being the first Bruneian sea captain to challenge the warships of a major sea power on the high seas for centuries.

April 25
10:12 A.M. Pacific Time

"**Y**OU'RE where?" Rod Llewellan's boss asked. "We're still in pursuit of the suspects on Interstate 5, approximately twenty miles south of Buttonwillow," Llewellan replied. "They are definitely headed toward Los Angeles."

Ever since they had driven out of the Santa Cruz Mountains, the FBI agent had remained in touch periodically with the field office, but there hadn't been much to say. It had been an uneventful, even boring, pursuit—nothing like the car chases in the movies. Between Tracy and Grapevine, the 250 miles of California's San Joaquin Valley through which Interstate 5 runs is as featureless as any section of the Great Plains in Kansas or the Dakotas. There are no towns of any size visible from a highway that is as straight and flat as Interstate 40 between Amarillo and Oklahoma City.

They had been watching their quarry inching south on the GPS, closing to get a visual confirmation every thirty minutes or so, then dropping back. The blue Honda Accord had stopped once, at the Buttonwillow exit, but only to buy gas. Erik Vasquez had remarked on the incongruity of it. Here were terrorists who had been responsible for violently upending the lives of a million people, and they had to gas up their car like anyone else.

"We've been in contact with Los Angeles field office, and they've been in touch with LAPD and CHP," Llewellan's boss explained. "They've all agreed that it would be best not to have any marked cars or choppers anywhere near the Accord, and to let you handle it for the time being. But the field office will be sending some agents north to try to rendezvous with you at Santa Clarita and help keep track of these people as they get into the LA Basin freeway grid."

"As I said before, I think it's important to see exactly where they're headed," Llewellan said. "There may be others involved."

"We agree, but up to a point. Los Angeles officials are edgy as hell. The Los Angeles police chief and the mayor have had a conference call with the director in Washington. They want to make sure that you're on top of them if and when they try to dope a water line. This just plain cannot happen."

"Understood," Llewellan promised.

The monotony of the past three hours changed abruptly as Interstate 5 began to climb abruptly over Tejon Pass. The Volvo was suddenly surrounded by coughing and groaning semis and slowed suddenly from around 70 mph to about 40 mph.

Rod Llewellan wondered aloud about what the family in the minivan up ahead or the trucker they had just passed would have thought if they had known the real identity of the two men in the innocuous blue car that was hardly noticed in the southbound lane that day.

April 26
12:17 P.M. Brunei Time

A S had been the case the night before, the lunch conversation was dominated by an exchange between Sultan Omar and the professor. He had begun with a monologue about the importance of Suvarnadvipa to his country's place in the world, but gradually it came down to the importance of the site to his own importance in the world. Anne responded by embellishing every story she had ever read about Suvarnadvipa, even making up a few stories off the top of her head, especially involving the tantalizing possibility of buried treasure. She explained at length the things that he would see when they went out to *his* Suvarnadvipa later in the afternoon.

As had been the case the night before, the sultan finally pulled Anne off to another room to speak with her in private. This left the Raptors and Ambassador

Incpaduka in the dining room with Tweedledum and Tweedledumber.

Though the sultan's appetites gravitated toward teenaged bodies, he had found himself dreaming about this lovely woman. He found her physically exquisite in a way that his teenagers were not, and he was also enthralled with the idea of her becoming the front person for the archaeological institute that he imagined for Suvarnadvipa, *his* Suvarnadvipa.

He had watched her during lunch. As he had noticed the graceful movements of her body in her blue crocheted dress, and as he had listened to the superlatives that she had used to describe *his* Suvarnadvipa, he'd become certain that he had to make his move.

"Professor, you asked me last night whether I was making you a 'proposition,'" he said when they were alone. He had brought the margarita pitcher with him, and he topped off her drink as he spoke. "I suppose that I was really not being as clear as I might have been."

"How so, Your Majesty?"

"I do, in fact, wish to make you a proposition. I told you that I would build an archaeological institute here at Suvarnadvipa, and I will. I encouraged you to consider being here and being part of that institute. Today, I wish to formally ask you to be the head of that institute."

"Hmmm," she murmured thoughtfully, playing the role to its hilt. "The head of your institute?"

"You pick your own title, Professor. Do you wish to be director? Chairperson? President? Any title you wish. *Anything* you wish, it's yours. The same with the facilities. You want a state-of-the-art laboratory? Consider it yours. A library? Done. You tell me."

Anne smiled. "That's very generous."

"And your salary?" Sultan Omar began. "I'll offer you one million dollars per year. Is that enough? How about a two-million-dollar bonus after three years?"

"I'm honored, Your Majesty." Anne blushed. It didn't seem real. Although nothing in the past six weeks had been anything close to what had been her reality a year ago.

"Your Majesty, may I interrupt?" Hudim Incpaduka said, stepping into the room and breaking the mood. "I must speak with you . . . privately."

"Please excuse me, Professor." Sultan Omar smiled as he followed Incpaduka out of the room. She noticed that he turned slightly as he passed through the doorway. His 322-pound body was too wide to walk straight through. "I'll let you consider my proposition for a moment."

"While you are planning your theme park, your navy is headed for a confrontation with the Seventh Fleet," Incpaduka scolded the monarch. "Pardon me for being one of Your Majesty's most impertinent subjects, but I think your attention is better focused on the very delicate situation that is at hand, rather than on planning a museum. This is as counterproductive as Uhtaud's casino scheme."

"I certainly beg to differ with you about its being counterproductive," the sultan retorted. "Suvarnadvipa will transform the image of this country and it will be a cornerstone of our greatness. Just as we are expanding our borders to their historical glory, so too are we restoring our cultural prominence."

"The Seventh Fleet . . ."

"Screw the Seventh Fleet!" Sultan Omar said impatiently. "Abiddijab has planned this encounter minutely. It is carefully timed to coincide with our second attack inside the United States. You and Yayah Korma are like women, running nervously as our moment of magnificence approaches. Within a matter of a day or so, President Livingstone will be humbled and defeated, and you will lead the delegation that lands in Guam to plant our flag there. I sincerely hope that you will be up to the task."

April 26
12:56 P.M. Brunei Time

ANNE McCaine found herself alone in the room, alone with the warm rattan wall coverings, the overstuffed floral-print furniture, and the view of the waves breaking on the shore in the distance. She found herself alone, with the half-filled margarita pitcher that Sultan Omar had set on the table.

She glanced into the other room. He and Incpaduka were in a heated conversation in the other room and paying no attention. Her hands were trembling as she opened her canvas tote bag and carefully took out the four plastic vials.

Last night, when they had returned to the hotel, Anne had waited until they were in the elevator to open her purse and show the colonel the cluster of tubes that she had pilfered from the package in the sultan's office. He nodded quietly, not wanting to say anything in an elevator that was probably bugged. They both knew what they *probably* were, but they had the means to find out.

When they got back to her room, she opened her makeup bag and pulled a piece of paper from a packet of lens-cleaning tissue and laid it on the top of the desk. In fact, the tissue was a piece of filter paper impregnated with dimethylamino-benzaldehyde. Anne then carefully opened one of the vials and let a couple of drops of the colorless, tasteless liquid fall on the paper. Next, she opened a small bottle containing hydrochloric acid and placed a few drops at the edge of the blotter paper. As she and the colonel knew, if LSD were present, a purple ring would form, turning blue within about half an hour. In fact, the entire piece of paper had turned blue before their eyes.

They silently made note of the fact that this was LSD of exceptional purity and concentration.

Now, her hands were trembling slightly as she uncorked the first vial and emptied it into the margarita pitcher.

She looked back into the other room. The sultan and Incpaduka were still talking.

Anne opened a second vial and dumped it into the pitcher.

She looked again. They were still at it.

Taking a deep breath, she opened the third, and its

contents joined those of its predecessors in the pool of blue agave tequila, Grand Marnier, and lime.

There was a sudden commotion. Anne quickly capped the third empty vial and dropped it back into her bag. She picked up her own, full margarita glass and stepped away from the pitcher.

"Professor, please pardon our rudeness," the sultan purred as he waddled back into the room, the sober-faced United Nations ambassador in tow. "I wish to propose a toast to Suvarnadvipa."

He poured himself a full glass of the mixture and found a glass to pour one for Incpaduka. Anne held up her full glass, indicating that she didn't need any more.

"That tasted a bit watered down," Sultan Omar said as he downed his glass in two gulps. "We must have more."

He refilled his glass and that of the ambassador, but Anne shook her head, indicating that she still had plenty.

"I would like to drink a toast to the Suvarnadvipa Archaeological Institute," the jolly sultan said happily. Ambassador Incpaduka raised his glass and drank the toast, although he was clearly preoccupied by other issues.

"I'd like to drink a toast to His Majesty's choice of museum directors," Anne said with a wink.

"I'll certainly drink to that." Sultan Omar laughed, touching Anne gently on the arm.

The sultan offered two more toasts, draining his glass each time. The ambassador had drunk a couple of glasses, but was now declining refills. Anne noticed that the pitcher was nearly empty.

April 26
12:56 P.M. Brunei Time

A small, innocent-looking red-and-blue helicopter cruised over the western edge of the main runway of the Brunei's international airport, but nobody below at the main facility of the Tentera Udara Diraja Brunei, the Royal Brunei Air Force, paid much attention. They had become used to seeing the University of Colorado chopper flitting here and there over the past few days. They knew that it was in Brunei to work on one of the sultan's big projects, and that placed it beyond suspicion.

Over the past couple of days, Boyinson had been logging a lot of flight time, making sure that the red-and-blue helicopter was a familiar sight in the skies over the capital. The people of the city, and the people living in the houseboats along the river, were used to seeing it. The air traffic controllers at the airport tower were used to seeing it. The sailors over at the Jalan Tanjong Pelumpong naval base at Muara were used to seeing it.

As Boyinson was buzzing around town making the Little Bird a familiar sight, Brad Townsend was carefully monitoring the comings and goings of the air force. From the hangar that had been assigned to them across the runway from the main terminal, the Raptors could see it all. The main Brunei air force base on the west side of the international airport was home to four squadrons with the majority of the helicopter fleet.

Two of the squadrons operated helicopters, and the third had a mix of choppers and utility aircraft. The fourth operated four CN-235 maritime patrol aircraft. They were armed with air-to-surface rocket launchers and they could carry 30mm cannons, but they were far away from their base most of the time, committed to the chore of monitoring the sultan's vast new exclusion zone.

Separate from the air force fleet, but also based here at the airport, was the personal Gulfstream V belonging to the sultan himself. With a nonstop range of nearly 7,500 miles and Rolls-Royce engines, the plush aircraft was literally the Rolls-Royce of Brunei's official family of aircraft.

April 26
12:56 P.M. Brunei Time

FOR the Raptor Team, today was D-Day.

High atop the main telephone exchange building in the center of Bandar Seri Begawan, a low-velocity .50-caliber projectile smashed into a control box on a one-hundred-foot antenna. It was not an explosive round, but it did a great deal of damage. Because of its low velocity, it penetrated only the outer casing of the metal box, and instead of passing through the box, it ricocheted around within it, tearing wires, smashing connectors, and causing short circuits.

Three seconds later, a similar round impacted a VHF antenna. Within the span of two minutes, at least two projectiles struck every antenna and cell phone tower at the telephone exchange building. Inside, malfunctions and loss of communications were noted, and efforts were made to locate and trace the problem. Nobody had been close enough to hear the *pling* of bullets hitting the metal structures on the roof.

Because it was daytime, no one noticed as a tracer round struck a nearby electrical transformer. A woman walking along the street thought she saw the next tracer, but this was overshadowed by the sight of a second transformer exploding in a shower of sparks.

Lights went out across Bandar Seri Begawan, not everywhere, but in enough places to create confusion.

The fires in several transformers ignited the creosote-saturated power poles, and the fire department was summoned.

For the Raptor Team, today was D-Day, and the first step in any modern war is to degrade the opposing side's ability to communicate.

Will Casey carefully disassembled his Barrett M107 sniper rifle, gathered up expended shells, and packed away his unexpended ammunition. He chuckled about a conversation that he once had with his cousin who had been an F-15E Strike Eagle driver in the U.S. Air Force. His cousin had bragged about what the Air Force calls a "surgical strike." He had been part of the strike package that had "surgically struck" the main telephone exchange building in Baghdad with five-hundred-pound JDAM smart bombs back in 2003.

Will wished that he could tell his cousin about a *real* surgical strike. He wished that he could tell his cousin about the time he closed down most of the telephone communications in the largest city in Brunei with such surgical precision that it would take hours, if not days, for them to figure out how it had happened!

April 25
10:54 A.M. Pacific Time

"WHERE are we going?" Reid Arthur asked as Basim Rashid exited Interstate 5 and turned under the freeway onto California Highway 138. He had dozed off during the long and tedious drive through the San Joaquin Valley, but woke up as they climbed Tejon Pass. He had seen the road sign announcing that they were entering Los Angeles County. Rashid hadn't told him exactly where they were headed, but after they had passed the fourth big green sign with mileage to the City of Angels, Arthur had pretty much figured out that the next target for Rashid's wrath was not going to be Bakersfield. Glowering at the road ahead, Rashid guided the blue Accord eastward through the Tehachapi Range toward California's high desert.

They had spoken little since leaving the Santa Cruz County drug lab, and Arthur had had plenty of time to think. If he had any second thoughts, he'd had plenty of time to voice them, but he had no second thoughts. He had decided in a moment of revolutionary zeal that, like his heroes of another generation, he was not going to fear killing others to make the enemies of the people hear the message. He had made this decision emotionally, but he'd had the chance to reconsider. He had slept on it overnight, and had awakened with the same decision.

What would the Weather Underground have done? They'd turned an angry fist to the pig Nixon, and he would show his angry fist to the pig Livingstone!

This morning they had descended a narrow winding road among the mist-shrouded redwoods of the coast range. Now, the Pakistani left Highway 138, turning onto a narrow winding road among the manzanita and mesquite of the parched and arid Antelope Valley.

They drove for miles into the desert, kicking up choking clouds of dust. Occasionally, Rashid would stop, look at some notes on a scrap of paper that he carried in his shirt pocket, and squint at some landmark or other on the horizon. Then they were off again. They had passed a few houses shortly after they had turned off the main road, but beyond that, it was devoid of human habitation.

Finally, Rashid checked his map again, smiled, and turned off the road into a narrow gully where the car could not be seen from the narrow gravel road.

"Power to the people, Reid." He grinned broadly as he opened the door.

The Pakistani popped the trunk and carefully removed the nine gallon jugs, heavily secured with duct tape to keep them from coming open. Next, he took out the two backpacks that Arthur had tossed into the trunk yesterday. He carefully loaded four jugs into each of the packs, layering them with the old rags that they'd used to cushion the jugs in the trunk.

Without saying anything more, they each shouldered a backpack. Rashid nodded to Arthur to carry the ninth jug, while he picked up an old canvas bag that was filled with tools.

With that, the trunk was slammed shut and Basim Rashid marched into the desert with Reid Arthur close behind.

April 26
1:38 P.M. Brunei Time

"**A**IRCRAFT approaching from the north, Kapitan," the young ensign said nervously. Kapitan Adanan Vegawan watched as the blip on the radar screen approached the missile ship KDB *Sajuang*.

"Look!"

Vegawan looked.

It was a gray SH-60 Seahawk LAMPS helicopter coming in low and fast about a hundred yards off their port side. He heard the ripping sound of its engines as it passed and then suddenly, it was gone.

"Shall we fire, Kapitan?"

"No, hold your fire," Vegawan said as he had said a half-dozen times before. Ever since they had been on patrol out here in the vicinity of the Balabac Strait, the U.S. Navy had been watching them. The Seahawks would buzz them at low level and it made him nervous. His men would ask, almost beg, for a chance to open up with their Oerlikon 30mm cannon, and *this* made him nervous.

What made Vegawan very nervous today was that he was escorting a barge containing three Khomeini-6 missiles.

April 26
1:38 P.M. Brunei Time

"**I** would like to introduce the new director of the Suvarnadvipa Archaeological Institute," Sultan Omar
Jamalul Halauddin boomed as he came back into the
dining room with Professor Anne McCaine at his side.

The Raptors applauded politely and smiled. Ambassador Hudim Incpaduka also managed a narrow smile
and a polite couple of claps. Dave Brannan marveled at
how surreal this whole scene was, not knowing then
how very, very surreal it soon *would be* for the sultan.

The sultan lowered himself into his chair and
snapped his fingers for dessert to be served. The
Americans looked at one another. They had been eating for more than an hour. Never, on any operational
assignment, had these former Special Forces comrades
eaten so much and so well. They had barely touched
the last two courses, and now *more*. Thinking to himself, Jason Houn wondered if perhaps they could wait
long enough and the sultan would simply eat himself
to death.

Brannan glanced at the professor. She winked, nodded to the sultan, and glanced down into her bag. He
understood and stifled a grin. Yes, it would soon be very
surreal.

Sultan Omar enjoyed the spice cake and the papaya
ice cream, and didn't notice, when he asked for more,
that the rest of the people at the table had barely
touched their firsts. He *did* notice how terribly rich the
light in the room had become. Could it be sunset already?

Instinctively, he glanced out the window. The sky was very dark and very blue, and the clouds were very distinct shapes. He remembered as a child, when he had looked at the clouds and had imagined elephants and tigers. He couldn't remember when such images had ever seemed as clear as they did today. The clouds appeared so real, so distinct, and so perfectly focused, and when he glanced back to the people in the room, everything in the room was clearer than it had been a moment ago. Everyone was in perfect focus. No, they were in more-than-perfect focus. It was as though he could see inside them. He felt as though he could read the minds of the people in the room.

He looked at Professor McCaine and saw the most beautiful woman in the world. She smiled, and the radiance of her smile bathed him in the most satisfying warmth. She was his. He could tell by the way that their eyes met. She was more than his museum director, she was his goddess.

He started to laugh. He had imagined himself as a rather clever man. He had easily seized power in a coup d'etat. He had easily blackmailed the United Nations and humbled the United States. But he was just now beginning to realize how truly brilliant he really was.

Hudim Incpaduka stood and excused himself, but instead of walking out the door, he appeared simply to melt into the wall. What a coward! The sultan thought this was incredibly funny. He leaned back in his chair and laughed even louder.

He looked around the room again. Everything was so perfectly clear. Outside the window, he saw the swaying palms and realized that they were part of him.

They had no existence without him. He had not been conscious until that moment that they were really identical to him, as though they were all part of the same living being. He had not realized this before, but now it was perfectly clear. Their souls and his soul were but one soul. He had passed through what Aldous Huxley characterized as the "Doors of Perception."

As he looked around the room, he realized that his body had dissociated itself almost completely from his mind. He felt as though he was no longer primarily a physical organism. His arms and legs and his enormous body were inconsequential.

The man who had accompanied the professor to the dinner last night came over to him and sat beside him. He could see the details of his face and the rich color of his auburn mustache. It was like burnished copper.

The man took something from his pocket. It was a photograph. The sultan glanced at it and tried to reach for it, but his inconsequential arm did not answer his omnipotent mind. The man held the picture up for him to see. It was a baby. At first glance, just a little baby, but on second glance, he saw that the little brown eyes bulged goblinlike from the face. The expression was so horrifying that it brought chills to his spine.

He earlier had passed through Huxley's "Doors of Perception," and now he moved through the room to the doors on the opposite wall. They opened, and Sultan Omar stepped through the gates of hell!

The baby's mouth seemed to scream in terrible agony. Sultan Omar could hear the screams. The piercing shriek was deafening and terrible. He opened his mouth to demand that it stop, but he could not find the words. He could feel his tongue so clearly that he could almost see it. It had become a huge slug, coiling and squirming inside his mouth. It was a huge and disgusting slug. How did it get there? Did it crawl up from his stomach? He bit down on it in an effort to kill it or force it away, and he could feel it biting back. The pain was unbearable.

He looked back at the room. Everyone was looking at him, their faces so clear and so transparent that he could see their bones and blood vessels. Their faces became that of the baby. Each and every one was *screaming* at him.

On the table, the spaces between the dishes and the silverware seemed to turn into objects. It was as though the shadows were coming alive. They skittered about the table like cockroaches, moving so fast that he could not follow their movements. He felt a prickling sensation all over his body, as though the roaches were attacking him.

Between the roaches and the screaming, he forgot that he was brilliant. He forgot that he was omnipotent and he forgot that his soul was one with that of the trees. He felt only unspeakable horror, and the flames of Holy Fire that lapped at his body. Sultan Omar Jamalul Halauddin saw only an avalanche of stinging, colored light spilling over him.

SEVEN

April 25
2:02 P.M. Pacific Time

"**T**HEY'VE left their car, and they're hiking into the desert with the acid," Erik Vasquez said as he studied the two men with his binoculars. "I'd hate to be there if they get thirsty and have to take a swig."

The two FBI agents were on their own, at least for the time being—alone with the bad guys in the desolate high desert of the Antelope Valley. They had been expecting the two terrorists to drive south into Los Angeles, and they had planned to meet their backup in Santa Clarita, but that was more than fifty miles south of the Highway 138 turnoff. Backup was on the way, but for the time being, it all came down to Llewellan and Vasquez.

"Well, whatever they're doing, we *will* have to be

there," Rod Llewellan said, climbing out of the car. "And we'll have to double-time it to stay within sight of 'em."

"We should be able to do that pretty easy," Vasquez observed. "Those clowns are really struggling. Their packs each must weigh thirty or forty pounds."

The agents had driven as close as they dared. They didn't want Arthur and Rashid to hear them, or to see the dust that was produced by a vehicle on this gravel road. Their pursuit would now be on foot. Each man grabbed a water bottle and an extra clip for his Glock 9mm, and they headed out across the high desert country following two men and more than thirty-three million micrograms of LSD.

Just as they apparently had with San Francisco's water supply, these men were evidently planning to unleash an act of mischief designed to send many of Los Angeles County's ten million residents on acid trips.

Somewhere out there—and Llewellan wished he had a map that showed him exactly where—was part of the complex and far-reaching Los Angeles Aqueduct system, the southern California equivalent of pipelines that crossed the San Joaquin, carrying water from Hetch Hetchy to San Francisco. The huge and often very controversial water project that served the West's largest city dated back to the original aqueduct designed by William Mulholland and finished in 1913. More than two hundred miles in length, this part of the system had essentially drained the water table of the remote Owens Valley to feed the demands of the rapidly growing Los Angeles. Through the years, it was supplemented by other water projects, including a second California

Aqueduct in the San Joaquin that came online in 1970, and the Colorado River Aqueduct that now provides over half of Los Angeles's water. By the beginning of the twenty-first century, the Los Angeles Department of Water & Power was America's largest public utility, delivering two-hundred-billion gallons of water annually through 7,226 miles of pipe, most of it running through deserted arid land far from the LA Basin.

The agency had reacted to the attack on the Hetch Hetchy system by tightening security throughout Los Angeles, and around the reservoirs that lay north of the city, as well as its open aqueduct through the San Joaquin and the Colorado River system. The old aqueduct leading from the Owens Valley was a remote and enclosed pipeline that they apparently hadn't gotten around to patrolling.

The FBI agents followed the two men for close to an hour, taking care to maintain a distance at which they could see, but not be seen. Reid Arthur and Basim Rashid moved slowly and deliberately. Arthur tired easily and stopped occasionally to remove his pack, rest, and have Rashid urge him to keep moving. Finally, they reached a point where Rashid stopped and took off his own backpack.

"This is it," Llewellan whispered. "Let's get as close as we can."

Arthur pulled off his pack and sat down to wipe his brow, while Rashid walked back and forth, scraping the desert floor with his foot. As the two agents got closer, they could see what he was kicking. Buried just beneath the surface, and partially visible in several places, was a large rust-colored pipe about a foot in diameter.

Rashid got down on his hands and knees, and brushed the dirt and gravel away from a section of pipe. It looked very old, having been constructed of rounded metal plates held together with parallel rows of large rivets. It was indeed old, dating back to the section of the aqueduct system completed in 1913, but it still carried a rushing river of water into Los Angeles.

As Llewellan and Vasquez watched, Rashid began banging on the pipe with a hammer and chisel. He had taken a large hand drill out of his bag of tricks, and was pounding an indentation in the pipe to start the drill.

Meanwhile, Arthur began methodically removing the gallon jugs from the backpacks. Two, four, six, eight, *nine*. The two agents looked at one another. Nine gallons! Even if the stuff was heavily diluted, this was the makings of a catastrophe of staggering proportions.

"FBI," Llewellan called, identifying himself. "You're under arrest. Hands clasped behind your heads and down on your knees."

Reid Arthur was stunned. Still wasted by the physical exercise to which he was unaccustomed, he took a moment to process what was going on. How could this have happened? Where did the FBI come from? How could they have been followed?

Still crouching over his bag of tricks, Rashid hissed angrily. Arthur saw his hand slowly slide inside the bag. The FBI agents were about twenty-five yards away and approaching with guns drawn when Rashid pulled his own gun.

He fired two shots in rapid succession and took off running.

The two agents returned fire, but Arthur couldn't see whether Rashid had been hit. In the confusion, however, he did notice that they had taken their eyes off him. Adrenaline surging, he grabbed one of the plastic jugs and clawed the heaving taped lid off. The colorless liquid in the jug looked like water, and it sloshed like water. It also spilled like water as he upturned the jug over the indentation in the pipe where Rashid had been banging.

"Don't shoot, you'll hit the pipe," Llewellan shouted as he ran toward Reid Arthur at top speed.

Arthur felt the impact of the agent's shoe in his kidney and he felt his body tossed through the air for several feet. He fell facedown and tried to get up, but a foot slammed down, impacting him square between the shoulder blades.

Rod Llewellan handcuffed the suspect, taking care not to allow his own skin to come in contact with any of the liquid that was splashed all over the bearded man. He searched the bag for further weapons and found some bailing wire, with which he secured the suspect's ankles.

Having subdued the man, Llewellan next turned his attention to the pipeline. To his immense relief, the indentation that had been pounded into it was just that. There was no hole. The contents of the jug had spilled harmlessly into the dirt.

In the distance, he heard the *pop-pop* of gunfire, and started running toward it to aid Vasquez.

The other man was now about a hundred yards away and still running through the sagebrush. Erik Vasquez had gone about half that distance, and was also running. Though shots had been fired, none had connected.

Basim Rashid was running for his life. He had always been prepared to die a martyr's death, but to be shot out here in the middle of nowhere accomplished nothing. He had to either get away, or kill the agents and go back to finish what he had started.

His lungs were on fire. His legs ached. He couldn't continue running much longer, and there was no place to run anyway. This corner of the Antelope Valley was like the flat bottom of a huge frying pan. There were mountains on every horizon, but they were many kilometers distant. He could not escape. He would have to fight.

Rashid needed to take cover, but there was nothing but knee-high sagebrush for as far as he could see. It would have to do. He hit the ground and immediately crawled away from the place where he had gone down so that the American couldn't tell exactly where he was. The FBI man had dropped to his knee about fifty meters back, and was looking for him. He couldn't see the other agent, and guessed that he was still with Arthur.

The Pakistani had fired three shots, two as the agents arrived and another as he made his escape. His Walther P5 9mm had an eight-round magazine, so he would have to make the last five shots count. That was two for each agent, plus one spare—or was it one for himself?

Erik Vasquez kept his eyes on the place where the suspect had gone down. He had glanced back earlier and had seen Llewellan coming, but he didn't dare look for him now. He had to keep his eyes forward, trained on the slight movement in the brush.

He inched forward, watching carefully.

He watched. He waited.

He moved gradually closer and closer, wishing that he knew how much ammo the guy had. He had counted three shots, or was it four?

Vasquez thought about Quantico, and he thought about the hours of marksmanship training. He still remembered what the instructor had said about how the closer you get, the better your accuracy, *but* that conversely, the closer you get, the better the accuracy of whoever is shooting back.

Now's the time, Vasquez thought.

He pointed, aimed, and fired two rounds.

There was some scuttling in the bushes and the suspect popped up to return fire.

April 26
1:46 P.M. Brunei Time

"I think that the sultan has bitten his tongue," Dave Brannan said, feigning concern. Neither Tweedledum nor Tweedledumber had been paying much attention to what was going on at the table. They had been so bored as Sultan Omar Jamalul Halauddin railed on and on about Suvarnadvipa and his grandiose plans

that they hadn't noticed that he'd bitten his tongue.
Nor had they seen Brannan showing him the picture of
little Don Junior lying quietly in his crib.

They stood up when Brannan called to them, and
moving quickly when they saw the small rivulet of
blood dripping from the corner of the sultan's mouth,
they hurried to his side. The professor stood up and
backed her chair away so they could get to him.

"Your Majesty," said Tweedledum.

"What's happened?" Tweedledumber asked.

Sultan Omar looked at Tweedledum. He opened his
mouth, but did not speak. He looked as though he'd
seen a ghost.

"Maybe he's having a panic attack," Brannan suggested calmly.

"What did you do to him?" Tweedledumber demanded.

"I think it's all in his mind," Anne said.

Tweedledum and Tweedledumber turned away to
look at her, and Ray Couper raised his Heckler & Koch.
As the .45-caliber round smashed into Tweedledum's
head, Tweedledumber was knocked off guard by a similar projectile fired by Jason Houn. The two Raptors had
taken the opportunity of the earlier distractions to screw
the silencers onto their weapons.

They each put a second round into their targets and
glanced at the large man with the trickle of blood on
his chin. His eyes had rolled back into his head and his
breathing was labored and shallow. As they watched,
his body suddenly shook in a single violent spasm.
Anne was so startled that she jumped.

The colonel laid a finger on his neck to feel his pulse as Jason Houn placed the muzzle of the silencer against the big man's temple.

"Let them remember him this way," Brannan said, shaking his head.

Couper placed the photo of Don Junior on the sultan's chest and snapped a couple of photos of the two faces with his camera phone.

"Well, boys, its been a lovely lunch," Anne said, grabbing her tote bag and walking toward the door. "But I think it's time to get back to the city."

April 25
3:01 P.M. Pacific Time

AS Rod Llewellan had watched Erik Vasquez slowly and methodically moving in on the place where the suspect had taken cover, he had done the same, moving far around to the left. When push came to shove, they would have the guy in a cross fire.

As Vasquez had fired two rounds in the general area where the suspect was, Basim Rashid had popped up and fired a quick shot. As he hit the ground, he had jumped straight toward Llewellan's position, apparently unaware that the second FBI agent was there.

"Drop it!" Llewellan demanded.

Rashid aimed. Llewellan fired.

The FBI agent's 9mm slug impacted just above his wrist, shattering his tibia and compelling him to drop the gun.

Basim Rashid had been startled by Llewellan. He cursed himself for not having seen him. He had been too anxious to keep track of the other man.

The excruciating pain in his arm took his breath away, but he couldn't let them stop him. The agent was moving forward, the gun at his side. The Pakistani lunged for his weapon, grabbed it with his left hand, and raised it. Just as he was squeezing the trigger, he felt another sharp pain in his shoulder that knocked him off balance.

Rod Llewellan kicked the gun away and ripped off a piece of the suspect's shirt to apply pressure to the shoulder wound. Erik Vasquez's bullet had done quite a bit of damage, and it was bleeding heavily.

Somewhere in the distance, they could hear the sound of a helicopter.

April 26
1:59 P.M. Brunei Time

"**THANK** you so much for your hospitality, Your Majesty," Professor Anne McCaine said graciously and mainly for the benefit of the guards outside the room. "We'll be looking forward to seeing you at the Suvarnadvipa site in about an hour."

She gently closed the door to Sultan Omar Jamalul Halauddin's private dining room and cast a disarming smile at the guard across the foyer who was leaning on the pillar and cradling an L85A1 assault rifle.

The professor and the Raptors strolled casually,

heading for the large front door, hoping to be as far away as possible when it was discovered that the sultan had not survived his lunch.

Suddenly, a scream echoed from a hallway that fed into the foyer from another part of the building.

"Get them off me!"

The guard with L85A1 ran toward the sound of the scream. Two others materialized from the shadows and dashed toward the yelling.

"Get them off me!" Ambassador Pehin Dato Hudim Incpaduka shouted as he staggered from the darkness of a side hallway, his voice a mixture of anger and confusion. The guards were confused. It was not apparent that anything was *on* him—not even his clothes.

"Get them off me!"

His shirt and jacket were missing, but strangely, he was still wearing his tie. His pants were around his ankles, but he was shuffling forward as quickly as he could under the circumstances. His body was covered with splotches of blood, and he was frantically scratching himself.

"Get them off me!"

The guards were dumbfounded.

As the four Americans made for the door, another guard with sergeant's stripes and an L85A1 emerged from behind them and ordered them to stop.

"Nobody leaves!"

Suddenly the Americans had a half-dozen automatic weapons trained on them.

"Okay," Brannan said, holding up the palms of his hands. "But this man needs immediate medical attention. Dr. Couper here was about to render first aid."

Incpaduka crumpled to the floor, and "Dr. Couper" rushed to his side. Couper had been the team medic back in the days when the Raptors were still in Special Forces, so Brannan had decided to throw him into the role of a "doctor" on the spur of the moment. After all, he knew all the right terminology, even if he wasn't wearing a white lab coat.

"He's having an allergic reaction," Couper diagnosed, immediately taking charge of the situation and redirecting the attention of the guards to the problem of dealing with Incpaduka. None of them was willing to interfere with the people who were coming to the aid of the United Nations ambassador.

"We need to get him to Bandar Seri Begawan immediately," Couper said.

Brannan and Houn immediately folded down a narrow bamboo screen to create a makeshift stretcher, while Couper and one of the confused guards held the main door open. As they exited with the stretcher, Brannan ordered the guards to locate the rest of the man's clothes and clean up the mess on the floor. The idea was to give them something to do to keep them from discovering the sultan, at least until the Raptors could reach the late monarch's helicopter.

As the Americans near Tutong were lugging Incpaduka toward the Bell 214, the Little Bird was making its last flight over Bandar Seri Begawan as an innocent-looking red-and-blue helicopter.

Will Casey returned to the Raptors' hangar from his "hunting trip" just as Boyinson was touching down. Even before the rotors had completely stopped spinning, they and Brad Townsend were at work, fitting the

M134 machine gun turret and the launch tubes for the AGM-114 Hellfire missiles.

For the Raptors, today was to be D-Day, and it was time to turn their Little Bird into the most heavily armed warplane in the country.

April 26
1:59 P.M. Brunei Time

JACK Rodgers stood at the helm, maintaining seven knots and keeping his compass heading aligned with the Balabac Strait. Somewhere out there, the Seventh Fleet knew they were coming. The Seahawk had gotten a very good look, and somewhere on a flag bridge somewhere in the Sulu Sea, somebody was looking at pictures of those three missiles and somebody was planning the demise of the barge and its escort.

Rodgers noticed that the missile ship KDB *Sajuang,* which had been shadowing the barge since it left Muara, had pulled back somewhat. It was now about an eighth of a mile away, but still off the starboard side keeping pace in the gentle swells. The skipper probably didn't want to be hit if the Americans decided to take out the barge.

The two Iranians aboard the barge had spent the cruise mainly lounging on the deck. One had had a terrible bout of seasickness, and it had almost made Rodgers sick to watch him. Otherwise, they had been doing nothing except lie around for the whole cruise, but now, suddenly, they were a beehive of activity. One of them had gone below, and the other was walking around looking over the side.

Suddenly there was a clunking, scraping sound belowdeck and the wheel spun loose in Rodgers's hand. He reached for the throttle and felt it jammed in place.

"What the fuck are you doing down there?" Rodgers screamed at the Iranian that had gone below. He had started toward the gangway when the Iranian emerged from below with a grin on his face.

"Allah Al-Akbar!"

The other Iranian repeated the call from across the broad flat deck, and started monkeying around with the brackets that were holding the missiles in their horizontal position.

It didn't take a great deal of imagination for Rodgers to realize that this guy had just turned the barge into a suicide boat. The barge would now continue on the same heading and at the same speed until it passed *out* of the exclusion zone and was intercepted by the U.S. Navy. At that point, these jokers would try to fire the missiles. In the meantime, they expected that American helicopters would have seen and photographed the American, and in Washington a statement would be released.

"Please fix the rudder," Rodgers pleaded. "I don't want to die."

The Iranian began laughing, and he shouted to his friend that the American was sniveling.

Rodgers knelt down and begged. The Iranian finally had enough and walked toward the wheelhouse to swat him and demand that this whelp shut up. As he raised his hand to hit the whimpering American,

Rodgers grabbed his foot, twisted it sharply, and tossed the Iranian toward the stern. By the time that he realized what had happened, the flustered Iranian found the American nearly on top of him. He had staggered and tried to stand, but lost his balance on the slowly undulating deck.

The next thing the Iranian experienced was an excruciating kick to the groin, and the sensation of the sea rushing up toward him. He felt the cool wetness of the South China Sea and tasted its saltiness. He flailed his arms and gasped for breath. He grabbed at the barge, but it was already twenty feet away and moving at seven knots. As his head bobbed up and down in the swells, he could see the KDB *Sajuang* in the far distance. He opened his mouth to scream, got a mouthful of salt water, and went under.

The second Iranian, the one who had been fussing with the missiles, had seen nothing of what happened because his line of sight was blocked by the wheelhouse. He shouted several times in Farsi and, getting no answer, he went to investigate.

As he came around the wheelhouse, he saw the American lying on the deck, but he didn't see the other Iranian. He shouted down the gangway, received no answer, and walked over to look at the American, who appeared to be unconscious.

Again, a would-be suicide bomber felt himself suddenly off balance on the heaving deck of the barge, and again, a man who couldn't swim experienced the sensation of plunging into the blue waters of the South China Sea.

April 26
2:14 P.M. Brunei Time

"**WHAT** happened to the ambassador?" the pilot of the Bruneian Bell 214 asked when the chopper was airborne and cruising toward the capital.

"We thought that he had probably experienced some sort of allergic reaction," Couper shouted over the sound of the big chopper's General Electric CT7-2A turboshaft engines cranking up. "But he may have been poisoned."

"Poisoned?" the pilot asked as he glanced back at United Nations Ambassador Hudim Incpaduka. He was seated in the back row between "Doctor" Couper and Professor McCaine, looking very, very sick, with his bloodshot eyes rolling from side to side and a drop of spittle on his chin.

In fact, he was very, very stoned and experiencing incapacitating hallucinations. While Sultan Omar Jamalul Halauddin was consuming a lethal dose of LSD, the ambassador had sipped a somewhat smaller quantity, but a quantity sufficient to turn him into a veritable zombie.

"Yes," Dave Brannan said, answering the pilot's question. He was sitting in the front next to the pilot. "The sultan and the ambassador told us in confidence that they feared a coup in the making. When the ambassador became ill, the sultan asked us to get Mr. Incpaduka to safety."

"What about the sultan?" asked the pilot.

"He said that it is a monarch's duty to stand up to

the threat," Brannan lied. "He said that it's like being the captain of a ship. If a coup *does* materialize, he wants to lead from the front."

The sultan's body would probably have been discovered by now, and Brannan wanted to stay ahead of the curve by crafting a plausible cover story. If anyone contradicted this fabrication, he could explain it as them having gotten misinformation from someone involved in the coup.

"Where should we take him?"

"The sultan told us that he wasn't sure that any place in Bandar Seri Begawan was safe," Brannan replied. "He thinks that we had better take him to Australia."

"Australia? This helicopter doesn't have the range to fly to Australia."

"But the sultan's Gulfstream V does," Brannan said calmly. "Take us to the airport."

"I need to contact my base for instructions," the pilot said nervously.

"Of course," Brannan said. He nodded to Jason Houn, indicating that they might have to be prepared to do some convincing with the pilot.

The pilot called his base, couldn't get through, and tried several alternate numbers. Finally, he got through to someone who told him that communications—landlines and wireless, as well as two-way-radio—were experiencing an unexplained disruption.

Turning to Jason Houn, but speaking loud enough for the pilot to hear, Brannan said, "That's the first thing that happens when there's a coup. They start cutting communications."

The pilot looked nervous and confused. They were now over the southwestern edge of the capital.

"Listen," Dave Brannan scolded. "The sultan specifically requested that we get the ambassador out of the country."

"Ambassador Incpaduka just told me that he wants to get out of the country," Anne shouted from the backseat.

With that, the pilot shook his head, banked to the left to circle around the city. They could see the airport in the distance.

As soon as the Bell 214 was on the ground at the Gulfstream hangar, Brannan, along with the professor and the helicopter pilot, went to look for the flight crew. They knew the helicopter pilot, and they recognized Anne from the brief television interview that she had done at the palace, so they were receptive to believing the story of a possible coup, as improbable as it might have seemed. They acknowledged that they had experienced the communications breakdown, and taking Brannan's suggestion, they readily agreed that a coup might have played a part in such a problem.

With this, they said that if the sultan wanted the ambassador taken to Australia, the pilots would be glad to take him to Australia. Brannan sensed that *they* would be only too happy to be getting out of the country. If the coup was successful, Brunei would not be a hospitable place for the sultan's personal flight crew. If not, they could always come back.

However, there was a problem.

"What problem?" Brannan asked. Ever since they

escaped from the sultan's beachfront pad in Tutong, everything had gone smoothly. Of course, he knew that it was axiomatic that just as you started to coast, you always hit a pothole.

"Well, the Gulfstream isn't exactly flight-ready," one of the pilots explained. Although the aircraft was theoretically supposed to be available to fly at the whim of the sultan, it wasn't. The pilot affirmed that the flight crew was ready to go at a moment's notice, but the problem lay with the *ground* crew.

"How long will it take?"

"Two hours. Maybe three. It also needs to be fueled."

April 26
2:29 P.M. Brunei Time

JAHAR Abiddijab had been in a good mood. By this time the American would know that there was no turning back. Just in case he had a case of cold feet, Abiddijab had arranged for the steering and throttle functions aboard the barge to be disabled. The barge would head straight out of the exclusion zone and straight into the Seventh Fleet. Whatever happened next, *whatever* the U.S. Navy did, would reflect badly on the United States—and anything that was bad for the Great Satan warmed the heart of Jahar Abiddijab.

The Iranian picked up the phone at his compound within a compound at the naval base. He dialed again, and again the call did not go through. Jahar Abiddijab had been in a good mood, but that was starting to change. He tried his cell phone again, and the circuits were *still* busy.

He was anxious to contact Sultan Omar and to give him an update on the barge operation, but he could not, and when things didn't go the way he liked, he got angry. He was angry with Brunei for having a Third World, third-rate telephone system. He was even angry with the sultan with his newfound obsession with this female American archaeologist and all of her mumbo-jumbo bullshit about cities of gold. Abiddijab was jealous of the sultan's new playmates.

Insulated within his compound within a compound, Abiddijab had not yet heard the rumors that were starting to fly around town about a coup. These rumors had not yet reached his compound, just as the capital city had not yet gotten word from Tutong that Sultan Omar Jamalul Halauddin had been found dead.

Just as he threw his cell phone down in disgust, Abiddijab heard the sound of a helicopter hovering very near.

He looked up to see a Bell 214 with the markings of the Tentera Udara Diraja Brunei. This was the aircraft that the sultan used. Could it be that the sultan was coming here to see *him*?

As the helicopter touched down in the large open area near the compound, Abiddijab ordered his Iranian guards to open the gate to the compound and he strode purposefully out to meet it.

Dave Brannan was the first to step out of the helicopter, followed by Jason Houn and Brad Townsend.

Abiddijab paused, waiting for others to emerge from
the chopper, but it was just the three Americans, each
of them carrying a gym bag.

"His Majesty sent us," Brannan said, trying to
smile his most disarming smile. "We need to talk with
you."

"Of course," Abiddijab replied, recognizing the
men. "Please come in."

He led them back into the paved open courtyard
area about the size of a basketball court that separated
the two reinforced-concrete buildings where the satellite photos had first showed the Khomeini-6 missiles,
and where Jack Rodgers had played cards.

There were about a dozen Iranians carrying AK-74
assault rifles here, and the big metal roll-up doors in
the larger building were both open. Inside, the Raptors
could see a long metal tube about eighteen inches in
diameter lying on wooden blocks. This was the fourth
Khomeini-6 missile, the last one left in Brunei. This
was what they had come for. That was the easy part,
but as the axiom goes, just as you start to coast, you hit
the pothole.

Only two of the Iranians noticed when the three
Americans reached into their gym bags. Abiddijab did
not. He had committed the oldest mistake in the book.
He had his back turned.

Three simultaneous explosions occurred in different
corners of the compound as three M84 stun grenades
went off. For those standing under the concrete over-
hangs of the buildings, the overpressure concussion was
crippling. For nearly all, the brilliant flash of the exploding metal-oxidant mix of magnesium and ammonium

was blinding. Everyone was disoriented, but that, after all, was why they invented stun grenades.

When the Bell 214 made a fast stop at the Raptor Team's Little Bird hangar to pick up Will Casey en route to the Muara compound, Dave Brannan had picked up the M84s along with other weapons. He decided to use these nonlethal, non-shrapnel-producing explosives rather than fragmentation grenades or MK3A2 concussion grenades because he wanted to minimize the amount of debris flying around a compound where a nuke was being stored. An important axiom of modern warfare that cannot be overstated is that being within fifty yards if a nuclear weapon goes off can pretty much ruin your weekend.

Before the first echo of the M84 blasts had finished reverberating across the compound, the three Raptors were sweeping up the human detritus with their Heckler & Koch MP5 submachine guns. One guy with an AK-74 tried to be a hero or a martyr, and consummated the latter as a three-round burst splattered across his face.

Lying prone in the chopper, Will Casey didn't have a clear view of the courtyard, but he was in a perfect position to cover the other Raptors as they egressed, and to keep the gate guards from getting involved. These guards were too far away to have been effected by the M84 blasts, but they certainly heard them. They also heard the ripping sounds of the MP5s hosing the place down. They shouldered their AK-74s and began sprinting toward the action. They didn't get far. One guard was flabbergasted to see the other guard's neck suddenly burst apart in a cloud of blood and shattered bone. He didn't ponder it for long. Casey took down both of the gate guards with his Barrett M107 sniper rifle. Using a .50-caliber round on targets such as this was overkill, but it sure got the job done.

Jahar Abiddijab had been knocked down by the concussion, but he caught himself. He glanced back, saw the Raptors opening fire on everything that moved, and began to run for an open door across the courtyard. For the first few seconds, he expected to feel himself being hit at any moment, but as he ran, and the closer he got to safety, the more he began to feel that he would make it.

Then he felt something hit his knee. It was not a sharp pain. It was more like bumping a table in the dark. It didn't really hurt, but suddenly his legs didn't work. His brain told them to run, but they just felt loose and became tangled. As he toppled over, his previous forward velocity threw him headlong onto the asphalt, smashing his shoulder and shearing the skin from the side of his face.

Abiddijab was no longer a part of the action; he was now just an observer. Dead men lay all around him. There was another blast. He could feel the concussion in the ground beneath him. The three Americans were throwing hand grenades through open doors.

Suddenly, the ground shook with another sound. Some of his people had gotten to the roof and were manning the huge 30mm antiaircraft gun on the roof. They had depressed the barrel and they were firing down into the compound.

The Americans were trapped!

April 26
2:29 P.M. Brunei Time

AS most of the team had headed out to retrieve the
nuke, the professor and the "doctor" remained
behind at the Gulfstream hangar to monitor prepara-
tions for their flight. Anne kept an eye on the ailing
ambassador, who they had parked in a small office on
the side of the hangar, while Ray Couper had gone
aboard the sultan's Gulfstream V to check out the ac-
commodations.

Glancing through the side window of the main
cabin, he saw a group of armed men entering the
hangar. An officious-looking little military officer in a
white dress uniform was followed by seven men in
Bruneian army uniforms carrying L64 assault rifles. He
watched as the officer spoke to one of the pilots, who
gestured toward the office where the ambassador was.

Couper headed toward the main door of the Gulfstream, but there were already two soldiers moving up
the air-stairs.

"Kapitan Haji asks that you leave the airplane," one
of the soldiers demanded as he met Couper in the
doorway.

April 26
2:32 P.M. Brunei Time

BEFORE the main Raptor Force had departed the
Gulfstream hangar in the Bell 214, they had been
in touch with Greg Boyinson to provide top cover for

their mission to extract the fourth nuclear warhead. By
this time, the AN/PRC-148 multibands that the Raptors carried were probably the only two-way-radio
system in the country that was operating flawlessly.

The Bell 214 had the Tentera Udara Diraja markings that would get the Raptor ground force *into* the
compound, but the Little Bird had the necessary firepower that could get them *out*.

The 30mm automatic cannon on the roof was in action for only a moment. Orbiting above at scarcely
150 feet, Boyinson saw the muzzle flashes and immediately targeted it with a Hellfire missile. The high-
explosive warhead pulverized the antiaircraft gun,
sending fragments of debris fifty feet into the air.

"While you're at it," Boyinson heard Brannan's calm
voice say on his AN/PRC-148 headphone, "there are a
couple of shooters in the building on the immediate
west side of your last hit."

A moment later, a second Hellfire slammed into the
building with a *whump*.

As the tinkle of pieces of metal falling to earth
faded, all was quiet but for the not-too-distant buzz of
the Little Bird. The popping sound of small-arms fire
had stopped. Abiddijab could hear two men running
and one man walking. He wiggled and tried to move.
He propped himself up on one elbow, and tried to crawl.
He had great difficulty moving his legs, but somehow
he was inching forward, sliding in something slip-
pery. He looked back and saw his shattered legs sliding in a large pool of blood. His femoral artery had
been ruptured by one of the 9mm slugs that took him
down.

A shadow fell across the pool of blood, and Abiddi-jab looked up into the expressionless face of the American with the auburn mustache. Strangely, his first thought was that the American was here to take him back to Guantanamo, but that assumption faded as the man raised his Mk.23.

As soon as the firing stopped, Houn and Townsend had dashed to the Khomeini-6 missile. Mainly, it was painted dark gray-green, but the forward section was bare metal. This was all the Raptors needed to see in order to know that a warhead was attached. Working quickly with their multipurpose tools, they pulled out the brightly colored flush screws. By the time that Brannan returned from turning Jahar Abiddijab into a martyr, they were ready to pull the sucker off.

"It's lighter than I thought it would be," Townsend observed as they lifted it off the blocks.

"About like an artillery shell," Houn said as they lowered it onto the makeshift carrying sling that they created by zipping two of their heavy-duty gym bags together.

"That's what these mothers *are*," Brannan said. "Most of the loose nukes running around the world today are Soviet artillery shells that got misplaced during the nineties."

Indeed, it was a frightening and sobering thought to ponder as the three men could easily transport a nuclear warhead from the compound to the helicopter at a fast walk.

"How long did it take us?" Houn asked Will Casey when they heaved the projectile into the Bell 214. Casey had stayed with the helicopter as much to make sure the pilot didn't stray as to provide cover. He had also been maintaining the mission stopwatch.

"Four minutes and twenty-three seconds," he said with a laugh as the helicopter lifted off. "Do you want to go back and try again for a better time?"

April 26
2:32 P.M. Brunei Time

"**U**NDER whose orders is this aircraft being made ready for flight?" demanded the officer in the white dress uniform.

"His Majesty's," one of the pilots assigned to the sultan's Gulfstream explained. "There have been rumors of civil unrest, and he has asked that Ambassador Incpaduka be flown out of the country at once."

The officer demanded to speak with the ambassador, and was led into the small office where he was sitting passively on a low couch in the corner.

Ambassador Pehin Dato Hudim Incpaduka, the former racketeer who had engineered the biggest shakedown of the United Nations in world history, sat there in an ill-fitting yellow sweatshirt staring intently at a noisily rattling air conditioner.

"Mr. Ambassador, I am Kapitan Mohammed Haji. I'm the military security officer for this area. I would like to speak with you."

The disheveled Incpaduka glanced at him blankly and looked back at the air conditioner, which seemed to interest him far more than the captain in the crisp and spotless uniform.

"Mr. Ambassador, have you spoken to the sultan?" Haji asked. "With the communications failure this afternoon, there are all sorts of rumors. . . . I need to know."

"We've all spoken with the sultan," the professor said, walking into the office. "The ambassador is ill and the sultan wants him taken to Australia for his own safety."

"And how are *you* involved in this?" Haji asked her suspiciously.

"Dr. Couper and I will be traveling with him," she replied.

"There is a national emergency under way," Haji asserted, turning to the pilot. "Security here is under my jurisdiction, and I will not permit anyone to leave until further notice."

April 26
2:44 P.M. Brunei Time

THE Bell 214 departed the area adjacent to the compound, flying low over the Jalan Tanjong Pelumpong naval base, and heading across Muara toward the airport. The Raptors looked down at the bewildered sailors as they watched the Royal Brunei Air Force helicopter fly overhead. They were as confused as anyone in the country, and were alarmed by the shooting within their own base. However, the one thing that they knew for sure was that this was the helicopter that Sultan Omar used, and *under no circumstances* do you fire on the sultan's helicopter!

Rumors of some sort of unrest, even a possible coup, had spread like wildfire, but with the communications breakdown, nobody knew anything definitive. Beyond this, nobody seemed to be in charge. Officers were afraid to give orders because none of them wanted to be on the wrong side of whoever prevailed in a coup when the dust finally settled.

As they were flying over the edge of Muara with the airport visible in the distance, a call came in on the AN/PRC-148. Will Casey answered it and passed it over to Dave Brannan.

"Colonel, you boys should be prepared for a situation when you get back here."

It was the professor. After the run-in with the security officer, she had calmly taken her ersatz MP3 player out of her bag.

"What's up?" Brannan asked.

"Security police. They don't want anybody leaving the country."

"How many?"

"One guy in a white uniform. Seven in camo with rifles. I gotta go."

Brannan quickly briefed the Raptors on the situation and they made ready to deal with this contingency.

Once again. the Bruneian chopper would prove to be one of their best assets. None of the military police even thought of challenging it when it touched down, practically in the doorway of the open hangar.

Three of the uniformed soldiers, half-expecting to see the sultan, instinctively stood at attention, holding their rifles in the port arms position. When three

Raptors tumbled out of the door, two soldiers swung their L64 assault rifles up to fire, but the third just stood there with his mouth open. All three crumpled to the pavement almost instantly.

A fourth soldier was inside the hangar and slightly obscured by some equipment. Being much more resourceful than his three comrades, he knelt and took careful aim. Unfortunately for him, Will Casey had him in the scope of the elephant gun. Naturally, the soldier never saw the .50-caliber round coming, nor anything at all after it came.

The fifth soldier was on the air-stairs arguing with Ray Couper when the other Raptors egressed the helicopter, and Couper dispatched him with one .45-caliber round from his Mk.23.

The sixth soldier ran into the hangar and grabbed one of the pilots as a human shield. This was a clumsy move with an assault rifle, and Dave Brannan was on him almost before he knew what was happening.

"I count six," Brannan said, standing over the last dead soldier. "Where are the other two?"

"Gone," said the pilot that Brannan had just rescued. "They left just as you were landing. They took the woman and left in the police car."

April 26
2:44 P.M. Brunei Time

JACK Rodgers reemerged on the deck and squinted into the sun. After he said bon voyage to the two Iranians, he had gone below to make an attempt at undoing their mischief. The jammed throttle had been a relatively straightforward fix, although it had taken him a long time to find a pry bar to do it with.

The broken tiller was a major problem. The Iranians had cut the shaft that led from the wheel to the rudder. It had probably been cut most of the way before they had even left port. That damned Abiddijab!

When the shaft was severed, the lower part had slid down through the hole, and it was at least two feet below the lowest part that he could reach. The solution was to try to pull off one of the steel plates on the shaft housing. He had kicked and banged and searched for a wrench. He found a wrench that fit some nuts, but they were rusted, and disintegrated when he tried to turn them. There were other nuts that were in better shape, but the goddamn wrench didn't fit them. That damned Abiddijab!

He gave up on the rudder shaft and spent the next half hour chopping and ripping control cables on the missile platforms, so that the missiles couldn't be launched if a crew from the missile ship KDB *Sajuang* came aboard and tried. He threw enough stuff overboard that the launch system was effectively destroyed.

When he had finished, he looked out at the distant horizon and tried to intuit what the Seventh Fleet would do. There were a number of possibilities, none of them good.

Rodgers couldn't turn the barge, but he *had* regained control of the throttle. The only option in his power was to simply throttle back and stop the damn thing. If the Iranians could jam the throttle wide open, he could certainly jam it closed, shut the engine off, and end this whole game of chicken right here in open water.

The *Sajuang* was still hanging out there off the starboard, too far away to have noticed Iranians diving off the fantail of the barge, but close enough to notice if he throttled back and stopped.

Jack Rodgers was pondering whether to take his chances with the U.S. Navy or the Bruneian Navy when he heard the sound of another helicopter. As with the previous Seahawk pass, it was on the port side, away from the *Sajuang*. Unlike before, however, it was coming up from behind, and it was not a Seahawk. The sound was more of a buzzing than a rattling.

It was not a Seahawk, it was a Little Bird. It was Greg Boyinson!

Rodgers watched as Boyinson banked sharply and came in low to get a good look at the barge. Jack throttled back to about three knots, stepped out of the wheelhouse, and waved his cap. Boyinson throttled back and nudged the chopper forward until it hovered about three feet above the undulating deck of the barge just forward of where the missiles lay motionless and guaranteed to stay that way.

Jack sprinted to the front of the barge, grabbed the handles on the side of the Little Bird, and pulled himself into the helicopter.

"What kept you?" Rodgers grinned at Boyinson.

"Shit, man, you're a fuckin' mess," Boyinson growled. "Careful you don't get any of that grease and crud on my upholstery."

"Gimme a break, I've been workin' below, trying to fix my damned yacht."

As Boyinson lifted off, they noticed that the *Sajuang*
had changed course and was steaming toward the barge
at top speed. Its twin-barrelled Oerlikon 30mm antiaircraft gun opened up with a hail of tracers. They missed
the helicopter by a wide margin, but as the Little Bird
moved aft of the barge, the gunner was quickly correct-
ing his angle of fire.

"That bastard's starting to piss me off," Boyinson
observed. Instead of pushing the throttle and blazing
off toward the horizon, he banked the Little Bird and
prepared to engage the missile ship. He scooted to the
left, circling the ship and staying one step ahead of the
rotating turret.

The Little Bird circled the ship like a contender in a
knife fight, hovering and teasing, then jerking ahead
faster than the gunner could turn. Finally, the Little
Bird was directly aft of the *Sajuang,* the gunner's sole
blind spot.

On the bridge, Kapitan Adanan Vegawan had
watched the Little Bird as it slowly circled, deftly
avoiding the stream of fire from the ship's gun mount.
Vegawan turned the wheel sharply to the starboard,
trying to take evasive action, but the helicopter pilot
easily matched his turn. The Nakhoda Ragam-class
patrol vessels were armed with Seawolf surface-to-air
missiles, but the *Sajuang* had only the 30mm gun for
defensive armament. Until today, Vegawan had always
figured that against a helicopter, this would be adequate.

The helicopter came closer and closer, so close that
he could see the pilot's face and the American flag

stitched to his jacket. That flag! What it represented angered and disgusted Vegawan. He wanted to strike that flag and the man wearing it. As he angrily cursed the American flag, he strained to turn his ship so that the 30mm could resume firing.

Still watching Vegawan and the desperately turning *Sajuang,* Boyinson thumbed the trigger of his pair of M134 six-barrel Gatling guns. A surging hail of 7.62mm rounds gushed into the bridge of the missile ship. As they pulverized Vegawan's chest, showering everything around him with his blood, the bullets splintered the bridge from the controls to the radio.

Vegawan didn't even have time to remember that in the excitement, he had forgotten to report the arrival of the Little Bird to his bosses at Muara.

As Greg banked away from the *Sajuang,* the gunner struggled to line up a shot. Well away from the arc of his fire, Boyinson turned the Little Bird to again face the ship for one last tip of his hat.

The Hellfire missile impacted the *Sajuang* amidships on the starboard side just at the waterline, ripping a hole big enough to drive through with a tractor-trailer rig. The secondary explosion of the fuel tank threw up a spectacular ball of fire and debris, but before all the burning pieces had fluttered back to the South China Sea, the ship was listing heavily and taking on water at a horrendous rate. Rodgers's earlier concern over what to do about the missile ship after he secured the Khomeini-6s had been answered—in a flash.

Boyinson orbited the flaming, fast-sinking wreckage once, and jammed the throttle forward.

"We better get goin', we got a plane to catch," Greg said.

"It's about time," Jack Rodgers replied, leaning back in the seat and putting his hands behind his head as the Little Bird accelerated across the wave tops. "I was wondering when you were going to stop playing."

April 26
2:59 P.M. Brunei Time

MAYBE if she hadn't kicked Kapitan Mohammed Haji in the crotch, she wouldn't now be sitting in the backseat of a Bruneian military police car headed for a military police lockup somewhere in Bandar Seri Begawan.

Maybe if the little man in the white dress uniform had not been so damned condescending.

Maybe if the little man in the white dress uniform hadn't decided to grab her by the arm and try to man-handle her.

Maybe if there hadn't been some grins and giggles from some of his own men when he toppled onto the concrete floor of the hangar, clutching himself and losing face.

Whatever the maybes, Professor Anne McCaine was in custody and destined for who knows what or where.

The military police car was headed west on the frontage road that ran behind the line of hangars and other buildings that line the side of the runway opposite the main terminal at the Bandar Seri Begawan Airport.

He wasn't traveling very fast, and there had been a couple of stop signs.

Maybe she could jump out?

That was just another one of those maybes. She tried the door handles. The doors were locked from the outside.

Anne was pondering what it might take to kick out the side window when there was suddenly a jolt, the sound of screeching tires, and an abrupt jerk to the left as the car came to a stop. It looked as though another car had run them off the road and had stopped immediately ahead. She couldn't see very well. Both the windshield and the pane of Plexiglas that separated the backseat from the front in the police car were filthy, and there was a great deal of glare from the sun.

As she squinted ahead, trying to figure out what was going on, the driver opened his door, pulling out his sidearm as he began to climb out.

There was a loud gunshot. The driver quivered and went motionless against his seat, one leg sprawled outside the car. Almost immediately, a large shadow covered the passenger side of the car and the door next to Kapitan Mohammed Haji was jerked open with tremendous force.

Colonel Dave Brannan grabbed Haji by the front of his uniform jacket and dragged him out of the car, his filthy powder-stained fist badly staining the crisp white jacket.

"Was that any way to treat a lady?"

Kapitan Mohammed Haji squirmed and struggled, but the big man with the auburn mustache had him firmly in the grip of his enormous hand. He was truly frightened of this huge American with the viselike grip.

With his other hand, Brannan opened the rear door, and Anne climbed out of the backseat. She smoothed her blue crocheted dress, folded her arms, and cast a disgusted glare at the captain.

"Are you going to apologize to the lady?" Brannan asked the trembling officer.

The officer glanced at her nervously, but said nothing.

This was not the answer that Dave Brannan had in mind. This bastard had played bully with the wrong woman. He jerked Haji forward so abruptly that they could hear his neck pop, then slammed him back against the car so hard that they could hear ribs cracking. Even Anne winced at the sound.

"Are you going to apologize to the lady?" Brannan asked again.

This time Haji opened his mouth to speak, but instead a stream of blood spilled out, splattering down the front of the crisp white jacket. He tried again, but he only heaved, sputtered, and coughed up another stream of blood.

Brannan released his grip and the man crumpled onto the ground.

Kapitan Mohammed Haji stared at the man and woman as they moved away. More than the damage done to his body, Haji was angered by the humiliation. He must have revenge. He reached down to his holster, struggled with the flap, and got his hand around the grip of his revolver.

Just as Anne leaned forward to embrace her hero,

his expression changed and he pulled away from her. The terrible day had seemed to have reached its climax, and everything seemed downhill from here, but as the axiom goes, just as you start to coast, you hit the pothole.

The colonel took two steps toward the writhing captain, and with his third, he stomped on his hand and the partially holstered revolver. With his fourth, he kicked the man's head. The sound was like that of a jug of wine breaking on a carpeted floor. The colonel reached down, picked up the pistol, and tossed it as far as he could into the field adjacent to the frontage road.

EIGHT

"**C**AN we get a video feed on the bridge?" Rear Admiral Walter Briscoe demanded. The commander of the Seventh Fleet's Task Force 70 was wound up like a coiled spring. His ships had been patrolling the Sulu Sea for the past month, playing chicken with the goddamn Bruneian Navy, and the bastards had been out there with three nukes aimed at him for nearly thirty-six hours.

"We have it, sir," Captain Roland "Roach" Rouche said, looking at the video monitor on the bridge of the USS *Ronald Reagan* (CVN-76). "The choppers are directly over it."

The task force had been monitoring the barge since it had left Muara yesterday, and when the pass by the

SH-60 Seahawk LAMPS chopper gave them visual confirmation that it was carrying three Khomeini-6 missiles, all of the ships had gone to general quarters.

Then, all of a sudden, late yesterday afternoon, the barge abruptly slowed to barely three knots and the Bruneian missile ship just as abruptly disappeared from the radarscopes. It hadn't slowed and it hadn't turned around. It had just disappeared. There had been a helicopter in the area at the time, but it had returned toward Brunei about the time that the ship disappeared.

Exclusion zone or not, Briscoe had ordered Seahawks into the area to take a closer look. What the choppers found surprised him. There was a debris field where the ship had disappeared from radar, but no survivors. Apparently the ship had blown up and sunk very quickly. Briscoe didn't care. Thanks to the ground rules imposed by the exclusion zone, this was one boatload of bad guys that he didn't have to worry about.

The Seahawks had surveyed the barge, and they had shadowed it all night long. During that time, they detected nobody on board, and no deviation in the progress of the barge except what could be attributed to wave action. It simply plodded along at a nonthreatening two or three knots. Jack Rodgers's plan to hand the nukes to the U.S. Navy on a platter had worked.

Now that the barge had chugged up to the edge of the exclusion zone, Briscoe had ordered a Marine Corps landing party to board it and take charge.

As Briscoe, Rouche, and a dozen others watched on the video feed, ten heavily armed Marines rappelled onto the deck of the barge. As countless sailors aboard the USS *Ronald Reagan,* the USS *Cowpens,* and three

Arleigh Burke–class destroyers strained to watch at the absolute limits of the power of their binoculars, the Marines spread out across the deck. One man went below, and then another, and a third.

Moments later, they emerged and gave a prearranged signal. There was, in fact, nobody aboard. More time passed as the Marines swept the ship for booby traps, and two sailors experienced in operating barges went aboard to take the helm. These men discovered, as Rodgers had, that the vessel could be stopped, but it couldn't be turned. Briscoe ordered them to shut it down, and stand by for his ordnance people to go aboard and prepare for the recovery of the three nukes.

"What do you suppose happened to the crew, and to that other ship, sir?" Rouche asked. "This is like one of those ghost ships that you read about."

"A goddamn ghost ship with the weapons to turn a million people into ghosts," Briscoe said sourly, still staring at the distant horizon.

April 27
6:12 A.M. Eastern Time

"**D**ID you and Buck Peighton have something to do with this?" Joyce Livingstone asked her husband as they watched the breaking news story on the flat-panel television screen mounted on the bedroom wall in the White House living quarters.

"I don't know," President Thomas Livingstone said, shaking his head slowly. "I honestly do not know."

The large type at the bottom of the screen read, "Attempted Coup in Brunei."

The news channel showed footage—just in—of a building catching fire from a burning power pole, and the announcer spoke of shooting and looting. Mainly, there was just confusion. Amid a flurry of unconfirmed reports, the only thing that seemed to be known for sure was that Sultan Omar Jamalul Halauddin was dead.

There had been a gun battle between rival factions at his beachfront villa near a place called Tutong. Apparently, each side blamed the other for the death of the sultan, but subsequent medical tests had confirmed that the 322-pound monarch had died of a massive heart attack.

The international airport at Bandar Seri Begawan had been closed after some shooting occurred near one of the hangars. The burned-out wreckage of the helicopter operated by a University of Colorado archaeological team had been found nearby, but there was no word on the fate of the Americans who had been part of that team.

A group calling itself the "National Unity Council" was reported to be meeting to choose a new sultan who could restore the calm and stability that the tiny nation had enjoyed prior to the death of Omar Jamalul Halauddin's predecessor.

The U.S. Navy's video feed of the Marines going aboard the barge was on all the cable channels, but the closest that the embedded reporters had gotten was the flight deck of the USS *Ronald Reagan*, from which they had been reporting for the past month. As he watched, the president counted the three missiles over and over. In the satellite photos there had been *four*. What happened to the other one?

As Livingstone made his way toward the bathroom to brush his teeth, a different announcer came on. Or maybe his wife had just changed the channel. This announcer had a different breaking story. It seemed that the ecoterrorists—the announcer didn't use that word— who were believed to have been responsible for the LSD attack on San Francisco had been apprehended. Apparently, they had been caught in an unsuccessful attempt to do the same thing to Los Angeles.

It was strange, Livingstone thought, that the media had failed to connect the two big breaking news stories of the day. Maybe they would, but probably not. A connection was just too implausible.

April 27
8:38 A.M. Eastern Time

WHEN Joyce Livingstone had asked her husband whether he and Buck Peighton had something to do with what had gone down in Brunei, he had said that he honestly did not know. Two hours later, when he got a call from Peighton on his personal cell phone, he did know.

The people who were part of the first public White House tour of the day hadn't noticed when a nondescript older gentleman lingered behind while they filed out of the Green Room. Neither did they notice that President Thomas Livingstone entered the Green Room. By then, they were two colored rooms away, listening to the guide explaining how President Rutherford B. Hayes took the oath of office in the Red Room in 1877.

"You've done it again . . . I think?" Livingstone told his old friend. It was more of a question than a statement. "I still remember that speech that you once quoted for me," Livingstone said. "The one that Theodore Roosevelt gave in 1910. The one about the men in the field."

"The men whose faces are marred by dust and sweat and blood." Peighton smiled.

"The man who strives valiantly; who errs, who comes short again and again, because there is no effort without error and shortcoming; but who does actually strive to *do the deeds,*" Livingstone continued.

"It's your American Volunteer Group, Tom," Peighton told him. "They're out there working for you, working for all of us, working to stop the rogues and criminals that think they can strike our homeland with impunity. They're striking back at the enemy that *nobody else* can touch."

April 27
7:38 A.M. Central Time

JULIA Girod set down her box of beignets and began dosing her steaming cup of coffee with honey. She didn't normally stop into Marie's at this time of day, but it was her day to bring treats in to the paper, and Marie's was the best place in town for those Louisiana-style square donuts that everybody loved.

As she snapped the lid on her cup, her eyes caught sight of a familiar short stocky man sitting near a window with his back to the room.

"Whoa-ooh," Greg Boyinson stammered as someone's hands gripped both his shoulders. He was startled, and about to react as startled Special Forces men react, when he smelled the aroma of a familiar cologne. It altered his mood faster than a NASCAR driver jerking an emergency brake.

"It's good to have you back, big guy," Julia Girod said, caressing the helicopter pilot's ear with her tongue. "I thought you said you were going to be gone until next week."

"The job wrapped up quicker than we expected," he explained, putting his arm around her waist and pulling her close. He was still seated, and the narrow band of bare flesh immediately above her belt buckle pressed against his cheek. Naturally, it had to be kissed.

"What exactly were you doing?" Julia asked as she sat down next to him and put her hand on his thigh.

"Helping out an old friend who needed a chopper pilot for a few days."

"Was it here in Louisiana?" she asked. He just loved the way that Louisianans pronounced "Louisiana." Even if Julia Girod hadn't been drop-dead gorgeous—and she was—he'd probably just stay around for the sound of her voice.

"Naw, it was out west," he answered, gesturing with his thumb in the direction of Beaumont—and Brunei.

"How *far* west were you doing your chopper work, big guy?" Julia asked as she caressed his rough hand and noticed the recent scuff marks across his knuckles.

"Pretty far, why?"

"Hmmmm," she said, casting him a knowing smile. "You know, *Captain,* I don't just write for a newspaper. I also *read* them."

April 27
8:27 A.M. Pacific Time

"**D**ID that guy Arthur ever recover?" Rod Llewellan asked, nodding to the newspaper that Erik Vasquez was reading at the truck stop diner in Lost Hills, California.

In California this morning, the media was saturated with news reports of the apprehension of the ecoterrorists responsible for the LSD attack on San Francisco. The coup in faraway Brunei was definitely second-page news in the Golden State.

As soon as the California Highway Patrol and Los Angeles authorities had been alerted to the attempt at a repeat performance on the Los Angeles water supply, police scanners picked it up. The news choppers for the Los Angeles television stations had been over the Antelope Valley within fifteen minutes of the arrival of the backup that Llewellan had called for.

"Yeah, he finally came down," Vasquez replied,

taking another bite of toast. "He absorbed enough acid through his skin to get him higher than a kite, but he's going to be better off than a lot of those people up in the Bay Area. Right now he's saying that it was all the other guy's idea."

"His troubles are only beginning," Rod said as he flagged down the waitress for more coffee.

Having discharged their weapons, and with Basim Rashid dead, the two FBI agents were no longer on the case pending the intradepartmental investigation. However, this was a mere formality. When the dust settled, they would be in for commendations and a little something extra in their pay envelopes.

As he took a sip of the fresh hot coffee, Llewellan marveled at how nobody in the media had made the connection between all this and the Brunei story. Maybe it would come out later, or maybe not. Maybe the truth had died with Rashid. Who knows? It didn't really matter. Both stories had wound to their conclusion.

April 27
11:27 A.M. Eastern Time

"**T**HEY'VE located the fourth nuclear weapon," Director of National Intelligence Richard Scevoles said as he arrived at the hastily convened Oval Office meeting late and out of breath. His tardiness would be forgiven by the good news that he bore.

"Who? Where?" asked Admiral Michael J. Felth, the chief of naval operations. He had just finished giving President Livingstone a briefing on the recovery of the other three nuclear warheads by the USS *Ronald Reagan* and Task Force 70.

"Middle of nowhere in northern Australia," the director replied.

"How on earth did it get there?" Livingstone asked.

"It was on a plane," Scevoles told the president. "It was on Sultan Omar's private Gulfstream V. The tower at Darwin got a distress call last night from an aircraft inbound over the Arafura Sea. The pilot said he was going to try to make an emergency landing in Arnhem Land . . . that's the big dry desert east of Darwin. The Aussies sent choppers out and they finally found the plane."

"Had it crashed?" Livingstone asked.

"No, and that's the funny thing," Scevoles said. "It had made a perfect landing on a narrow dirt strip about a hundred miles from anywhere."

"Who was on the plane?" Secretary of State John Edredin asked.

"Nobody," Scevoles replied.

"Nobody?"

"Nope, nobody." Scevoles shrugged. "The aircraft still had plenty of fuel. They could have flown all the way to Sydney easily. And there were no detectable mechanical problems."

"Just like that damned barge that my people picked up," Admiral Felth observed. "It showed up with nobody aboard, and the missile ship that was shadowing it just sank without warning. It was there on one satellite image and missing on the next."

"When the Australians searched the Gulfstream, they

found the nuke," Scevoles continued. "It was just sitting there in the passenger cabin. They didn't make a public announcement about it being aboard, but ASIS—the Australian Secret Intelligence Service—has contacted my office. We're sending some people out there this afternoon. They'll look it over tomorrow."

"Did it look like they were planning to attack an Australian city with the weapon?" Felth asked.

"The Aussies are sure looking into that possibility, but if whoever it was wanted to, there is no technical reason why they couldn't have at least tried. As I said, the plane had plenty of gas and there was nothing wrong with it."

"If that's what they had wanted to do, why didn't they at least try to reach Sydney or Melbourne instead of just landing as soon as they could after they reached Australia?"

"It's a mystery."

"Maybe they weren't running *to* Australia, but *from* Brunei," Livingstone suggested. "Remember, there was a coup of some sort under way in Brunei."

"But it was the sultan's airplane, and *he* never left Brunei," Felth reminded them.

"Do you have any idea what actually happened in Brunei?" Livingstone asked the secretary of state.

"If there was a coup," Edredin responded, "it was the funniest coup that I've ever heard of. There was an electricity failure and the phones went down, which is something that often happens when somebody stages a coup, but aside from some isolated incidents, nothing much happened. The sultan died of natural causes, and there was no opposition party trying to seize power."

"There were only two major shooting incidents," Scevoles interjected as he unpacked a large portfolio of fresh satellite images that he had brought with him. "There was one near the villa where the sultan died. It was between units of the army and the sultan's personal bodyguard. They each thought the other was responsible. There were about eighteen people injured, and two bodyguards were killed. They agreed to a cease-fire for a doctor to examine the sultan's body."

"There was also a report of a firefight here at the naval base," Felth said as he examined a photo of the Jalan Tanjong Pelumpong base in Muara.

"Actually, it was confined entirely to the compound within the base where we had previously seen the nukes being stored," Scevoles said. "There are conflicting reports about what happened, but apparently a Brunei Air Force helicopter touched down there for about five minutes, and when it took off again, about two dozen people were dead. They were mainly the Iranians who were managing the nukes for Omar. You'd be interested to know that one of those who was killed is our old friend Abdulla Maloud."

"Abdulla Maloud?" Edredin questioned. "That's Jahar Abiddijab, the character with the British passport who we had to release from Guantanamo Bay. The same one who Steve Faralaco met right here in Washington."

"The world's a better place with him out of the way," Felth asserted. "I only wish that *our* guys would have had the pleasure of taking him out."

"I'm sure that our British cousins would have something to say about that," Edredin said. "We'll probably be accused of complicity regardless of who killed him."

"I don't think that we need to worry about that," Scevoles said. "He was active in both this country and Brunei under the name Abdulla Maloud. He was living as Abdulla Maloud, and he died as Abdulla Maloud. Jahar Abiddijab had a British passport, but Abdulla Maloud did not."

"Do we know who was behind the coup?" Livingstone asked. He knew, but it was best that no one in this room knew that he knew.

"The word on the street in Brunei is that Hudim Incpaduka was involved somehow," Scevoles replied. "We have reports that he left the sultan's villa not long before the sultan was discovered. One story has it that he was sick and was carried out on a stretcher. Another story has it that he left in the same helicopter that landed at the naval base. There are a lot of stories going around, but you know what they say about eyewitnesses. . . ."

"They almost never remember things exactly the way that they really happened," Felth said, completing his sentence.

President Thomas Livingstone leaned back in his chair pondering this notion of things not always being as they seem. He was momentarily lost in thought, unnoticed by the others as they studied the satellite photos and chattered among themselves. Livingstone thought about his three-minute meeting with Peighton this morning, and especially about the photographs that he was shown.

One was of a little dark-eyed baby, his face twisted in pain. The other was of Omar Jamalul Halauddin. His face was gruesomely contorted, and his eyes bulged from his head. The expression was that of a man experiencing unspeakable terror. The president could almost hear him scream. The line of blood dripping from his chin seemed to point to a photograph lying near his collar. It was the same photo of the baby.

The president had handed the pictures back to Peighton. He knew that they were his to see, but not his to keep. Now, he was contemplating them more than he cared to while he continued looking at the satellite photos that were now being passed around the Oval Office. Peighton's snapshots had more to say.

Thanks to the Raptors, Omar Jamalul Halauddin had truly gotten a taste of his own evil medicine, and that taste was on his lips as he breathed his last.

April 27
1:09 P.M. Eastern Time

"I was expecting someone else," Ambassador Pehin Dato Yayah Korma said, staring at the man in the car.

"You were expecting Steve Faralaco from the White House?"

"Yes, I was."

"You were expecting to talk to him about political asylum in the United States?"

"Yes," Yayah Korma answered hesitatingly.

"Well, he couldn't make it. I came instead," General Buckley Peighton said with an affable grin. "C'mon, get in. Let's take a drive. Want some chips?"

Peighton poured himself a handful of corn chips and passed the bag to Yayah Korma.

"Where are we going?" the ambassador asked.

"I've been instructed to take you to the safe house in West Virginia where you'll be processed for asylum."

Korma relaxed. The last few days had been a whirlwind. He'd had a press release to send out, but he had simply burned it in the fireplace at the embassy. There was supposed to have been an American on a barge, but there wasn't. He had seen that on television. Then there had been a coup. The sultan was dead, and Korma decided that he had best look for another life. Faralaco had been amazingly cooperative. He had been very willing to help, and to let bygones be bygones. Those crazy Americans! Korma tossed another bunch of chips in his mouth. They hit the spot, but *ouch,* they were spicy.

"I'd like to live in a place with a good view of the ocean," the ambassador said, daydreaming of his new life.

"Of course."

"I'll need a sizable household staff. I think that a retired ambassador deserves a large staff, don't you?"

"Absolutely."

Unable to stop himself, Korma ate another handful of the chips, and stared longingly at the water bottle from which Peighton was sipping.

"They're pretty hot, huh?" Peighton laughed, reaching behind the seat and handing the ambassador a water bottle identical to his own.

Yayah Korma snapped the seal, unscrewed the cap, and took a long refreshing gulp of the water.

He felt relaxed now, and considered himself very, very lucky. Soon he would have a new life, a new and comfortable life. He made small talk with Peighton as they drove through the Virginia countryside.

As they drove, he inhaled the beauty of the warm spring day. He took another long gulp from the water bottle, and noticed that the sky seemed very, very blue today. It was unusually blue, almost *luminescent* blue.

EPILOGUE

A shadow passed in front of the doorway, blocking the sunlight streaming into the Ridgy Didge Tavern in Runaway Bay, Australia. The eyes of the surfies drinking at the bar glanced instinctively to see who it was. It was a sheila in a short bougainvillea-colored sundress and a faded denim jacket. A pair of sunglasses was perched atop her head, and her long, dark hair swept across her shoulders. The perfect shape of her legs and the flawless contours of her body were accentuated by her being silhouetted in the open door.

Grinning like a pack of shot foxes, half-a-dozen men stepped away from the bar to greet her with a casual g'day. When they noticed the size of the man in

the blue Hawaiian shirt who was about three steps behind her, they quickly turned back to their stubbies.

As Colonel Dave Brannan ordered a couple of pints
of Burragorang Bock from the bartender, he and the
professor momentarily glanced at the television set that
hung above the bar. There was a news flash. A man
who had now been identified as Hudim Incpaduka, the
former Bruneian ambassador to the United Nations,
had been found wandering aimlessly along a dirt road
in Northern Territory about eighty kilometers west of
the Stuart Highway. He had no idea where he was, nor
did he have any idea *who* he was.

As Anne McCaine and the colonel walked through
the back of the bar to an outside seating area with a
few tables under a rusty tin roof, the voice of James
Douglas Morrison echoed from the jukebox. "There's
a killer on the road," sang the Lizard King. "His brain
is squirming like a toad."

Brannan took a long, satisfying sip of his beer, and
Anne leaned over to lick the foam from his lips. This
was followed by a long, mutually satisfying kiss.

Neither of them was in much of a hurry today. They
had awoken early, but had stayed in bed until nearly
noon. No, they were not in much of a hurry to do anything. The colonel had gotten his money for his last
job wired to a bank in Sydney. The professor had
phoned Asa Henderson from her area-code-720 cell
phone to tell him that she had unilaterally resumed her
sabbatical. She had been "terribly traumatized" by being in Brunei during the coup, and told the chairman
that she didn't know whether she could ever go back.

He had agreed. He had seen it on television. He would find someone else.

Maybe she and the colonel would go surfing this afternoon, or maybe they'd go back to that bungalow that they had rented by the week and just go to bed early.

Anne kicked off her flip-flops, put up her feet, and leaned her head against the colonel's shoulder. He kissed her on top of the head and casually picked up a newspaper that was lying on the table. His eye was drawn to a photograph of the grinning Bruneian heritage minister, Dr. Awang Uhtaud, standing next to the newly installed Sultan Ahmad Tajuddin II.

The new sultan had announced that he was trading his predecessor's stick for a carrot, terminating the exclusion zone in favor of what he called the "Inclusive Zone," a tourist-friendly Brunei. He and Uhtaud were pictured at the groundbreaking ceremony for what was described as the future crown jewel of the Inclusive Zone—an ambitious new tourist facility near Tutong that would be called Suvarnadvipa.

Brannan chuckled and handed the paper to the professor.

"The Sultan of Brunei is dead." Anne smiled, taking another sip of her beer. "Long live the sultan."

ABOUT THE AUTHOR

Bill Yenne is the well-established author of numerous nonfiction military histories. *Publishers Weekly* has described his work as "eloquent." The *Wall Street Journal* recently called another of his military histories "splendid" and went on to say that he writes with "cinematic vividness." Gary Sheffield, professor of War Studies at the University of Birmingham in England, wrote that one of his earlier Penguin novels, *A Damned Fine War*, "succeeds triumphantly.... It is an excellent read."

Don't miss the page-turning
suspense, intriguing characters,
and unstoppable action that keep
readers coming back for more from
these bestselling authors...

Tom Clancy
Robin Cook
Patricia Cornwell
Catherine Coulter
Clive Cussler
Dean Koontz
John Sandford

Your favorite thrillers
and suspense novels
come from Berkley.

penguin.com